Dying for Devil's Food

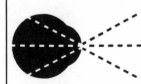

This Large Print Book carries the
Seal of Approval of N.A.V.H.

Dying for
Devil's Food

Jenn McKinlay

WHEELER PUBLISHING
A part of Gale, a Cengage Company

Farmington Hills, Mich • San Francisco • New York • Waterville, Maine
Meriden, Conn • Mason, Ohio • Chicago

Copyright © 2019 by Jennifer McKinlay Orf.
A Cupcake Bakery Mystery.
Wheeler Publishing, a part of Gale, a Cengage Company.

Wheeler Publishing Large Print Cozy Mystery.
The text of this Large Print edition is unabridged.
Other aspects of the book may vary from the original edition.
Set in 16 pt. Plantin.

LIBRARY OF CONGRESS CIP DATA ON FILE.
CATALOGUING IN PUBLICATION FOR THIS BOOK
IS AVAILABLE FROM THE LIBRARY OF CONGRESS

ISBN-13: 978-1-4328-6342-5 (softcover alk. paper)

Published in 2019 by arrangement with Berkley, an imprint of Penguin Publishing Group, a division of Penguin Random House LLC

Printed in the United States of America
1 2 3 4 5 6 7 23 22 21 20 19

For my sisters-in-law, Susan Orf Johnson and Katie Orf Wener. You are two of the funniest, smartest, loveliest women I know, and even though we never get enough time together, I am so grateful for the times we do share. You two were my super awesome bonus prizes when I married your brother. Much love always. XOXO

ACKNOWLEDGMENTS

Major thanks to my editor, Kate Seaver, and my agent, Christina Hogrebe. They didn't even blink when I said I was going to send the cupcake girls to their high school reunion. Ha! Also, big thanks to Sarah Blumenstock for her attention to the details. And as always, I am in awe of the original cover artist, Jeff Fitz-Maurice. You never let me down with these amazing covers. To the rest of the team at Berkley, especially Tara O'Connor, how can I ever thank you? You consistently come up with new and amazing ways to share my books with the world, and I am ever grateful.

And, as always, big hugs to my men, the Hub and the Hooligans. You three give me so much material, seriously, the books practically write themselves. Love you forever.

ONE

"Squeee!"

At the screechy noise, Melanie Cooper squeezed her pastry bag too tight and frosting shot out of the tip into a big glob on top of the cupcake she was decorating for a wedding the next day.

"Angie DeLaura, what was that?" she asked. She blew her blond bangs off her forehead as she glared at her business partner, who had just come running through the swinging doors from the front of the bakery into the kitchen, where Mel was working.

"That's Angie Harper to you, and" — she paused to strike a pose and fan herself with a large envelope and fancy-looking invitation before she continued — "to everyone else we graduated high school with fifteen years ago."

"Huh?" Mel frowned at her recently married petite brunette friend.

"Our fifteen-year reunion," Angie said. She pointed to the envelope in her hand. "It's coming up and guess who they want to bake cupcakes for it?"

Mel stared at her childhood friend who was the sister of her heart. How could she put this as tactfully and delicately as possible?

"No." Mel used a rubber spatula to scrape the glob off the ruined cupcake and flicked it into the large garbage bin to her right.

"What?" Angie froze in mid-fan. "What do you mean, no?"

"I have no intention of baking cupcakes for those people," Mel said.

She bent over the cake in front of her. It was a red velvet cupcake with cream cheese frosting. She was keeping it simple and working the frosting in a thick smooth swirl that she then sprinkled with small red hearts. Just the thought of going to her high school reunion made her want to mainline the frosting and shove a whole cupcake into her mouth like a boss.

"But . . . but," Angie stammered. It was clear she hadn't anticipated this sort of response, which boggled Mel, but she continued on.

"No buts," she said. "You're welcome to go to our reunion but I refuse."

"Mel, I don't think you're grasping the big picture here."

"Oh, I'm grasping it and I'm tossing it away."

"But look at us," Angie said. She swung her arms wide to encompass the kitchen and beyond. "We're hugely successful. We have franchises all over the country. That gives us a moral imperative to show up at our reunion."

"No."

"Mel, I know there were some people who hurt your feelings back in the day —"

"Hurt my feelings?" Mel straightened up. She grabbed a pinch of heart-shaped sprinkles and didn't so much sprinkle them as threw them onto the freshly piped frosting. She stared at her friend. "Angie, they called me 'Melephant,' they bullied me about my weight, and Cassidy Havers, in particular, wrote my name in all of the boys' bathrooms with my phone number. She was vicious and mean and cruel and if I never see her again, it will be too soon."

"She's Cassidy Havers-Griffin now," Angie said.

"Griffin?"

"Yes, as in Daniel Griffin."

"She married Danny?" Mel asked. She felt her old high school crush spread its wings and rise out of the ashes of her adolescent heart like a phoenix. "When?"

"A couple of years ago," Angie said. "I think you were in Paris at culinary school at the time."

"And you didn't mention it?"

Angie just looked at her and Mel nodded. Yeah, she wouldn't have told Angie if her high school crush had gotten married, either. Oh, wait, her crush had been Tate Harper and he had gotten married six months ago. To Angie.

"But you're going to marry Joe," Angie said. "And you had a much deeper and longer-lasting crush on Joe than on Danny, right?"

"Well, of course, but I can't believe he married *her,*" Mel said. She shuddered. "I mean, he was captain of the basketball team and totally out of my league in high school, and she was the homecoming queen, so I guess it makes sense, but I always hoped he'd meet someone . . ."

Mel's voice trailed off. She was not going to say it out loud.

"More like you?" Angie guessed.

This was the problem with besties, they knew you too well.

"No, not like me," Mel said. She felt the need to protest even though they both knew she was full of it. "But someone more like me than her."

"Uh-huh," Angie said. She lowered her head and glanced at Mel through her eyelashes. "I can't believe you're going to let Cassidy Havers keep you from our reunion."

"Don't even try it," Mel said. "You can't manipulate me into going. You're not that good."

"But what about the commission?" Angie asked. "Five hundred cupcakes with little fifteens on them and we can do them in the school colors of gold and black. They will look so cool and we can use them on our website for advertising and get even more reunion jobs."

"Nope," Mel said. "I'm not interested."

She frosted several more cupcakes and added the sprinkles. Angie didn't move. She just stood there, glaring. Mel knew she was formulating her argument to get Mel on her side. It was never going to happen. Not only because Angie didn't have her older brother Joe DeLaura's lawyerly gifts but also because Mel would not be budged on this. She had less than no interest in seeing anyone from her graduating class. Ever.

"So, the idea of strutting into our reunion, looking amazing, as a successful business owner and renowned pastry chef doesn't

13

appeal to you in the least?" Angie asked.

"Not even a little," Mel said. "I could not care less what those people think."

"And the thought of sashaying into the room on prominent assistant county attorney Joe DeLaura's arm, while flashing that dazzling sparkler of a ring he gave you, does nothing for you, either?" Angie asked.

"Not a thing," Mel said. "I'm thrilled to be engaged to Joe but he's not a trophy husband."

"You sure about that?" Angie asked. "Because I'm pretty sure every woman in our high school, including a few of the teachers, had a thing for Joe."

It was true, Mel had to concede that, but she wasn't about to say it out loud or Angie would have her at the reunion so fast her cupcakes would have whiplash.

"I'm sure Joe would be flattered to hear that," she said.

She hefted one large tray of cupcakes onto her shoulder and carried it to the walk-in cooler for delivery tomorrow morning. When she came back out, she noted that Angie had her chin set in a defiant tilt. Oh, boy, she wasn't going to let it go. Mel lifted the second tray and carried that one into the cooler as well.

There was no avoiding Angie as Mel

began to clean the steel worktable. Cupcakes were a gloriously messy business. She glanced down at her apron to find some dollops of frosting stuck on the front. She smiled.

Despite what she'd said to Angie, she was thrilled with how successful their enterprise Fairy Tale Cupcakes had become and would have loved to brag about it. When she had started the business with her two childhood best friends, Angie DeLaura — now Harper — and Tate Harper, a few years ago, she had never envisioned the level of success they had achieved. She knew a lot of it was because of Tate's brilliant business acumen, but she didn't think he could have made them a success if the product she toiled over, the cupcakes, wasn't top notch.

"You realize you're forcing me to go there," Angie said.

"Go where?"

Angie blew out a breath. "Mel, don't you want to show off *you*?"

Mel tipped her head to the side. She felt like a dog hearing a high-pitched whistle. "Come again?"

"You. Look at you," Angie demanded.

Mel glanced down. She noted the hot pink apron, the frosting blobs. Oh, there was a sprinkle stuck in a glob. She flicked it off

15

into the garbage. Beneath the apron, she was the same old Mel in denim capris, slip-on Vans in the chevron pattern, and a plain blue T-shirt. Sexy, she was not. Comfortable, she most definitely was.

"I'm not seeing where you're going with this," she said. She gestured to her ensemble. "This is not exactly show-off worthy."

"Yes, it is. Mel, this is your chance to show them what you look like now," Angie said. Her voice was soft as if she was trying to say it in a way that wouldn't offend Mel. Sadly, there was no way to say it without offense.

"You mean I should go to the reunion because I'm thinner than I was back then," Mel said. Her voice was tight. "I should hold my head high, wearing a size six, sometimes eight, and trot around the room, letting everyone have a good look at the new and improved Melanie Cooper? Is that where you're going with this?"

Angie shrugged. "Maybe."

"Aw, come on, don't be bashful. You opened this can of worms," Mel said. "What do you think will happen if I do that?"

"You'll have the last laugh," Angie cried. There was a fierce light in her brown eyes. "You'll arrive a hugely successful pastry chef, about to marry a gorgeous district attorney, and you will positively stun them with how beautiful you are."

They stood staring at each other. Mel gave her friend a small smile. "I love that you see it playing out that way. You really are such an idealistic optimist. Here's the problem. That's never going to happen."

The kitchen doors banged open and Marty Zelaznik, the bakery's octogenarian counter help, stood there with his scrawny arms on his hips and his bald head glowing like a beacon.

"Hey, Ange, how about a little help out there? The lunch rush came and you vamoosed. I've got people lined up to the door," he said. He looked at Mel. "Wouldn't kill you to come out and help, either."

"Fine," Mel said. She walked around the table to follow him back into the bakery.

"Oh, no, you don't," Angie said. She was hot on Mel's heels. "We're not done here."

"Yes, we are."

"Walk and talk, people," Marty barked. "We have customers waiting."

They pushed through the swinging doors and sure enough, there was a line now going out the door. Most were calmly waiting but a few of them looked irritated. Never a good thing.

"Hi, how can I help you?" Mel asked the

17

first person in line.

"I need a dozen cupcakes," the woman said. She was twenty-something, dressed in a pale green suit that brought out the red in her blond hair. "But I don't know what kind to get. I'm meeting my boyfriend's parents for the first time and I'm terrified. Cupcakes will help, right?"

"Absolutely," Mel said. "If his parents don't appreciate a dozen cupcakes from us, then you're far too good for them."

The girl laughed and Mel guided her in picking out a solid dozen with a dairy-and-gluten-free option thrown in just in case there were some dietary intolerance issues. Then it was on to the next customer and the next. The business did not stop Angie from badgering her about the reunion, however.

"We could rent a limo," Angie said while boxing up an order.

"No."

Mel tried to avoid the discussion but Angie was persistent.

"How about we get Mean Christine to do our hair and makeup?" Angie asked while Mel rang up a customer. "She always makes us look amazing."

"No."

"Oh, I've been to Christine's," the customer said. "She can roll back the years like nobody's business."

Mel shoved the box of cupcakes at the woman, who lifted her eyebrows, took the box, and left.

"Angie, I am not going," Mel said. "I don't know how many ways I can say this to make you understand."

"You're just being difficult," Angie said. She crossed her arms over her chest with such a look of immovability she could have sprouted roots.

"No, I'm not," Mel protested. "You can go with Tate. You don't need me there."

"Yes, I do," Angie cried. "You're my best friend. Besides, our whole business is successful because of you. We need to be there together to represent."

" 'You know, even though I had to wear that stupid back brace and you were kind of fat, we were still totally cutting edge,' " Mel said.

"*Romy and Michele's High School Reunion,*" Angie identified the movie quote. It was a longtime game between them as movie lovers to stump each other with movie quotes. "I have been waiting for you to bust that out since I mentioned the reunion."

"What reunion?" Olivia Puckett, Marty's squeeze, asked as she entered the bakery, which had finally cleared out.

"Our fifteen-year high school reunion," Mel said.

"Fifteen?" Olivia looked them up and down. "I'd have thought you were on twenty by now."

Angie emitted a low growl from her throat. Mel instinctively stepped in front of her to block her from Olivia.

"Why are you here?" Mel asked Olivia with narrowed eyes.

"I'm taking my honey out for a late lunch," Olivia said. She blew a kiss at Marty and he leapt into the air, pretending to catch it. Mel hoped he didn't slip a hip with that maneuver.

"Gagging," Angie said. "I'm actually gagging."

Olivia gave her a dark look. "What's the matter, short stack? Is the bloom off your newly wedded rose?"

This time Mel wrapped an arm around Angie's head and pulled her in close. She supposed it could technically be called a headlock, but it prevented Angie's wildly swinging fist from connecting with Olivia's nose, so Mel figured it was for the greater good.

"Now, Liv, be nice," Marty said. "Mel is having issues because she's too chicken —

bock bock — to face her old classmates at her reunion."

Mel dropped her arm and Angie careened forward. Olivia side-stepped behind a table just in time.

"I am not chicken!" Mel protested.

That brought Angie up short and she whirled around to look at Mel as if she could not be serious. "Yes, you are! Otherwise, why don't you want to go? Brittany Nilsson is coordinating the whole thing and she says just about everyone has RSVP'd yes. She was so excited about your cupcakes."

"Like I care what Brittany Nilsson thinks of my cupcakes," Mel scoffed. "I have no reason to go. I don't care about high school or any of those lame people. I kept in touch with the people who were my friends and that's all that matters."

"That's me and Tate," Angie said. She held up two fingers.

"Exactly," Mel said. "Why do I need anyone else?"

Olivia glanced back and forth between them like she was watching a ping-pong match.

"You're talking about turning down a job for five hundred cupcakes!" Angie raised her hands in the air as if she had hit her exasperation breaking point. "Most of these people we graduated with are local or still have family here. The potential for more business from this reunion is huge."

"I don't care," Mel said. "I don't want to do it. I don't want to go. I don't want to see any of those people ever again."

"You're just being stubborn," Angie said.

"No, I'm not."

"Yes, you are."

"Well, I'm going to lunch," Marty said. "Liv, you ready?"

Mel glanced at Olivia, who was suddenly quiet. She had her back to them and was whispering into her phone. Mel stepped closer so she could hear.

"Yes, I'm the owner of Confections bakery. I hear you need five hundred cupcakes," Olivia whispered.

Angie's eyes went wide. She waved her arms like she was indicating that the bridge was out. "Now see what you've done? Olivia is going to scoop our job."

"Not on my watch," Mel said. She stepped around Olivia and snatched the phone out of her hand. "Hello?"

"Hi, Ms. Puckett? Is everything all right?"

"There's no Ms. Puckett here," Mel said. "This is Melanie Cooper, owner of Fairy Tale Cupcakes."

"Oh my god! Mel! Hi, this is Brittany Nilsson, remember me? Go Devils!"

Mel closed her eyes. It was impossible not to remember Brittany. She was the most school-spirited person Mel had ever known. Short, stout, and with a walk that was militarily precise, she chanted peppy slogans that sounded more like orders being barked. During spirit week, she positively ruled school-color day, crazy-hair day, and dress-like-twins day. She was in two words: too much.

"Hi, Brittany," Mel said. "Of course I remember you."

Olivia made to snatch her phone back but Mel turned away from her. She heard a grunt and an oomph and guessed that Angie had blocked another attempt.

"Angie tells me you're quite the culinary wizard, so here's what I'm thinking: five hundred cupcakes with little glittery fifteens on them," she said. "And could you make a variety of flavors? Chocolate cake with vanilla icing is so 2010."

Mel glanced over her shoulder. Marty and Angie had each hooked one of Olivia's arms, holding her back. The light in her eyes was fierce, and Mel realized she could give this huge order to Olivia and walk away but, no, she couldn't. They'd been baking rivals ever since the day Mel had opened her shop and even though Olivia was dating Marty, it hadn't changed one bit. Mel would be frosted by her own pastry bag before she'd willingly give Olivia her business.

"That sounds great, Brittany," Mel said. "I'll e-mail you an invoice."

"Fantas—"

She hit end on the call and tossed the phone back to Olivia, who yanked her arms free and caught it. Mel then glanced at Angie. "You win. We're going and we're making the cupcakes."

"Yay!" Angie jumped up and down and clapped. Then she turned to Olivia and the two women exchanged a high five. "Nice work, Puckett."

"Thank you," Olivia said.

"What?" Mel snapped. "This was a setup? You two set me up?"

Olivia shrugged. "Sometimes you just need a hard shove to the back to do the right thing. Come on, handsome, I'm so hungry I could eat a bear."

"Right behind you," Marty said. He glanced at Mel. "For the record, I had no idea about any of this."

Mel turned to Angie. "Oh, the betrayal! How could you?"

"How could I not?" Angie asked. "Mel,

it's our fifteen-year high school reunion and we're getting paid a fortune to show up and show off. Honestly, if you hadn't caved in under the Olivia competition maneuver, I was planning to clunk you on the head and drag you to the reunion bound and gagged if I had to."

"You're mental." Mel shook her head. "This is really that important to you?"

"Yes." Angie studied Mel's face and added, "Cheer up, this is a huge event and we are going to rock it. I mean, it's been fifteen years since we've seen any of those people — what could possibly go wrong?"

Two

"How did you get talked into this again?" Joe asked as he straightened his tie.

"Your sister manipulated me with Olivia Puckett's help," Mel said. They were parked in the large lot adjacent to the resort where the reunion was being held. "I'm still mad at her."

"It's been weeks. That's a pretty long time to hold a grudge," he said.

Mel gave him a dark look.

Joe raised his hands in the air in a gesture of surrender and said, "But, of course, I'm completely on your side." He leaned over the console and kissed her quick. "Have I told you that you look beautiful tonight?"

"Three times," Mel said. Then she smiled at him. "Thank you. But fair warning, you may have to say it a couple hundred more times to get me through this evening. I can't believe I'm doing this."

"Nervous?" he asked.

"Terrified," she said. She made no move to get out of the car and Joe seemed to be waiting to follow her lead. She loved that about him. He never rushed her. She took his hand in hers and said, "There's something I need to tell you."

"All right," he said. He paused with his head tipped to the side, as if he had all the time in the world for her to be ready. As the middle of Angie's seven older brothers, Joe was the family mediator and a master at patiently guiding people where they needed to go. Oh, how she loved this man.

Mel shifted in her seat, trying to find her courage. She hated this. She didn't want to have to tell him all of the humiliating stuff from her teen years. A flash of anger toward Angie flared up in her. She could have just gone on with her life, never admitting any of this but, no, here she was getting ready to face her old nemesis and there was no way she couldn't prepare Joe for the drama that was likely to unfold. It would be like sending him barefoot into a snake pit.

"The thing is, I wasn't exactly homecoming queen material back in the day," Mel said. "In fact, I was more likely to be confused with the float that the homecoming queen rode on, or at least that's what our homecoming queen, Cassidy, liked to say to me."

Joe blinked. Mel knew she had just changed his perspective of her entirely. He probably didn't remember that when she was a teenager she was on the heavy side — understatement — and that her weight had been a burden for her throughout high school and most of college, until she nearly starved herself to death. If anything, he remembered her as Angie's chubby friend, not the most flattering image but not entirely accurate, either. She'd been more than chubby.

After a miserable stint in the corporate world, she decided to follow her bliss and quit the insanity of crazy starvation diets and went to Paris to study cooking. It was there that she learned to have a healthy relationship with food. And it was after that that she reconnected with Joe, who was four years older, and who now knew her as a grown-up and a woman who knew who she was and how to manage her emotional eating — mostly.

"Cassidy?" Joe asked. One eyebrow was lowered in what she recognized as his unhappy face.

"Havers," Mel said. "Although Angie told me she's Cassidy Havers-Griffin now."

"And she was your homecoming queen?"

"Yes," Mel said. "I know she was four years behind your class but you probably saw her at the annual homecoming football game. She was a vivacious redhead, with big bazooms and a cute little button nose, and huge blue eyes. She looked like a fairy princess."

"Sounds like she was more the villainess in this story," he said. "Please tell me you shoved her face-first into a bowl of pudding or stuck a *kick me* sign on her back."

Mel burst out laughing. "No, I was too shy and timid back then. Mostly, I remember trying to shrink myself in all directions. I used to walk with my elbows tucked in and my head down."

A soft look came over Joe's face. "I wish I had been there. I would have protected you."

Mel was horrified and shook her head. "Oh, no, that would have done me in. I could barely string together a sentence whenever I saw you at your parents' house as it was. You were Angie's older brother, the impossibly handsome and kind Joe De-Laura, and I was crushing on you so hard. It would have killed me if you'd witnessed any of my humiliation."

He raised his eyebrows. Mel was not going to get into it. She waved her hand and said, "Dumb stuff. No big deal."

"It doesn't sound like no big deal," he said. "Especially if it still hurts you. Do I have to punch someone into the ground tonight?"

"No, really, it doesn't hurt me anymore," she said. "I just want you to be prepared if we go in there and people don't remember me or they're not kind; it's because I was definitely an outlier in high school, as were Angie and Tate, which is why we're such good friends."

"And yet Angie is very excited to attend the reunion," Joe said. "Why is that?"

Mel glanced down at her hands in her lap. "Because Angie probably would have been popular if she hadn't chosen me as her best friend. I was the fly in the pie there. But Angie is so loyal, she always put me first. I think she's eager to show everyone how successful we are, whereas I —"

"You what?" Joe asked.

Mel felt her throat get tight. Damn it. She didn't want to cry but this whole thing was much harder than she'd expected. The truth was she'd been bullied mercilessly by Cassidy and her squad and the wounds still cut deep.

"I just don't want to get hurt," Mel said. "I don't want to be that sad girl who felt so ugly and unattractive all through school. It's taken me so long to leave her behind me, and I'm afraid if I walk in there, I'll be her again."

Joe cupped her cheek and pulled her close. He kissed her forehead, her cheek, and then her lips. "Listen, I don't think you should let go of that girl. She made you who you are, who, for the record, is funny, smart, kind, and a stunner of a woman. That girl needs you to embrace her and love her."

"But she was weak," Mel said. "You know, I realized when I got older that I wasn't bullied because I was overweight — okay, I was — but it was more because I was sensitive. The bullies enjoyed torturing me because they knew they would get a response. They knew they could make me cry. I was such a target because my feelings were so easily hurt."

"I'm so sorry that happened to you, and I would go back in time and save you from that if I could," he said. "Even if you hadn't wanted me to. But that sensitive girl, that shy young lady who was so easily hurt, she's one of the reasons I love you."

Mel rolled her eyes. She knew a bunch of bologna when she heard it.

"Hear me out," Joe said. "You are a beautiful woman, and I've thought that for a very long time, even before you and Angie teamed up to open the bakery and I had an excuse to see you every day."

The love in his warm brown eyes made Mel's heart pound triple time. Only Joe had ever been able to do that. He took her hand in his and laced their fingers together.

"But it's not the pretty package that made me fall completely, stupidly, can't-breathe-without-you in love with you," he said.

"Really?" Mel's voice was high and tight and she had to clear her throat and say again, "Really?"

"Mel, I've watched you throw yourself in harm's way repeatedly to help people of all sorts," he said. "You hired Oz, a scary-looking teen, and Marty, a cranky old man, and you've taken on all six of my brothers when it was warranted. You give so much of yourself to everyone who meets you and you do it with humor and grace and kindness. You are one of the most amazing people I've ever met and no mean girl from your high school days will ever change my opinion of you. Clear?"

Mel felt a grin burst across her face. "Crystal."

"Good, now let's go show them who's who and what's what," he said. He climbed out of the car and walked around it to get

Mel's door.

She took one moment to glance up at the sky and say, "Dad, I know you've been gone more than ten years and I don't know if you have any sway with the forces above, but if you could just make sure I don't humiliate myself tonight that would be totally rad. Love you." She kissed the tips of her fingers and touched the roof of the car.

Charlie Cooper, her larger-than-life dad, had passed away when Mel was fresh out of college. There was not a day that went by that she didn't feel the lack of his bear hugs and booming laugh and she knew if it was at all possible, he would keep her from falling on her face tonight. Feeling marginally better, she took Joe's hand as he helped her out of the car.

Mel had spent the better part of the day at the beauty salon. Her short blond hair had been poofed, fake eyelashes attached, and smoky eye applied. She was as ready as she'd ever be. She'd even splurged on a blue Shoshanna midi cocktail dress in floral guipure lace, which accentuated her figure and made her feel as if she cleaned up okay. Strappy sandals and a small black clutch completed the look. The narrow heels made walking a challenge and she was happy to have Joe's arm to lean on.

"Come on, gorgeous, I want to go show off my girl," he said.

Mel giggled, actually giggled — it was mortifying — but she let him lead her up the stairs and into the resort.

Tate and Angie were waiting for them. Angie raced forward, wearing a darling red cocktail dress and platform stilettos.

"Oh, thank goodness," she said. "I was just getting ready to text you. I thought you might have decided to ghost."

"I might still," Mel said. She hugged her friend. "But I'm here for now. You look fantastic, by the way."

"Me?" Angie asked. "Look at you. Wowsie wow wow."

Mel laughed. She glanced at Tate. Like Joe, he was in a dark suit, which made him look like a grown-up, but the mischievous glint was still in his eye when he said, " 'That is so fetch!' "

" 'Gretchen, stop trying to make "fetch" happen. It's not going to happen!' " Mel retorted.

"*Mean Girls,*" Angie identified the movie quotes. She looked at her husband. "How appropriate."

Tate shrugged. "I thought so."

Mel hugged Angie and then Tate. When she was close enough, she whispered in his ear, "Speaking of mean girls, have you seen her yet?"

"Cassidy?" he asked. He gave her a mock look of horror. "No, not yet. Maybe we'll get lucky and she won't be here."

"Oh, she'll be here," Mel said. "She's probably been waiting for this night since we graduated. It's another opportunity to put on her tiara and lord it over the rest of us."

"Who are you two whispering about?" Angie asked.

"Code name: Regina George," Tate said.

"Oh, you mean Cassi—" Angie began but he interrupted.

"What is the point of having a code name for her if you go and use her real name?" he asked.

"Are you talking about Cassidy somebody or other?" Joe asked.

Angie gasped. "How do you know about her?"

"Mel told me," he said.

"You told him?" Angie went wide-eyed. "About how she wrote your name and number in all of the boys' bathrooms?"

"What?" Joe's head whipped toward Mel.

"I didn't get into the particulars," Mel said to Angie. Then she looked at Joe. "It wasn't that bad. My brother, Charlie, took

35

care of it."

"Did he?"

"Yes, he apparently scribbled out my number and then wrote odes to Cassidy's generosity with her charms and included her phone number. My dad raised his allowance for that one," Mel said.

"I knew I liked him," Joe said. But his lips were tight and Mel knew he hated that she had been bullied in school. She wrapped an arm around his waist and rested her head on his shoulder.

"I'm okay," she said. "Really. I have you and Tate and Angie. Plus, our cupcakes look amazing. Let's go see them, then if it's weird we can skedaddle."

"Sounds like a plan," Joe said.

They began to walk toward the registration table. Mel was halfway across the floor when she caught a glimpse of red hair out of the corner of her eye. Some survival instinct must have kicked in because she turned toward Joe.

"What is it, cupcake? You have a weird look on your face," he said.

"Weird?" she asked. "Must be allergies."

"Mel, what's going on?" he asked.

"Oh my god, is that you?" a shrill voice cried across the crowded lobby. Had Cassidy's voice always been that screechy? Mel couldn't remember. "It *is* you! Angie De-Laura, well, look at you. You haven't changed a bit. You're just as short as ever."

There was a beat of silence. Mel guessed that Angie was trying to decide if this was a compliment or not. Given the source, Mel was betting not.

"Neither have you," Angie said. The disdain in her voice left no doubt that it wasn't a compliment.

"And, Tate, you're still hanging out with little Angie? Isn't that precious?" Cassidy asked.

"Well, given that she's my wife, yes, I'd say it is very precious," he said.

Mel smiled. The warmth and affection in Tate's voice was the perfect bucket of dirty water to be tossed onto the wicked witch.

"Huh, if I remember right, you always traveled in the threesome," Cassidy said. "Where's your third? What was her name? You know, the big girl?"

Her voice was getting louder as she came closer. Mel felt her chest get tight as she realized Cassidy Havers-Griffin was closing in. She looped her arm through Joe's and tried to tug him out of the lobby, but he was busy getting their name tags from Brittany Nilsson at the sign-in table. Brittany was gushing over Joe like he was the president of their class instead of the one four years ahead of theirs.

"I remember you, Joe DeLaura. Go Devils!" Brittany cheered.

"Are you ready, honey?" Mel asked him. "We should go."

"Sure, just a second. I'm still looking for your name tag," he said.

Mel glanced at the table in front of them. It was massive and it was covered with badges. They could be here all night and the enemy was closing in!

"That's okay," she said. She forced a bright smile. "I don't need one."

"Everybody needs one," Brittany said. She tucked her chin-length black hair behind her ear and gave Mel a flat stare. Brittany was short and sturdy and barked orders a lot, more like a tank commander than the leader of the pep squad, or so Mel had always thought. "How will people know who you are if —"

"Are you kidding me? I know who she is!" A man jostled up next to Mel. He smelled of beer as he thrust his buzz-cut head and lantern jaw into her personal space. "Give me an M!"

"Oh, god," Mel said. She blinked. It had been years but she'd know that deep voice anywhere. "Dwight Pickard."

"Give me an E!" he cried. "Hey, Cassidy, look who's here!"

With a squeal, the tall redhead who'd been talking to Angie and Tate approached. Mel closed her eyes for a moment, hoping that this wouldn't be as horrible as she feared and wishing she had a cupcake or four in her hand to help her get through it.

"Is that — ?" Cassidy asked. Her long red hair was as smooth as water and it flowed around her shoulders like liquid fire. Her big bazooms and button nose were the same, as was her tall, tiny-waisted figure. She was wearing false eyelashes and her makeup was a bit on the heavy side, but otherwise Cassidy Havers looked exactly the same. She even wore the same vibrant pink lipstick she'd worn in high school. Mel felt as if she was time-warping back to the absolute worst days of her life.

Cassidy peered at her with a narrowed gaze. She leaned back and studied Mel, then she moved around her and checked her out from every angle. It made Mel feel vulnerable. She half expected Cassidy to pants her, or worse.

"Well, well, well, can you believe it, Dwight?" Cassidy asked her longtime partner in bullying. "It looks like Melephant finally tried a diet that worked. Honestly,

Mel, I didn't recognize you. I mean where is the rest of you? What are you, a fourth or a fifth of the size you used to be?"

"A tenth," Dwight said and then laughed.

Mel felt her throat get tight. This. This right here was exactly what she'd been dreading. That feeling of being made to feel worthless, ugly, rejected. Oh, how she hated it.

A pair of arms slipped around her from behind. Joe. He pulled her back against his front, lowered his head, and propped his chin on her shoulder. He eyed Cassidy and Dwight with one eyebrow raised as if he had no idea who they were but was quite certain they weren't important.

"Hey, cupcake," he said loud enough for everyone to hear him. "They made a mistake on your name tag."

"They did?" Mel asked. She was half afraid he was going to slap a badge on her that read *Melephant.* She saw Cassidy watching them through suspicious eyes.

"Yeah, they put you down as Melanie Cooper and not as Mrs. Joe-DeLaura-to-be," he said. "Clearly an oversight. I want the entire world to know how lucky I am that you've finally agreed to be my wife."

Then he kissed her. It wasn't a friendly kiss, either. It was full of passion, affection, and love. If high-school Mel had known this moment was waiting for her through all of the bullying, she would have gone through it all with a smile just to get here to this moment.

When he pulled back, she blinked at him and said, "I love you so much."

"Marry me *right now,*" he said.

Mel burst out laughing. Ever since Tate and Angie had gotten married, Joe had been teasing her daily with random "let's get married *right now*" suggestions. One of these days, she was going to shock him and say yes.

"Whoa, whoa, whoa. Let me get this straight." Cassidy held up two perfectly manicured hands in a stop gesture. "You two are together, as in a couple?" She glanced at her bestie, the same one she'd had in high school, Megan Mareez, who had just arrived, and asked, "Did you know about this?"

"About what?"

"Mele . . . Melanie Cooper is dating Joe DeLaura," Cassidy said. She waved her hand at them as if Megan might have missed them.

"We're engaged, actually," Mel said. She patted Joe's arm with her left hand, making sure her ring was visible, while she relished every stinking syllable.

"It's true. You could say I'm 'the rest of her,' " Joe said. "The less beautiful, less brainy part of her." Mel glanced at his face. The look he cast Cassidy was positively glacial.

"Well, that's — I mean — how — but you —" Cassidy's ability to speak left her but the look of disgust on her face was pretty easy to interpret.

"Congratulations? Is that what you're trying to say?" Joe offered. "Thank you." Then he kissed Mel again. Out of the corner of her eye, she saw Cassidy storm away, the points of her heels punching into the wooden floor as she went.

"That's wonderful news," Megan said. She stepped forward and squeezed Mel's hand. "I'm very happy for you both."

Tall and slender with black hair that hung halfway down her back, Megan was a beautiful woman. In high school, she had been Cassidy's best friend but if Mel remembered right, Megan was the one person in Cassidy's pack who didn't just follow. She'd even comforted Mel a time or two when Cassidy's bullying was just too much. Mel had always wondered why Megan had hung out with the other woman.

"Megan, are you coming or what?" Cassidy snapped from across the lobby.

Megan cast them a sheepish glance. "Excuse me."

"Of course," Mel said.

"See you around, Mele—" Whatever Dwight had been about to say was stopped by a glare from Joe. He didn't follow Megan and Cassidy but turned and headed for the bar.

As they watched Cassidy storm off, Joe leaned down and whispered in Mel's ear, "I don't think I've ever wanted to hit a woman as much as I wanted to slug that Cassidy woman. She's a nightmare."

"Truly," Mel said. "But you handled her brilliantly." Then she rose up on her toes and kissed him. It was supposed to be swift and sweet but Joe had other ideas.

"All right, all right, enough with the canoodling, you two," Tate said. "We're the newlyweds here. That's our job."

"Yes, but that's my sister," Joe said. "No canoodling for you."

"All right then, let's drink," Tate said. "Beers for the gents and what for the ladies?"

"Champagne," Angie said. She linked her arm through Mel's. "We're celebrating."

"We are?" Mel asked. She looked at her friend in confusion.

43

"Yes," Angie said. "The day Melanie Cooper broke out of her cocoon and became a beautiful butterfly."

Mel looked at her three nearest and dearest. Then she smiled. "All right, I'll drink to that. You know, Ange, I think you were right. I think this may just be one of the best nights of my life."

THREE

Mel and Angie staked out one of the tall tables by the wall while Tate and Joe elbowed their way up to the bar.

"Fifteen years, can you believe it?" Angie asked. She scanned the room. "Look, there's Rachel Gunderson."

Mel looked in the direction Angie indicated but she didn't see Rachel anywhere. "I'm not seeing her."

"Stop looking for her head gear," Angie said. "She's in the green dress with the really cute shoes, and she's got her hair up in a ball on her head."

"Oh, there she is." Mel spotted her. "You're right, the shoes are super cute."

"Oh, look!" Angie said as she saw someone behind Mel. Then she grabbed Mel's hand and held her still. "No, scratch that. Don't look."

"Okay? Help me out. Who am I not looking at?"

"Danny Griffin," Angie said.

Regardless of Angie's hold, Mel's head whipped around in the direction Angie had been looking.

"Oh, wow, he looks terrible," Mel said.

"What?" Angie asked.

"I mean look at him, he's all saggy and sad," Mel said. She studied the man in the gray suit leaning against the bar. His hair was thinning and he had a serious paunch hanging over his belt. What had happened to her teenage heartthrob? This was just depressing. "I thought he was a newscaster for some sports channel. Shouldn't he be more polished than that? Oh, gees, I'd better ask Joe to make my drink a double."

"But —" Angie began but Mel interrupted.

"I mean, how did the hottest guy in our class fall apart like that in fifteen years?" she asked. "Do you know how many times I wanted to kiss him while I was tutoring him in English? Too many to count and now, oh, it's just sad to see how he's unraveled."

"Um, that's not Danny at the bar," Angie said.

"It's not?"

"No, that's Wayne Pillock."

"Oh, hey, that makes sense," Mel said. "He looks just like his dad, the track coach, remember?" She turned around to face Angie and came nose to necktie with a very tall man. She slowly lifted her head as she glanced up and felt her tongue get stuck on the roof of her mouth.

"And this, right here, would be Danny Griffin," Angie said. Her words came out a breathy sigh because Danny, unlike Wayne, looked ah-mazing.

His sandy blond hair still fell over his forehead in a thick wave. His pale blue eyes sparkled with laughter and a touch of mischief. The dimple in his right cheek when he smiled was there winking at Mel just like it did when they were teens, and he still had his basketball player's body: long, lean, and all muscle. Oh, dear.

"Hi," Mel said. She tried to think of something else to say, but this had been about all she had ever managed to say to Danny other than explaining how to diagram a sentence. She was just relieved she was actually able to say *hi* and not *ger-duh-ugh* or some other equally embarrassing unintelligible sounds.

"Melanie Cooper." Danny grinned at her. Ack, there was the dimple again! "It's been forever."

She nodded, as she was still trying to unstick her tongue.

"Come here," he said. He opened his arms wide for a hug and Mel stepped into his embrace as naturally as breathing. She caught a whiff of a scent that was pure Danny, a citrusy smell with subtle notes of sandalwood and leather. Divine. How many times had she sat next to him just breathing in his scent because it made her dizzy? Too many to count.

When he finally let her go, he said, "You look as beautiful as ever."

And that was the thing with Danny Griffin — she really believed he meant it. He had been unfailingly kind to everyone in high school even when he was a star athlete and could have been a real jerk. It was one of the many reasons why she couldn't believe he had actually married Cassidy Havers. She had always believed he would end up with someone better than that.

A slow song started to play, and Mel expected Danny to make an excuse and beat a hasty retreat to go find his wife. Instead, he held out his hand to her and said, "Come dance with me."

A million high school daydreams had started and ended with Danny Griffin asking her to dance. Mel stared stupidly at him until she felt a hard shove to her back. She glanced behind her and saw Angie making a shooing motion with her hands.

"Have fun, kids," Angie said. "Don't worry. I'll hold the table."

Mel would have protested but Danny was already taking her hand and leading her onto the dance floor. There had been so many high school dances spent in the shadows with Tate and Angie, watching from the bleachers as Danny danced with Cassidy. Mel had always wondered what it would be like to feel his hand on her waist as he pulled her close and rested his cheek on her hair. And now here she was. Incredible.

The DJ was playing "Someone Like You" by Adele, and Mel could hear the poignancy of her voice as she crooned about long-lost love. She knew she couldn't have picked a better song to dance to with Danny. No, she hadn't been in love with Danny, but she had sure crushed hard. She felt as if everything was coming full circle. She was here, engaged to the love of her life, while enjoying a dance with the heartbreaker of her graduating class. Again, she wished fifteen-year-old her could have known this was going to happen. She would have sailed through high school with much less angst.

"Tell me, Mel, what have you been doing for the past fifteen years?" Danny asked.

49

Mel wondered if he was just being polite or if he really wanted to know. Her thoughts must have been clear on her face, because he said, "Yes, I really want to know."

She laughed and he grinned. "Okay, well, I went to college in LA, then did the corporate thing, which was awful. So I quit and went to culinary school in Paris and opened up my own bakery with my friends Tate Harper and Angie DeLaura-Harper. Now we're franchising all over the United States. It's pretty awesome. But the best part of my life is that I'm engaged to Joe DeLaura, which is amazing because I've had a crush on him since I was twelve."

"What?" Danny looked shocked. "I thought I was the guy you were crushing on in school."

Mel gave him a look that was part embarrassment and part worry that she'd offended him.

"I'm sorry," she said. "But Joe is . . . Joe."

Her face must have softened when she said his name because Danny grinned at her and said, "Aw, Mel, I'm just teasing you. I mean, Joe DeLaura was a god on the basketball court. Who wouldn't want to marry him? Besides, I know you never liked me that way."

"Didn't like you that way?" she cried. "I

totally did."

"But you never spoke to me unless it was directions about what we were studying," he said. "You were quite the taskmaster. I thought you thought I was just a big dumb jock."

"No!" Mel protested. "Not at all. You were lovely."

Danny made a face. "Lovely? That makes me sound like a total loser."

Mel laughed. "Hardly, Mr. Championship Shot at the Buzzer, no less."

"Well, there is that," he said. He twirled her around the floor a bit more. "It's cold comfort but I'll take it." He studied her face. "I'm really very happy for you, Mel. You deserve the best guy in the world."

"Thank you," she said. "And no worries, I found him."

A shadow passed over his face. It was gone so fast, Mel wasn't even sure she saw it and then he said, "Make sure you hang on to him then. When you find the one, you don't ever want to let them go."

"I will," she said. She wanted to ask him what he meant. It sounded as if there was so much more to it than he was letting on, but she didn't push it. "What's happening in your life now? I heard you're a local sportscaster on the news. That has to be thrilling."

"It is, but I'd rather be a player," Danny said. His look was rueful but then he forced a smile and said, "Not that I'm complaining. After I blew out my knee in my fifth season with the Phoenix Suns, I thought I'd never work in sports at all, so I'm thrilled to be a part of it even if it's from the sidelines."

They smiled at each other and Mel was amazed at how equal the footing felt between them now. And it wasn't because he wasn't the star basketball player anymore or because she had lost weight since the last time he'd seen her, but rather they were grown-ups, doing interesting things and living their best lives. It felt . . . nice.

"So, when is the wedding?" he asked. "The groom looks ready."

He tipped his head to the side and Mel saw Joe standing on the edge of the dance floor, chatting with Brittany Nilsson. Well, Brittany was chatting; Joe was sipping his drink and watching Mel. Their eyes met and he toasted her with his glass. It took everything Mel had to keep dancing with Danny and not leave him on the floor to go to her guy.

"We haven't pinned down the date exactly," Mel said. "Trying to work around both of our schedules has been challenging."

"I know what you mean," he said. "When Cassidy and I got married, we had to wedge it in between games and my time on the road. I swear we had fifteen minutes to pull the whole thing off."

"How long have you been married?" Mel asked.

"It'll be six years in a few months," he said.

"Wow." And because she couldn't stop herself, Mel asked, "Cassidy, huh?" She just had to know what Danny saw in her that Mel didn't. Surely, he was beyond the curves and perky nose by now.

"Yup," he said. He nodded and for the briefest moment, a nanosecond really, Mel saw regret in his eyes as surely as she could see the dimple in his cheek when he pushed down whatever he was feeling and forced a smile and said, "Helluva gal, that Cassidy. You know, she stood by me when I was injured and my whole life seemed to be over. I'll always be grateful for that."

It was clear that was his story and he was sticking to it. Mel would have let it go — she should have let it go — but she couldn't.

"Are you happy, Danny?" she asked. "Being married to her?"

"Sure," he said. "I mean I'm on the road a lot, so it's hard on her. She gets lonely and a little . . . angry. I tried to tell her when we got married that this was my life, but I don't think she really understood. When I got picked up to cover baseball season, too, well, I don't think marriage to a man who was always gone was exactly the life she'd pictured for herself."

"So, things are complicated?" Mel asked.

Danny looked at her and a grin split his face. "That's it exactly. Leave it to you, Mel, to know just how to say what my life is right now. *Complicated* covers it."

Mel grinned back at him. Truly, with his Hollywood good looks, a woman would have to be in a coma not to respond.

"Stop it!" a voice snapped. "Just stop it right now, Melephant."

Two arms were thrust in between Danny and Mel, shoving them apart. Mel stepped back in surprise. Danny didn't look surprised at all.

"Cassidy, I was dancing with Mel," he said. He looked supremely annoyed.

"Why?" Cassidy snapped. "Why would you dance with *that*?" She waved her arms in the air as if she was gesturing to an enormous wooly mammoth in the middle of the dance floor. Mel crossed her arms and one eyebrow ticked up higher than the other. Enough was enough.

"I'm not a *that*, I'm a *who*," Mel said. Looked like her days tutoring English weren't done.

"No one is talking to you, Mele—"

"Stop," Danny said. "Do *not* call her that ever again. Mel is my friend. You will not bully her. You promised me that you would behave tonight. I won't listen to you call her or anyone else names. Honestly, that childish behavior is beneath you."

Cassidy's lip curled and she mimicked Dan's words in a high-pitched, squeaky voice. " 'Mel is my friend.' Listen to you. What happened to the basketball star I married? He was the most popular boy in school. Now look at you. You spend your nights reporting about others doing what you can't anymore. My god, you're a waste of space."

FOUR

Mel gasped. There was a level of viciousness in Cassidy's words that sucked all of the air out of the room like a flash of fire. Two bright red patches of color highlighted Danny's cheekbones and he glared at his wife.

"How much have you had to drink?" he asked. "I asked you not to do that tonight."

"Whatever," she snapped. "You're not the boss of me." She tossed her red hair and turned back to Mel with a scowl. "You need to go sit in a corner where you belong. No one wants you here and you'd better stay away from my man. If I catch you near him again, I'll —"

"Be overly dramatic and ridiculous?" Mel asked. She looked Cassidy up and down. She could see it now, the drunkenness. Cassidy wobbled on her feet. Her eyes had a glaze to them and her pink lipstick was smeared. She looked, frankly, a bit rough.

"Why, you —" Cassidy started toward her with her claws extended.

Danny made a grab for Cassidy but she slipped past him. Mel dodged to the right and slammed up against a solid chest. She glanced up. Joe.

"Hey, cupcake, I was looking for you," he said. "Come on, let's dance."

He led her into the shelter of his arms away from Cassidy, and Mel leaned against him, relieved. "Thanks."

"Hey, hey!" Cassidy shouted at them. She gestured wildly from herself to Mel. "This isn't over. It's not over until I say it's over!"

Mel stopped and turned around to face the woman who had made her teen years so horribly unbearable. Cassidy was a drunken, shallow, vain caricature of a person and she couldn't harm Mel, not anymore.

"You're wrong, Cassidy," Mel said. "It *is* over, because you can't hurt me anymore. You simply don't matter to me."

With that, she turned back into Joe's arms and he whisked her away. They danced until the song ended. Mel could feel everyone's eyes go from her to Cassidy and back again. She didn't care. She tipped her chin up and focused on Joe.

"That's my girl," he said. "Sorry you had to deal with that."

Mel shrugged. "Don't feel sorry for me, I'm not the one who married her." She shuddered.

Joe nodded. "He seems like a nice guy, but his taste in women, oof, is not so good."

"Agreed."

As they left the dance floor, Angie stood on tiptoe and waved them over to the table. She and Tate were holding the real estate, as tables were hard to come by in this venue.

"What happened?" Angie asked. "What did that viper say? Do I need to go punch her in the mouth?"

"Nothing," Mel said. "Nothing important, at any rate, and no. There will be no punching."

"I have to agree with Mel there," Tate said. "No punching, much as I love your feisty side."

Angie narrowed her eyes and studied Mel's face. "Did she make you cry? Are you going to cry? If she did, if you do, I am absolutely punching her, I don't care what you say."

Mel laughed and hugged her friend hard. "No, she didn't. In fact, I just had the most cathartic reunion moment. I looked her right in the eye and told her she couldn't hurt me anymore because she simply didn't matter to me." Mel sighed. "It was glorious."

"And she's got me, keeping watch," Joe said. "Don't worry. 'No one puts Baby in a corner.' "

"Ah!" Angie cried. "My brother did not just quote *Dirty Dancing.* "

"Oh, yes, I did," he said. He buffed his nails on his suit coat and then blew on them.

"Not bad, newbie," Tate said to Joe. Then he looked at Mel and added, "You have been such a good influence on him."

"I try," she said. She turned to Joe. "That was beautifully executed, hon."

He gave her a half bow. "Just for you."

"All right, let's get 'em up and get 'em down," Tate said. He handed out the cocktails that were waiting on the table. "To old friends, best friends, and new friends."

"Here, here." They clinked glasses and sipped their beverages.

"Okay, so while you were taking on the class bully, I was gathering the scoop on our classmates," Angie said.

"Isn't that what social media is for?" Mel asked.

"Please, that's all lies and image crafting. It should be called Fakebook. No one's life is as good as they make it seem," Angie said. "But here I got the dish, the dirt, the poop, the skinny, the goss—"

"All right, I get it," Mel said. She took a sip of her drink. It was a fruity concoction with some kick. "Lay it on me."

"Okay, so, do you remember Tiffany Peterson?" Angie asked.

"Yeah, she was in my Algebra class," Mel said. "Really smart but super shy."

"Well, you won't believe it, but she is now . . ."

Angie's voice faded to the background as Mel's gaze strayed to Cassidy and Danny. They were still standing on the edge of the dance floor. Cassidy was hissing through her teeth and waving her arms wildly. Dan looked like he wanted to run far, far away. His teeth were gritted and his head hung down in defeat. It made Mel sad to see him that way.

Cassidy leaned in close and snarled something at Danny. It must have been particularly nasty because his head shot up and there was a fierce light in his eyes. For a second, Mel was sure he was going to take her drink out of her hand and dump it on her head.

"Can you believe it?" Angie asked. "And then how about Erin Highsmith? She is doing so well in New York . . ."

"Wow, really?" Mel said. She nodded and

gave Angie her most attentive face while she tried desperately to hear what was being said between Cassidy and Danny. Curse this DJ and his loud music. She glanced back at them to see Dan shaking his head while Cassidy wagged a finger in his face.

"And then there's Kristie Hill," Angie was saying. This brought Mel's attention back. The Kristie-Cassidy scandal had been huge during their senior year.

"Is she here?" Mel asked.

"Oh, yeah," Angie said. "Over there."

She pointed at a table across the room from theirs. Mel glanced that way. Sure enough, there was Kristie Hill with two of her friends. She looked the same with her long dark hair and curvy figure.

"Have any words been exchanged?" Mel asked.

"Not that I know of," Angie said. She leaned close and said, "But I heard from Tami Cohen that Kristie was planning to snatch the crown right off Cassidy's head if they invited her up on stage as the homecoming queen tonight. Apparently, Kristie is still rather bitter about the crowning debacle at homecoming our senior year."

"No way," Mel said. She looked at Kristie, who was looking at Cassidy, who was still fighting with Danny.

Kristie's eyes were narrowed and she looked like she was ready to brawl. Mel couldn't blame her. During homecoming their senior year, Kristie was supposed to be crowned homecoming queen but there was an envelope "mix-up" and Cassidy was crowned instead. By the time they did a recount, the principal had decided to let Cassidy keep the title. Kristie had raged about it for the rest of the year.

If Kristie went after Cassidy, well, Mel did not want to miss a second of that. She turned her attention back to Cassidy and Danny. It was not going well. Cassidy was red in the face and it looked as if she was ripping Danny a new one. For his part, he was staring over her head at some distant point as if he was trying to find a happy place.

Just when it looked like Cassidy was going to throw a punch or her drink at him, Tucker Booth arrived and grabbed her arm, amazingly keeping her drink in the glass. Cassidy glared at him, but Tucker wasn't deterred.

Tucker was the class smarty pants and he looked the part. He had short-cropped, tightly curled light brown hair, rectangular dark-framed glasses, and pants that never seemed to fit him quite right even though the crease in the front looked lethally sharp. He had spent all of high school following Cassidy around like a lovesick puppy, managing all of the sticky situations she got herself into like he was her personal assistant. He didn't look like a puppy now. Instead, he was shaking his head at her, the expression on his face clearly one of disapproval. Maybe some people did manage to grow out of their crushes.

Mel glanced back at Tate and Joe. The sight of Joe laughing at something Tate had said made her insides flutter. Nope, she was never getting over this crush. Not ever.

"And then here is the best gossip of all," Angie said. "Tucker Booth, remember him?"

Mel turned her attention back to Angie and pointed to the dance floor where Tucker was escorting Cassidy to a table on the opposite side of the room, thank god. Dan followed behind them, looking depressed.

"That Tucker?" she asked.

"Yes! Him! Are you ready?" Angie asked. "Tucker is a webpage designer for high-tech companies in Palo Alto, including labs that were researching cures for cancer, and he's dating that supermodel over there!"

"Supermodel?" Mel's head snapped in the direction Angie pointed. The woman was easy to spot as she stood over the crowd by four inches, easy. Naturally tall, she was wearing platform spike heels that added five inches to her height. That, plus the black leather dress she was rocking and her long waterfall of glorious raven hair made her impossible to miss. "Dang, she's fine."

"Right?" Angie asked. "I'm so glad I'm married now. Can you imagine being out on the market and having to compete with women like that?"

"Um, still not married yet," Mel said.

"Well, you might want to get on that, I'm just saying," Angie said.

"Agreed," Mel said. She glanced back at Tucker, Danny, and Cassidy. Tucker had his hands on his hips, giving Dan the business. Cassidy wobbled behind him. It was clear from the way Tucker was defending her that he was putting the blame squarely on Danny. Mel felt bad for Tucker. Despite having the most gorgeous woman in the world on his arm, he was still following around the popular kids and managing their business.

Mel glanced around the room. So many of her classmates seemed hung up on their glory days. She did a little self-assessment. Maybe facing down Cassidy had been worth all of the angst of this night, because suddenly none of this mattered. She was happy, successful, and her life was full of people she loved, who loved her in return. What more could a woman want?

She wasn't living in the past. She was full-on looking forward to the future, which promised more culinary adventures, opening even more franchises, and the cherry on top — marrying Joe.

"Hey, Cooper, I gotta say — great cupcakes," Dwight Pickard said through a mouthful of cupcake. He was two fisting, one in each hand, and the grin he sent her made him look like a little kid embarking on a fabulous sugar rush.

"Thanks," Mel said.

She had outdone herself on the cupcakes. She knew it. The school colors were black and gold so she had made a variety of cupcake flavors and then topped them with buttercream, over which she had rolled a smooth black fondant, which was decorated with edible glittery gold fifteens. Set up in an enormous tower, they looked spec-freaking-tacular.

Angie nudged her with an elbow. "Looks like you're a hit."

"We're a hit," Mel said. "None of this would be possible if you and Tate hadn't jumped in when I said I was going to open a cupcake bakery."

"Yeah, you're right," she said. "You totally would have failed without us." Then she rolled her eyes and shook her head, letting Mel know what she really thought of that.

Mel laughed and then asked, "Do you feel like you got to strut your stuff enough?"

Angie nodded. "Yes, I do, and it was everything I'd hoped it would be."

"It was, wasn't it?" Mel asked. She glanced around the room one more time. "I don't know about you, but I think I'm done here. I'm going home now."

"So soon?" Angie asked.

"Yes," she said. "I really don't think this night can get any better; plus, I miss Captain Jack and Peanut."

"Those pets have you wrapped around their little paws," Angie said.

"Absolutely," Mel said. "But Joe is even worse with them."

"I know." Angie laughed. "He shows their pictures like they're his kids. Hilarious."

Mel hugged her friend and said, "Thanks for making me come. See you at work tomorrow."

"Bright and early," Angie said.

Mel joined Joe and Tate, and when their conversation paused she looked at Joe and asked, "You ready to go?"

"It's your show," he said. "Whatever you want is fine with me."

She leaned into him and gave him a smile that she hoped read like an invitation. "Let's go home."

Joe dropped his drink on the table and patted Tate on the shoulder. "Good seeing you, bro. Gotta go."

Tate laughed. He hugged Mel while Joe hugged Angie. As they walked to the door, Joe paused by the bar to pay his tab and Mel took the opportunity to use the restroom. She wanted to freshen up, or more accurately, wash the dust of this place off.

She pushed into the women's room, relieved to find there was no line. The lighting was low and the restroom posh, with floor-to-ceiling mirrors, a sitting area that included a lounge chair, and stalls with doors that also ran from floor to ceiling, offering complete privacy. Mel would have enjoyed those back in high school. If she'd needed a cry she could have been assured that no one would peek under or over and then blab to the whole school that she was bawling her eyes out because of something Cassidy had done.

She shook her head. Nope, nope, nope. She wasn't going to think about that stuff anymore. She was done with high school and all of the bad memories that came with it. Now she would focus only on the good.

Mel passed through the sitting area. It was empty. Wait. She saw a foot sticking out from the lounge chair. She circled around it. Cassidy Havers-Griffin was sprawled on the lounger, looking like she was taking a power nap with a cupcake in one hand and her lipstick in the other. Mel froze. If Cassidy woke up and saw her, she had no doubt that the woman would start up again, and Mel was not going to be involved in another scene. No way, no how.

She took one step back. Cassidy didn't move. She took another. No response. And another. She took two more steps back. She was almost at the door. Freedom beckoned. She could still escape.

Mel turned around and slammed right into Brittany Nilsson. The tiny woman caught Mel in her surprisingly strong arms when Mel pitched backwards. Brittany looked her up and down.

"Are you all right?"

"Yeah, thanks," Mel said. She saw Lianne Marsten standing behind Brittany. "Hi."

"Hi, Mel," Lianne said. "Great cupcakes."

"Thanks."

"You really outdid yourself," Brittany said. She plowed past Mel and strode into the lounge area. Mel cringed, hoping that Cassidy didn't wake up from all of the noise. Brittany wasn't known for her quiet voice.

"Hey, Cassidy's here," Brittany said. "Did you know she was here?"

"I just saw her when I came in," Mel said. "I think she's taking a power nap."

"I don't think that's allowed," Lianne said. "The resort people will want her to get a room if she's sleeping."

"Hey, Cassidy, wake up," Brittany said. Cassidy didn't respond. "So rude."

Brittany strode up to her and reached out to tap her on the shoulder. "Cassidy, wake up."

"I think she had a bit too much to drink," Mel said. She gestured to the empty drink glass on the floor beside her.

"You think?" Lianne asked. "She got busted for a DUI six months ago. Danny had to take her car away when she refused to quit drinking. He was worried that her drunk driving would get someone killed. Of course, it would destroy his career, too."

"Honestly, the woman is the homecoming queen of our class — and married to the homecoming king," Brittany said. She tossed her chin-length black hair to get it out of her face. "You'd think she'd show some self-respect."

"I'm just going to go . . ." Mel said. She didn't want to be there when they roused the bear.

"Cassidy!" Brittany clapped her hands in Cassidy's face. Sharp, cracking noises that made Mel jump. Still there was no response. No jump start. Nothing.

Mel frowned. Even a drunk could be roused a little. This seemed like it was more than an alcoholic stupor.

"Cassidy." Brittany patted her face, and then snatched her hand back and looked at Lianne. "She feels weird."

"Weird how?" Lianne asked.

"Cold, like, really cold," Brittany said. She reached down and shook Cassidy by the shoulder. Both the cupcake and the lipstick slipped from Cassidy's hands and fell onto the carpet at her feet. Brittany jumped back. In a voice that could have raised the departed, she shrieked, "She's dead! Cassidy Havers is dead!"

FIVE

"No." Mel shook her head. "That's not possible. I just saw her outside."

Lianne hurried around the couch. She put her ear to Cassidy's chest. She then put her fingers on Cassidy's neck where her pulse would be. "She's not breathing. There's no pulse or heartbeat. Brittany's right. She's dead."

Mel felt as if her tongue suddenly swelled in her mouth. This was not happening. No, no, no, no, no. She had to get out of here. She had to call her uncle Stan. She had to find Joe. She turned and ran for the door, digging her phone out of her purse as she went.

Joe was standing just outside the ladies' room waiting for her. Something like sheer panic must have shown on her face because he grabbed her by the arms and pulled her into a bracing hug. It was just like the hugs her late father used to give her and was one of the many reasons she loved her man.

"What happened? Are you all right?" he asked. He released her and studied her face.

"Nope, not all right. Cassidy is dead," Mel said. "I went into the bathroom and I thought she was passed out but then Brittany and Lianne came in and tried to wake her. Oh my god, I mean I couldn't stand her but I certainly wouldn't wish this on anyone."

"Are you sure she's dead?" he asked.

"Positive."

Joe took the phone out of Mel's hand and put it back in her purse. He reached inside his jacket pocket and pulled out his own phone, thumbing the display and holding it up to his ear.

"Stan, it's Joe," he said. "We have a situation. I'm at Mel's high school reunion at the resort and one of her classmates was just discovered dead."

There was a pause and Mel tried to hear what her uncle Stan, who was a detective in the Scottsdale PD and a long-time friend of Joe's, was saying. She could only hear bluster but not any words coming out of the phone.

"Well, yeah, it was Mel who found her," Joe said. He reached down and took Mel's hand in his and squeezed. The volume on the other end of the phone increased but Mel still couldn't understand what Stan was saying. Probably for the best.

"Yeah, we'll be here," Joe said. "Thank you."

Mel studied his face. It looked grim. "What's happening?"

"Uncle Stan is on his way and he alerted dispatch to send over any cars they have in the area. In the meantime, we need to keep everyone out of the bathroom," Joe said. "Whether she died of natural causes or not, the scene is to stay as untouched as possible."

"You!" Brittany came rocketing out of the bathroom. She saw Mel and pointed a stubby finger at her. "You were in there with her. What happened? Did she call you *Melephant* one too many times and you killed her?"

"No!" Mel cried. "I would never."

"I'm going to have a look," Joe said. He moved toward the door but Brittany held up her arm, blocking the entrance.

"Step aside, please," he said. "I'm a county prosecutor and as such I'm an officer of the court."

"Yeah, and you're also her fiancé," Lianne said. She moved so that she flanked Brittany and together they made an impenetrable wall of women. "So, no, we'll just wait for the police."

"Are either of you a medical professional?" Joe asked. "Because she might need—"

"I'm an ER nurse," Lianne said. She shook her head. "There's nothing that can be done. Cassidy is dead."

"What?" Jillian Kemper, who was standing nearby, whipped her head in their direction. "What did you say?"

"Cass—" Lianne began but Joe cut her off.

"No!" he said.

"What? Like they're not going to find out the minute the police get here?" Lianne asked. She turned back to Jillian. "Cass—"

"Is unconscious," Mel cut in. "Can you go find Danny?"

"Oh." Jillian made drinking motion with her hand. "I gotcha. It's sad when the pretty ones end up drinkers. Sloshed is never a good look, you know what I'm saying?"

"Yeah, I do," Mel said. She made a shooing motion with her hands and Jillian frowned at her. Then she spun on one pointy heel and sauntered off into the crowd.

"What did you do that for?" Brittany asked. "She's going to send Danny over and

74

he'll be upset to find out she's worse than unconscious."

"I'm pretty sure we can't avoid the upset part, but better he hears it from us than as a rumor circulating through the crowd," Mel said. She rubbed her forehead. She felt as if she was living a nightmare. She turned to Joe. "Any idea how long until Stan gets here?"

"He was at your mom's so it should be pretty quick," he said.

"My mom's?" Mel asked. Her uncle Stan had been dating her mother for the past few months. While she was happy for them both, it was still weird. Uncle Stan was her dad's younger brother. And when her father had passed away, he had stepped in as a father figure to her and her brother and a support system for her mom. It had taken over ten years, but he and her mom had fallen in love. Mel really was happy for them, but still, it was weird.

"Yes, so less than ten minutes, depending upon traffic," Joe said. Clearly, he was not consumed by the weirdness of the new relationship.

"I feel like someone should be in there with her," Mel said. "I mean, she's all alone in a bathroom."

"She doesn't care," Lianne said. Her face

75

was implacable. The harsh truth of Cassidy's demise was etched in the fine lines around her nurse's eyes. Mel wondered how many loved ones Lianne had to coax into understanding that their person was gone and that there was nothing that could change that.

She nodded. A ruckus at the entrance to the resort brought their attention around. Two uniformed officers pushed past the reception desk. One was middle-aged, good-looking in a rugged sort of way, the other was younger, lanky, and looked a bit freaked-out. A rookie, Mel was guessing. The older one saw Joe and waved.

"DeLaura," he said. They shook hands. "Stan said you'd be here. What have we got?"

"Thirty-something female, deceased," Joe said. "Or at least, that's what I've been told." He gestured to Lianne. "She's a nurse and was one of the first on the scene."

"Follow me, Officers," Lianne said. She turned and walked back into the bathroom. The two officers followed. Brittany did not, nor did she move aside so that Joe and Mel could follow.

"The police are here," Joe said.

"Yes, they are," Brittany said. She sounded relieved but she didn't move.

"I think you can step aside now," Joe said. "Clearly, they know me."

Brittany looked from him to Mel and then shook her head. "No."

Joe opened his mouth to protest but just then Danny Griffin arrived. He looked a little irritated and a bit resigned. Mel wondered how often he had to collect his wife when she'd had too much to drink. There was no surprise on his face, so she figured it was a pretty regular event.

She wondered if she'd handled it right. Maybe they should have had Jillian tell him the truth, but then the news would have spread through the reunion like wildfire, and for poor Danny to be on the receiving end of the news like that . . . No, this was better. As it was, they were already getting looks from some of the people standing nearby.

"Is she in there?" Danny asked. He looked at Mel.

Mel nodded. She was about to let him walk in there and see for himself, but then she just couldn't do it. What if the situation was reversed? Would she want to walk in and find her partner dead? Or would she want to be forewarned?

"Wait, Dan," she said.

"Yes?"

Mel felt her throat get tight. Impatient, Danny moved to step around her, but Brittany grabbed his arm. "Wait. Danny, the thing is . . . Cassidy is, well . . . she's dead."

Danny frowned. He blinked and then looked at Brittany as if he thought she was telling a really tasteless joke.

"I'm sorry, Danny," she said. "So very sorry."

He shook her off and then stormed past Mel into the women's room. Even from outside they could hear his shout. It was a horrible sound, a cry of disbelief mingled with outrage and dusted with horror.

Mel leaned into Joe and he put his arm around her. He must have heard the same anguish in Danny's voice that she did. It made her want to hug Joe and keep hugging him, where she knew they were both safe.

"He must be distraught," Brittany said. "I should go in and comfort him, don't you think?"

"No," Mel said. She looked at Brittany in disbelief. Was Brittany seriously thinking of making a play for Danny right now? "The police are in there. They'll take care of him."

Brittany raised her hands in frustration. "You know, it should have been me that he dated in high school instead of her. Then we wouldn't be here now. I mean we'd be here but it wouldn't be like this. Danny and I should have been the homecoming king and queen. It just made sense. I was the captain of the pep squad and he was the captain of the basketball team. We would have been perfect together, a real power couple. I could have made him happy."

Mel stared at Brittany. Was she for real? Was this conversation for real? Maybe it was the shock.

"I don't really think this is the right time to be talking about that," Mel said. She looked at Brittany and shook her head. Brittany shrugged and tossed her short dark hair as if she was shaking Mel off.

"Mel! Joe!" Uncle Stan came charging into the resort. He had a roll of antacid tablets in his hand, but Mel suspected it was more out of habit than necessity. Since he'd been dating Joyce, her mother, he'd been eating better and exercising and in fact looked ten years younger than he had just a few months ago. That made Mel happy.

"Uncle Stan," Mel said. She left Joe and hurried forward and hugged him tight.

"How're you doing, kid?" he asked.

"All right," she said. She pulled him toward the entrance. "But this is turning into a bit of a nightmare."

"I'll bet," he said. "Joe said you found the body."

"Yes."

"Were you in there alone?" he asked. His tone was serious and Mel knew he was hoping she hadn't been.

"At first," she said. She gave him a side eye.

"At first? What? Why were you in there alone? Why wasn't Angie with you? I thought you gals always went to the restroom in pairs."

"We didn't this time."

"Well, I hope you've learned your lesson. There's a reason you're supposed to go in pairs," he said. He sounded mad but Mel knew Uncle Stan well enough to know that he was just concerned. Worry manifested as surly in Uncle Stan.

By now a small crowd had gathered, probably because Danny had been seen disappearing into the ladies' room and word had spread. Mel and Stan weaved their way through the bodies. Joe was still at the entrance to the bathroom with Brittany. Stan shook his hand and they exchanged a world-weary, grim look that Mel knew was shared by most of the people who worked in law enforcement of any kind. Then Stan looked at Brittany.

"Who are you?" he barked.

"I'm Brittany Nilsson, the reunion co-ordinator," she said.

"Well, Brittany, you're in the way, so move it," Stan said.

She gasped and pressed herself against the side of the wall.

Satisfied, Stan said, "Stay here," to Mel and Joe and strode into the restroom.

An ambulance arrived. Two EMTs swooped by with a stretcher. The people nearby, sensing something was really wrong, surged forward, getting thicker and deeper and, Mel didn't think she was imagining it, more menacing.

Tate and Angie pushed their way through the small horde. There were a few grunts and some swearing but when Angie was on a mission there wasn't much point in standing in her way.

"What's going on?" she asked.

Mel leaned close to whisper in her ear but the chatter of the people around them was loud so she had to speak up. "Cassidy is dead."

"What?" Angie cupped her ear and leaned closer. "It sounded like you said 'Cassidy is dead.'"

"I did." Mel met her stare with a worried

one of her own.

"But we just saw her," Angie protested. "I mean, she looked ready to rip your head off when you were dancing with Danny. Cassidy can't be dead."

"Well, she is," Mel said. She shivered.

"What's going on?" Tate leaned down so he could get in on the conversation.

Angie turned toward her husband and said, "Cassidy is dead."

Tate's eyes went wide. "Dead? Cassidy is dead?"

Of course, just as he repeated the horrible news, the DJ ended the song and his voice came over the public address system, announcing that it was time for the dance between the homecoming king and queen. Mel felt her eyes go wide and she looked at Angie in a panic. The king and queen were Cassidy and Danny, both of whom were in the ladies' room right now, and only one of whom was ever going to dance again. Mel thought she might throw up.

"Hey hey hey, now, don't be shy," the DJ crooned over the microphone. "Where are our royals? It's time for them to don their crowns and get this party started!"

"This is awful," Angie said.

"Horrible," Mel agreed. She looked at Joe. "We have to stop him."

"I'll go talk to him," Tate said. "Wait here."

He dove back into the crowd, making his way to the stage.

"I'll go get an update from Stan as to what's happening," Joe said. "I don't like that they're taking so long."

He headed into the bathroom, looking at Brittany like he'd step on her if she gave him a hard time. She wisely stayed where she was, pressed up against the wall.

Mel glanced over the heads of the people in the crowd. Most were waiting for the king and queen to appear, while the lesser crowd hunkered around the bathroom, wanting to know who was having sex, who had overdosed, or who was sloppy drunk. Mel didn't think they'd caught on that there was a death amongst them — yet.

Waitresses were trotting through the crowd, handing out the cupcakes Mel had spent the better part of the past two days laboring over. They were lovely, with their black fondant and dazzling number fifteens on top. Mel noticed that phones were whipped out as people clustered with their high school pals and took selfies with the cupcakes. She wondered if they'd still value these selfies when they saw Cassidy get wheeled out of here in a body bag.

"What's going on?" Megan Mareez

popped out of the crowd. She looked anxious, and Mel knew there was no way they were going to be able to keep her out of the loop about her best friend.

Mel glanced at Angie. She couldn't imagine having someone tell her Angie was dead. The mere thought of it made her feel faint. She noticed that Megan looked a bit pale and wondered if it was just the bad lighting or if Megan had some sort of best-friend psychic connection going. Maybe way deep down, she just knew that something had happened to Cassidy.

"Megan." Mel waved her in close. "Listen, there's been, well, I don't know what happened but I've got some bad news."

Megan leaned in. "What? Did something happen to Danny? I saw him go in there." She pointed to the restroom.

"No, not him," Angie said. "Cassidy."

Megan looked confused. "What do you mean?"

"She's . . ." Mel struggled for words.

"Not well," Angie supplied. Mel looked at her and she shrugged.

"What do you mean not well?" Megan asked. Her voice was tight and it was clear she was getting upset. "Was she drunk?"

"She's dead," Brittany broke in. She looked at Mel and Angie with a look of disdain before she continued, "I'm sorry, but Lianne and I went into the bathroom and we found Mel and Cassidy in there, but Cassidy wasn't moving. When Lianne checked — she's a nurse — we discovered she was dead."

Megan put her hand over her heart. She sucked in a breath or two and then went pasty pale. She staggered on her feet and then dropped to the floor. Angie caught on quicker than the rest and leapt forward, catching Megan before she hit the ground, probably saving her from a broken nose.

"Help," Angie cried as she staggered under Megan's weight.

Mel stepped forward and crouched so that she could loop one of Megan's arms over her shoulders. Then she half dragged, half carried her with Angie's help over to a chair in the corner. She looked at Brittany, who was standing there as if she couldn't believe what had just happened, and snapped, "Go get help. Get Lianne."

Brittany glanced from the bathroom back to Mel and then back to the bathroom. It was pretty obvious she did not want to go back in there.

"Oh, for Pete's sake," Mel snapped. She propped Megan up against the wall and then grabbed Brittany's hand and yanked her over to one side of the chair while Angie watched the other. "Watch her, I'll get help."

She hurried down the short hall that led into the restroom. Inside, the atmosphere was grim. Lianne was standing off to one side, so Mel sidled up to her and said, "Megan Mareez just fainted. She's right outside and she seems okay but it might be best if you take a look at her."

"Oh, okay," Lianne said. "I'll go right now."

She dashed out the door without looking back and Mel realized she had been looking for a reason to leave. Mel glanced back at the group. Stan and Joe were standing together on the other side of the rest area talking to a man Mel recognized as a county medical examiner. Their expressions were grim. Dan was slouched on a chair. His hands were jammed in his hair and his head was down. He looked as if his entire world had just imploded on him.

The EMTs were standing off to the side and the two officers in attendance were snapping pictures and putting out the yellow markers that denoted a crime scene under investigation. So not an accident then. Mel felt her entire body go cold.

Someone in their graduating class had wanted Cassidy dead. But who? And why?

Six

Joe glanced up and saw Mel. The look he gave her did not reassure. He said something to Stan and the medical examiner and made his way around the edge of the room to get to her.

"You need to get out of here," he said.

"I know," she said. "It's a crime scene. I only came in because Megan Mareez fainted and we needed Lianne to take a look at her."

"It's worse than that," Joe said. "Come on."

He took Mel by the elbow and led her toward the door. He was moving pretty fast and she had to scurry on her high heels to keep up.

"Whoa, whoa, whoa," a voice called after them. "Is that Mel?"

"Don't look," Joe ordered.

But Mel had already swiveled her head back toward the room. "Too late."

Detective Tara Martinez, a spark plug of a

woman, stepped out of one of the bathroom stalls. She was wearing crime scene investigation gloves and holding a small camera.

"Trying to hustle your girlfriend out of the scene of the crime, DeLaura?" she asked. Her voice was unfriendly, per usual. "Wouldn't be because you think she's a suspect, would it?"

"Hey, that's my niece you're talking about," Stan said. He stepped forward. Tara was his partner, having taken the place of her cousin Manny Martinez, and while Mel knew Stan and Tara got along in a working capacity, he wouldn't tolerate her going after Mel, which Tara did frequently because she had a thing for Joe. In short, it was complicated.

"Well, your niece, or his girlfriend, has some explaining to do," Tara said. She glared at Mel, who decided she'd had enough.

"Actually, I'm his fiancée," she said. Tara's pinched features became even more so.

"Well, fiancée," Tara said. "Maybe you can tell us what our victim was writing on the bathroom wall with her lipstick right before she died."

"Huh?" Mel asked. She blinked. She had no idea what Tara was talking about.

"Really?" the detective asked. "That's all

you've got?"

"Come on, Mel," Joe said. "I don't think —"

"No," Mel refused. She'd dig her heels into the carpet if she had to but she wanted to know what Tara was talking about.

Stan blew out a breath. "Mel, I want you to tell me exactly what happened when you came in here."

"I came in," Mel said. "I found Cassidy on the couch. I thought she was asleep, so I tried to slip back out because she had been angry with me earlier for dancing with her husband and I didn't want another scene. I was backing up when I bumped into Brittany and Lianne, who were coming in. That's when we discovered she was dead."

"But you were in here with her alone at first?" Tara persisted.

"For mere seconds and not really," Mel said. "Because she was already dead."

Mel tipped her chin up. She really didn't like the way the pretty brunette was looking at her as if she'd finally got something on Mel. Mel didn't have anything to do with Cassidy's death. Why would she? She'd had her big life moment showing up Cassidy. Killing her would have been excessive and completely ruined it. Why would she do that? Fortunately, she had the presence of mind not to say any of this out loud.

"So you say," Tara said.

Mel didn't like the innuendo but she wasn't going to let the detective get to her. Instead, she turned to Joe and said, "Explain."

Joe glanced at Stan, who nodded and then waved Mel over to him. Mel left Joe and crossed the floor to stand beside her uncle. "What's going on?"

"The lipstick," Stan said.

"The one she had in her hand?" Mel asked. "What about it?"

Stan gestured toward the large stall at the end of the row. There was a crime scene tech in there taking pictures.

"It looks like Cassidy had begun to write, well, your name."

Mel turned from the tech working in the stall to her uncle. "I don't understand."

"M E L," he said. "That's what's written back there."

Mel went to go look, but he grabbed her arm and held her back.

"Are you sure she was writing my name?" Mel asked. "I mean it could be the beginning of something else, like, mellow or melancholy."

"Or Melanie," Tara added. She crossed her arms over her chest.

91

"Or melodrama," Mel countered. They all looked at her and she shrugged. "I have no idea why she wrote that, but don't you find it odd that she didn't write anything else?"

"Not really," Tara said. "Not if she did it to tell us who killed her."

"Hey, now," Stan snapped. "Easy, Detective, we're gathering evidence, not making wild accusations."

Mel put her hand over her chest. "Uncle Stan, you can't think that I —"

"No, I don't," he said. "Now that's enough, you two. We have plenty to do here without you baiting each other. Detective Martinez, if you don't mind, I think you're needed elsewhere."

Tara sent Mel a triumphant look. "No, I don't mind."

She turned and went back to where the crime scene techs were working on the body. Mel felt a surge of anger spike but she pushed it down. She refused to let this woman get to her. She hadn't done anything wrong and she wasn't about to let Tara Martinez make her feel as if she had.

"I had nothing to do with this," Mel said. She glanced at her uncle. "You know that, right?"

"I do," he said. He gave her a one-armed bear hug and Mel felt instantly better. "Still, you may want to call an attorney just in case."

And her peace vanished just like that. She turned to Joe and he said, "Come on, let's get you out of here. Stan, can I take her home or do you need her to go down to the station?"

"I think we're good for now," Uncle Stan said. "But be prepared in case I have to call you in, and, Mel, call your mother. Don't let her hear about this on the news."

"I will," she said. She put her hand in Joe's and he led her out of the narrow, cramped room.

When they got outside, the crowd from in front of the stage had joined those in front of the bathroom and they resembled an unruly mob more than they did a bunch of former high school students at a reunion.

Tate and Angie were off to the side, and Joe and Mel joined them. Angie took one look at Mel's face and hugged her tight. "It'll be okay."

"I hope so," she said. "Because this is actually a nightmare."

"You!" Dwight Pickard pointed at Mel. His cheeks were ruddy and his eyes were glassy. It was clear to Mel that he was schnockered, which not surprisingly did not make him more endearing and made her want to avoid him at all costs. She glanced in both directions. There was no path to escape.

Mel stiffened her spine and stared him down. "What about me?"

"Is it true?" he asked. He lurched forward and Mel felt Joe step up behind her, surrounding her with his own body and keeping her protected.

"Is what true?" Mel asked. She felt Joe squeeze her hip, and she knew he was trying to signal to her that she shouldn't engage, but how could she not? Dwight was coming after her in front of their entire graduating class. She had to defend herself.

"Did you kill Cassidy?" he slurred.

"No!" Mel protested. She didn't add "you idiot," which she thought she should get points for, but knew better than to point this out. "I would never do anything like that."

"Really, Melephant?" He dragged every syllable of her horrible nickname out and Mel began to grind her teeth. She'd never wanted to punch anyone so much in her entire life.

"Stop —" Joe began but Mel held up her hand. She didn't want him taking this fight for her.

"Because I'll bet you did," Dwight said.

"You made a play for her husband, we all saw you, and when he rejected you, you decided to kill her."

"You are insane," she said. "How could I kill anyone?"

"With your cupcakes," Dwight said. His eyes took on a crazy light as if he'd just had an epiphany. He lifted up his head and shouted to the crowd. "Don't eat the cupcakes! They're poisoned!"

"No, they aren't, you big jerk!" Angie snapped. She turned to the crowd and yelled, "Don't listen to him!"

It was too late. The damage was done. Mel watched in horror as people started spitting out the cupcakes. The ones who hadn't eaten theirs yet tossed them into the garbage and one woman, Millie Davis, was actually trying to make herself throw up the cupcake she had just eaten. For the love of frosting, had they all gone mad?

"Mel, don't engage," Joe said from behind her. "He's a bully and you can't reason with people like that. It's a waste of time."

"What's that, pretty boy?" Dwight goaded Joe. "You talking about me? Why are you hiding behind your girlfriend? Aren't you man enough to face me?"

Joe lifted Mel up and put her behind him.

"Oh, no," Mel said. This could play out a

variety of ways, one of which included Joe being disbarred. "Joe, don't listen to him."

" 'Joe, don't listen to him,' " Dwight said. He made his voice high-pitched and mocking. "So, DeLaura, what's it like to be whipped by a reformed chubette? You know, she could blow up on you at any point. One minute she's fine and the next she's packin' on an extra hundred pounds or so. Is that a risk you're willing —"

Kapow!

That was as far as Dwight got when Joe's fist connected with his face. Mel let out a tiny shriek and watched in horror as Dwight crumpled like a folding chair down to the ground. Mel thought it was very telling that no one jumped in to help him.

"Nice punch, Bro," Angie said. She slapped her brother on the back.

"What punch?" Joe asked as he shook out his fingers. "I was merely stretching my fist when he walked into it."

"That's how I saw it," Tate said. "Freak accident. Very unfortunate."

"Me, too," Angie chimed in. "It probably wouldn't have happened if Dwight wasn't so inebriated. It's a shame he's become such an unreliable drunk when he was such a stand-up kid in high school."

How she kept a straight face when she said

that, Mel had no idea. It was just then that the stretcher with a body bag on it came out of the ladies' room. Everyone stepped back to make room and also, she suspected, to avoid getting hit with the dead-body cooties. Some things don't really change from the playground days.

Mel glanced behind her and saw Danny following the stretcher, looking as if his insides had been scooped out. Megan Mareez rose from her chair and fell in beside him, looking equally hollow. In the face of their shock and grief, the crowd grew silent. Like her or not, the fact that Cassidy Havers-Griffin had died so unexpectedly reminded each of them of their own mortality and how quickly they could go from eating a cupcake to dead.

The reunion ended shortly after the medical examiner took Cassidy's body away. No one was feeling it, despite the DJ's repeated attempts to get the party started again. Mel wondered if he was just really into his job or if he was always that tone deaf to the mood of a crowd.

She glanced at Joe on their ride to the bakery and said, "I'm thinking a band for our wedding."

He was driving and he glanced at her

quickly, his grin a slash of white in the night. "That DJ was terrible. Band it is."

They were quiet for a while. By mutual agreement, everyone had decided to stop by the bakery on the way home to fortify with a cupcake. Mel was afraid she wouldn't feel better even if she ate an entire six pack of Black Bottom Cupcakes, a chocolate cupcake with a surprise cream cheese filling, all by herself.

They parked in the lot behind the bakery. It was closed now but per usual, Oz was in the kitchen already baking the next day's special. Oz had taken to culinary school like a champ and Mel knew it was only a matter of time before he left them to go work for someone else or to open a bakery of his own. She tried not to think about it. Losing Oz would be like losing her right hand, possibly her left, too.

Tate and Angie parked nearby and the four of them made their way to the back door. Tate used his key to let them in and held the door open for everyone before closing it behind them. The music was cranked, Logic rapping his hit "Under Pressure," while Oz opened the oven, bopping his head to the flow, completely oblivious to the fact that he was no longer alone.

Mel watched him for a bit, not wanting to

scare him when he was holding a hot tray. A well-muscled dude over six feet tall and rocking piercings and tattoos, Oz was no one's image of a cupcake baker, and yet he had an intuitive baking skill set that Mel hadn't seen in many chefs, not even when she was studying in Paris.

" 'But finally gettin' cake like a happy belated,' " Oz rapped with the song as he pulled the industrial-sized baking tray out of the oven. He turned around to find the four of them standing there and he let out a little yelp. The tray in his hands bobbled but he caught it, dropping it onto the large steel table in the center of the kitchen.

"Sorry!" Mel shouted over the music.

Tate crossed the room and lowered the volume on the mini-speaker so it was more background music and less main event. The swinging doors that led to the front of the bakery opened and Marty appeared, holding a mop in one hand.

"Who shut off the music?" he said. "It was just getting to the good part. I was going to bust out the floss."

Oz rolled his eyes. "You can't do the floss, you'll throw a hip out."

"Can so." Marty tossed down his mop and executed the dance move, alternating hip thrusts between his arms, which didn't go at all with the faint sound of Logic's rap still coming from the speaker.

"All right, all right," Joe said. "I'm never going to be able to unsee that, and we only stopped by for cupcakes, not a dance party."

"Hmph." Marty picked up his mop and snagged the speaker off of the shelf. "I'll be in front, finishing up."

"Make sure the shades are down; you don't want to scare off any passersby," Angie called after him. She was grinning, so Mel knew she was teasing.

Marty looked over his shoulder at her with one bushy gray eyebrow raised, and then with a wicked twinkle in his eye, he did the floss again. Angie laughed as the door swung shut after him.

"What are you making for tomorrow's special?" Mel asked Oz. She looked at the cupcakes in the tray but didn't recognize them as one of their regular flavors.

"Pineapple Upside-Down Cupcakes," Oz said.

He grabbed a bowl from the table and then sprinkled brown sugar on the tops of the cupcakes, which Mel noticed had pineapple rings and cherries baked into the top. Then he took a kitchen torch and caramelized each pineapple.

"Ah, the smell of burnt sugar," Joe said.

His sweet tooth was legendary and he began to look at the cupcakes Oz was working on like a hawk circling a ground squirrel.

"Oz, you've outdone yourself," she said. "Those look amazing."

"Thanks." He beamed. He looked at Joe and said, "You can have one. One. After I frost them."

"Sweet!" Joe said. Then he turned on his heel and went over to the walk-in cooler where they stored the cupcakes overnight.

Tate and Angie joined him and Mel watched as Oz took out two more trays of cupcakes and repeated the sugar and torch technique. The smell of cooking pineapple almost made her dizzy. Once he was finished, Oz headed over to their industrial mixer to start up a huge batch of vanilla buttercream.

Joe returned to the table, sitting on the end away from the cupcakes. He gestured for Mel to join him and she took the seat by his side. He put a s'mores cupcake in front of her and Mel remembered, again, why she was marrying this man. He knew what she needed when she needed it. She could look the whole world over and never find a man that in tune to her.

Oz looked from the cupcake to Mel and back to the cupcake. "Uh oh, s'mores. You only eat those when you're upset. What happened at the reunion?"

"What didn't happen?" Angie answered with a question as she and Tate joined them at the table.

"Bullies?" Oz asked. He'd had his own share of bullying to contend with when Mel had first met him. It was one of their bonds. The love of cupcake baking hadn't sat well with Oz's peers, but Oz had persevered as all heroes of their own stories do.

"Yeah, there was some of that," Mel said. She gave him a rueful look and bit into her cupcake.

Oz studied her for a second and then glanced at Joe. "So, did you knock him out?"

"Huh?" Joe asked. "How did you — ?"

"Your knuckles," Oz said. He turned away from the table and went to the small freezer they kept in the corner. He dumped some ice into a towel and brought it back for Joe.

"Thanks," Joe said. He plopped the towel on his hand and used the other hand to eat his cupcake. He'd gone all in on a margarita cupcake, with a chocolate cupcake chaser.

Oz turned back to Mel. "You okay?"

"Better than Cassidy Havers-Griffin at any rate," she said.

Oz's eyes narrowed in suspicion. "Wasn't she the mean girl? What happened to her?"

He glanced at Joe. "You didn't punch her, did you?"

"No," Joe said. "I would never."

"It's actually worse than that. She died," Mel said. "Right there at the reunion."

"What? Hold on," Oz said. He shook his head and fished his wallet out of his pants pocket. He took a five out and opened the door and called into the bakery, "You won."

"I did?" Marty slid into the open door with his hand out. "Hot dog!"

Oz slapped the bill into Marty's outstretched hand.

"Wait! You two had a bet?" Mel asked.

Both of them looked at her and then Oz shrugged. "It's been months since anything bad happened, we figured you were due. I just didn't think it would be tonight."

"I did," Marty said. "So, what happened?"

"A mean girl from our graduating class died," Angie said. "We don't know how yet. Mel found her in the ladies' room, sprawled out on a couch. Some people think she had a heart attack but I'd argue that's impossible since she didn't have one." They all looked at her in varying levels of horror. "Sorry, too soon?"

"A bit," Joe said. "No matter how awful she was, you really shouldn't talk about her like that, especially given that Mel is the one who found her and the police are looking at this as a possible homicide."

"But she was the worst, a total nightmare," Angie protested. "And I still don't regret cutting off all of her hair."

Tate burst out laughing. "I remember that! She had headphones on in language lab and when you heard her trash talk me, you cut off all of her hair in the back and she didn't know it until after class."

"I thought she was going to murder you," Mel said. "She had to get all of her hair cut to even it out."

"She deserved it," Angie said. "She was so nasty. Remember when she pretended to be bisexual and joined the gay and lesbian club at school just so she could out whoever attended in the school paper? I mean she actually printed their names even after an oath of privacy. She really messed up some lives there."

"Oh, that was awful," Mel agreed. "Then she tried to pretend that naming them in the school paper was her First Amendment right. One of the boys, Tommy Handler, was kicked out by his parents because of her reveal."

"What happened to him?" Tate asked.

"I know this one," Joe said. "He's a law professor at Stanford, specializing in the first amendment. We attended the same law school and, although he was younger than me, our paths crossed in a few classes. He's brilliant."

"Huh," Mel said. "Well, that's one way to turn the bullying around."

"Sounds like this gal had a lot of enemies," Marty said. He leaned close to watch Oz pipe his fresh vanilla buttercream onto a cupcake. His pupils practically dilated when Oz put a stemmed maraschino cherry on top.

Oz turned to glare at him. "Back up. You already took my five bucks, stay away from my cupcakes."

"If I lick it, can I have it?" Marty asked. He batted his eyelids at Oz, who did not look amused.

"Here." Oz handed him the freshly decorated cupcake. "Now shoo."

Marty plopped down on the empty stool on the other side of Mel. "So, given all of the people who hated this old classmate of yours, who do you think had the most reason to do her in?"

"No idea," Mel said. "Unfortunately only one of them found her. Me."

SEVEN

"Well, that's just bad luck, isn't it?" Marty said. "It doesn't mean you had anything to do with her death."

"Normally, it wouldn't," Mel said.

Oz lowered the piping bag. Joe reached for one of the fresh cupcakes and so did Tate.

"What do you mean 'normally'?" Oz asked.

"Well, I found Cassidy with her lipstick in one hand and a cupcake in the other," Mel said. "I thought she was sleeping it off and tried to sneak back out."

"Had the cupcake been eaten?" Tate asked.

"It looked like she'd taken a bite," Mel said. "But the lighting was dim in there. I couldn't be sure. I just wanted to get out of there before she lit into me again."

"But?" Marty asked.

"But before I could leave two other

women showed up," Mel said. "Brittany and Lianne. Lianne is a nurse and she's the one who determined that Cassidy was dead."

"Well, that doesn't mean any—" Angie began but Mel held up her hand in a wait-for-it gesture.

"I didn't get a chance to tell you this before, but in one of the bathroom stalls, it looks like Cassidy had been using her lipstick to write something."

"What?" Tate and Angie asked in unison.

"I mean, it could be anything," Mel said. She glanced at Joe. As if sensing an impending meltdown, he put his arm around her and pulled her close.

"Whatever it was, she didn't finish," he said. "But the beginning was the letters M . . . E . . . L."

"What?" Angie's eyes went round. "Why didn't you tell us this? What do you think she was writing?"

"Honestly, I was hoping it was *melody* or *meliorate,* but probably she was going to use her old nickname for me — Melephant. Then who knows what she would have added? I know she was furious with Danny for dancing with me, and I'm sure in her mind it was all my fault."

"Melephant?" Marty asked. Two red spots of color darkened his cheekbones. "Who are her parents? You get them on the phone with me right now. They have some explaining to do about that daughter of theirs, and I am just the one to hold them accountable. I will not tolerate bullying."

Mel smiled at him. "Aw, I appreciate it, Marty, I do, but her parents are getting the worst news of their lives right now, assuming they are still around. I actually feel really sorry for them."

"Me, too," Angie said. "And even if she was writing something mean about you, I don't think you have to worry about the police looking at you when so many people hated her, and I mean really, really hated her."

Joe's cell phone chimed and he pulled it out of his jacket pocket and looked at it. He glanced up at Mel and said, "Stan."

She nodded at him, knowing that there was only one reason Stan would be calling Joe. He pressed accept and lifted the phone to his ear.

"Joe here," he said. There was a rumble on the other end that Mel recognized as Uncle Stan's baritone. She was trying to determine if it was a happy grumble or an unhappy grumble, when Joe interrupted. "I don't care if they found Mel's fingerprints on a murder weapon with the handle still poking out of the victim's chest. She had nothing to do with this and you know it."

Mel glanced at Angie. Joe sounded angry. Joe never got angry. He was the DeLaura family mediator, born smack dab in the middle of the seven brothers. He was the keeper of the peace and as such never lost it. Never.

"Well, you can tell Tara that I said no, absolutely not. I am not bringing Mel in for a lie detector test or anything else," he said.

Mel could hear Stan's voice rise on the other end of the phone. He was not happy with Joe or the conversation or both.

"I know you know she's innocent," Joe said. "But I'd be remiss as her fiancé if I let her be put in a situation that might adversely impact her later so, no, no lie detector test, not unless you can come up with a hell of a better reason than her finding Cassidy first and some scribbles with a lipstick."

There was a long pause. Mel noticed that everyone in the kitchen had stopped moving as they listened to Joe's conversation.

"I know we're on the same side," Joe said. "Sorry I got testy." There was another pause and then Joe laughed and said, "Coming from you, I take that as high praise. I'll call you tomorrow."

He ended the call and pocketed his phone.

He reached for his cupcake but Mel grabbed the plate and moved it out of range before he could get it.

"Whoa, there, big fella," she said. "Explain that first."

"Not much to explain," he said. "Tara was pushing hard for you to come in for a lie detector test but Stan was balking. He called me so that I could say no and he couldn't be accused of favoritism since you're his niece."

"Do they have a reason to believe that she was murdered?" Mel asked.

"The medical examiner is running a tox screen," Joe said. "He seems to think she died from a heart attack but her husband, Daniel Griffin, says that she had no medical history of a heart condition. In fact, he says she was very fit since she was compulsive about working out."

This did not surprise Mel at all.

"Early to mid-thirties is awfully young to have a heart attack," Angie said.

"Unless someone helped her to have one," Tate said.

"And I'm their chief suspect because I found her," Mel said.

"Well, that and the fact that it looks like she was writing your name just before she died," Joe said. Mel knew she must have looked upset, because Joe forgot about the cupcake and hugged her instead. "Try not to worry. Uncle Stan is on top of the investigation and none of us are going to let you get busted for a crime you didn't commit."

"Except for Tara, who would love to have me behind bars, permanently," Mel said. She looked at Joe. "Then she could make a play for you without me in the way."

He shook his head at her. "Doesn't matter. I'll spend my life proving you're innocent if I have to. I'm a one-woman man, cupcake, so I'm afraid you're stuck with me."

"Good, because we need to stop by the station so I can take a lie detector test," she said.

"What?" Joe cried. "No, absolutely not. As your fiancé and your attorney I have to say no, as in no, no way, no how."

"But this is the only way I can remove myself at least partially from suspicion," Mel said. "Won't it make Uncle Stan's job a heck of a lot easier if I pass a polygraph?"

"Yes, but this isn't about —"

"Yes, it is," Mel said. "Everyone is going to believe I killed her. I have to do this not just for Uncle Stan but for me, too."

Joe heaved and sigh and hugged her close.

"For the record, I hate this."

"I know."

"This isn't going to zap me or any thing, is it?" Mel asked.

"Only if you lie," Don Jenkins, the polygraph operator, said. His voice was terse.

Mel glanced down at the equipment and then back up at him.

"I'm joking," he said. He didn't look like he was joking.

Don had arrived shortly after Mel and Joe. Uncle Stan had been resistant to Mel taking the polygraph test but when Mel insisted and Detective Martinez looked thrilled, Uncle Stan called in Don — his favorite examiner. Don was wearing a bright orange and blue Hawaiian shirt, untucked over a pair of jeans, and Birkenstocks. He looked as if he'd thrown his clothes on and rushed out the door, not even bothering to run a comb through his thick white hair. Uncle Stan, who was standing in the corner of the small exam room with Joe, was watching them with his usual roll of antacid tablets clutched in his fist. They were both staring at Mel with matching expressions of not happy. She gave them a little finger wave.

It was late. They were all tired but Mel knew there was no way she was going to be able to sleep tonight with the whiff of murderer hanging over her like a bad smell. She hadn't harmed Cassidy and if taking a polygraph would get Detective Martinez — and anyone else who thought she did it — off her back she was all in.

She tried to ignore the tubes strapped around her chest, the cuff on her right arm, and the sensors wrapped around the fingers of her left hand. She was afraid to breathe, move, or scratch any part that itched, which at the moment felt like her entire body.

"Sorry you had to come in so late," Mel said. She tried to meet Don's gaze but he was fussing with the computer monitor in front of him. When he did finally turn toward her, one white eyebrow rose above his black framed glasses and he said, "Really?"

"Yes," Mel said. Don looked back at the monitor and she felt herself panic, wondering if what she'd said had just registered as a lie. She started to freak out.

Her expression must have mirrored her thoughts because he looked suddenly sympathetic and said, "Relax, Mel. Remember what we talked about in our pre-interview. You're going to do just fine. I promise."

Mel relaxed against the cushion they'd put on her seat. She could do this. She hadn't done anything wrong. All she had to do was tell the truth.

She glanced at Stan and Joe. They both smiled but the smiles didn't reach their eyes, and she could tell they were concerned. Not that they thought she committed murder, she knew, but that this test wasn't going to help her in the end. Polygraphs had been proven faulty before, but Mel couldn't live with the possibility that anyone might think she'd murdered Cassidy, so it was a chance she was willing to take.

"Ready to start?" Don asked.

"Fire away," Mel said. She was going for levity but he didn't smile. She stifled a sigh.

"What is your name?"

"Melanie Cooper."

"Where were you born?"

"Scottsdale, Arizona."

"What do you do for a living?"

"Cupcake baker," she said.

Don glanced between her and the monitor as he asked the questions. His voice was calm; it matched his Hawaiian-shirt-hippie vibe, and Mel realized that this was probably why he was so good at this job. He managed to make her feel relaxed even though there was a part of her that was completely traumatized by the mere idea that she was taking a lie detector test.

The questions were all very basic. Mel glanced at Joe and saw him studying the computer monitor. She wondered if he knew how to read the results of a polygraph test. She couldn't tell by his expression, which made her feel anxious. She glanced away, not wanting to taint her test results.

"Did you attend your high school reunion tonight?"

"Yes."

"Did you speak with Cassidy Havers-Griffin?"

"Yes."

Mel kept her voice calm and steady. She could feel her heart rate increase and she felt a little sweaty but, surely, that was normal when talking about a murder. Don asked what felt like a million details about the reunion. Mel tried to keep all of the emotion out of her responses.

"Did you murder Cassidy Havers-Griffin?"

"No," Mel said. She was pleased that her voice was level and calm and perfectly controlled. She was ready to jump out of the hot seat now but the questions didn't end there. Instead, Don asked her several different ways if she had harmed Cassidy, had wanted to harm Cassidy, or had someone else harm Cassidy. It rattled Mel and she started to feel as if she was going to crack under the strain of repeating herself.

Finally, when she thought she might rip the gauges and wires off of her body and run screaming from the room, Don announced that they were done. Mel sagged back against her seat and she saw both Stan and Joe slump where they were standing. Mel glanced at the clock on the wall. She had been questioned for forty-five minutes. It had felt more like forty-five hours.

Don helped her out of the rig and then he said, "I'm going to review the charts and I'll have a result for you shortly."

"Oh, okay, thank you," Mel said. She crossed the room and Joe hugged her.

"I'm proud of you," he said. "That took guts." He kissed her head and Mel leaned against him.

What if she failed? Would Uncle Stan have to lock her up right then and there? She glanced at her uncle. He was chewing an antacid tablet as if it had done something to offend him. He stared at Don, who seemed oblivious to the three of them as he reviewed Mel's results.

Mel watched the clock. The room was silent. Don clicked through his monitor. He went back and forth, checked what looked like scribble lines of blue and red to Mel. What did it mean? Was that dark spot an indicator that she had lied? She felt herself begin to sweat even though the room was on the chilly side.

Finally, Don turned around and with a small smile, he said, "You passed."

"Thank god." Uncle Stan collapsed against the wall. Mel hugged Joe, burying her face in his neck. He squeezed her tight and then released her so she could hug Uncle Stan.

"I knew you would pass but on the very slight chance the test went wonky, I did not want to have to explain this to your mother," he said.

Mel laughed. She understood completely. Both she and Joe shook Don's hand and as they departed Detective Martinez entered the room. It was clear from her face that she was eager for the results.

"Well, am I taking her in?" she asked.

"No," Uncle Stan said. "Mel passed her polygraph. We can now focus our efforts elsewhere."

Tara glared at Mel. She stepped forward, blocking the exit. "These tests are only ninety percent accurate," she said. "So don't think you're completely in the clear as yet."

"Actually," Don said. "The test is only as

accurate as the examiner. I have a ninety-nine percent accuracy rate, and I'll be writing up a detailed report of this exam if you have any more questions."

Mel could have kissed him.

Tara was unmoved. "That still leaves a one percent margin of error."

Mel glanced at her. She was so over this woman being a pain in her behind. "I think it's pretty clear that I'm not in the one percent, but knock yourself out . . . please."

Both Joe and Don snorted at her play on words. Uncle Stan ducked his head and Mel knew he was hiding a smile.

"Come on, cupcake," Joe said. "Let's go home."

Mel put her hand on his cheek and then she kissed him. Just having him in her corner made her believe that everything was going to be okay.

"Yes, let's. I'm sure the kids are wondering where we are."

A few months ago, they had adopted a dog from an author who had been murdered. Her name was Peanut and she was a handful. Thankfully, the cat they had rescued prior to that, Captain Jack, had finally taken to the dog, but the two of them were prone to mischief when left unsupervised for too long. Mel wasn't sure who the ringleader was just yet, but if she had to place a bet, she would have said it was Captain Jack. At the moment, she'd welcome the normalcy of a shredded pillow or a puppy in the garbage, because even though she'd passed the polygraph, she knew the fallout from Cassidy being murdered at their high school reunion was far from over.

"This might be your craziest idea yet," Angie said. She was sitting shotgun in Mel's Mini Cooper. They were parked diagonally across from Danny Griffin's house, watching the comings and goings. They had borrowed tennis visors from Joyce, Mel's mother, so that their faces were covered and they looked like two ladies on their way to play tennis instead of two cupcake bakers on a stakeout.

"Oh, I don't know, I've had some doozies before," Mel said.

"True, but we've never done surveillance on a wake before," Angie said. "It feels wrong somehow, like we're stepping over some invisible line of decency — oh, hey, there's one of the mean girls now. Is that . . . nah . . . yeah . . . it's Betina Klipenger. Look at her! She was always so flat-chested in high school. Do you think she's had some work done?"

Mel glanced out the window at the lanky blond making her way down the sidewalk to the posh house set back from the road. Wow.

"I'm thinking her front side is going to get to the house five minutes before she does," Mel said. "So, that's an affirmative on the work."

"I heard she married an elderly podiatrist," Angie said. "He must have a fetish."

"And it ain't for feet," Mel said.

Angie snorted and held up her hand. Mel gave her a high five and they resumed watching the house.

"You know, it's helpful to see who's here, but we really need to know what's happening inside at the wake," Angie said.

"Yes, but if I go in, Dwight Pickard will probably freak out and I'm not sure that Brittany Nilsson or Lianne Marsten would be that thrilled to see me, either," Mel said.

"It's still early," Angie said. "I mean it technically doesn't start for another fifteen minutes. We could go in, give our condolences to Danny, and then hide so we could see everything that's happening."

"Because that's not weird or obvious," Mel said. "Hang on, here comes Megan Mareez."

"She looks awful," Angie said.

It was true. Megan was carrying a large

tray of what looked like bagels. Her long dark hair was twisted into a messy knot on the back of her head. She wasn't wearing any makeup and her eyes were red as if she'd been crying. Her dress was a long, baggy, sacklike thing in a muted print pattern of blue and purple paisley.

"Well, Cassidy was her best friend," Mel said. "It has to be an awful shock."

"Here's what I don't get," Angie said. "Megan was always an outlier in Cassidy's mean girl group. I mean, she was with them, but she wasn't one of them."

"I know what you mean," Mel said. "When Cassidy was at her worst, when she was vicious and cruel, Megan always seemed to be sympathetic to the victim. I always felt like she was trapped and didn't know how to break free."

"Well, trapped or not, she didn't do anything to help the victims of Cassidy's bullying," Angie said.

"No, that's not true," Mel said. "She did try to help, and she took no joy from Cassidy's meanness, not like some of the others."

"Like Betina?" Angie asked.

"Yeah, she was pretty horrible," Mel said.

"And yet, she was the first to show up at grieving widower Danny's door and no sign of her foot doctor husband with her," Angie said. "Interesting, don't you think?"

"You mean you think she's trying to make a play for Danny?"

Angie shrugged.

"Okay, so we're agreed that Betina is awful and possibly making a play for Danny, which wouldn't be a shock because of her old foot doctor husband," Mel said. "And what do we know about Megan?"

"I heard last night that she's been engaged twice but unable to wrangle either fiancé down the aisle," Angie said. "She's into high-end real estate and is making a fortune with her own business that caters exclusively to a wealthy clientele."

"So, she's living large," Mel said. "Any whispers about a rift between her and Cassidy?"

"None that I heard, but I'm not really in the inner circle," Angie said. "Most of what I picked up was from eavesdropping."

"Gotcha," Mel said. "Oh, man, hunker down."

Angie glanced out the window in the direction Mel was looking. Striding up the sidewalk in perfect sync was the pep squad with Brittany in the lead and Lianne just behind her to the right. Instinctively, Mel and Angie lowered themselves in the front seat of the car.

As Brittany and her crew marched past, Mel watched as they moved exactly as they had in high school at the pep rallies, with a purposeful stride in lock step with each other from the angles of their chins to the range of swing in their arms.

"I always felt like they were going to come up to me and yell, 'Be happy, damn it, this is a pep rally!' " Angie said.

Mel laughed. "I know. They are fierce about their cheer. I'm only surprised they didn't put on the uniform for old time's sake."

"Let's just hope they don't decide to do a human pyramid on Danny's front lawn," Angie said.

They craned their necks watching the women march up Danny's walkway, stopping only when they got to the front door. Mel could just see over Brittany's head that it was Danny who opened the door to them. He looked pasty pale and sunken-eyed, as if he hadn't slept at all; but was it from grief or guilt?

Mel watched as he hugged Brittany, Lianne, and then each of the pep squad women as they walked past him into the house. When he shut the door, Mel was immediately swamped by the same feeling she'd endured through most of high school, of being on the outside looking in. It made her feel petty and small. She hated it.

She glanced at Angie and noticed that she had a thoughtful look in her eyes. She wondered if Angie had felt as left out as she did in high school. She doubted it. Angie had always been more popular with their classmates than Mel was; in fact, there were many nights that Mel lay in bed worrying that her best friend was going to change her mind and dump her for the popular kids, but Angie never had. She never knew if it was her or Tate or the combination of her and Tate that Angie hadn't wanted to give up and right now she realized she really wanted to know.

"Angie, how come you never dumped me and Tate?" she asked.

"What do you mean?"

"You could have been in the 'in crowd,' " Mel said. "They always invited you to the parties and you got asked out by all of the hot guys. Why didn't you ever dump us for them?"

"Um, because they suck," Angie said. "I mean, seriously, why would I want to hang out with those creeps when I had you and Tate, his parents' home movie theater, all the junk food I could eat, and people who wouldn't talk trash about me the minute my back was turned?"

"Well, when you put it like that," Mel said. She was grinning at her friend like an idiot.

"Plus, I have seven, SEVEN, older brothers," she said. "The last thing I needed was another pack. I just wanted friends, true friends, real friends, best friends."

Mel reached across the seat and hugged her. Angie hugged her back.

"I'm so glad your parents moved to Arizona when they did," Mel said.

"Me, too," Angie agreed.

Mel glanced back at the house. She felt bad about doubting Danny. He might have been one of the popular ones, but he'd always been nice to Mel despite what Cassidy and the others said about her. She owed him for that. Then again, the man had married Cassidy.

How could he not have seen how awful she was to everyone else? Maybe he had walked into the marriage blind, but Mel was betting that he slowly came to realize what a nightmare he was married to, and maybe he had begun to feel trapped.

Perhaps he couldn't think of any way out besides murder. Could the boy she had known, the teen she had tutored in English, really have murdered his wife? She had a hard time believing it. Her inner teenager soundly rejected the idea that her former crush could be a cold-blooded killer, but it wasn't out of the realm of possibility. As Mel had come to realize over the past few years, you never really knew what a person was capable of when their back was to the wall.

She and Angie had resumed silently watching the house, when the door behind Mel was yanked open and a person jumped into the backseat. She and Angie both let out a startled scream and whipped around to find Tucker Booth sitting there, smiling at them.

"Tell me, ladies, what are we up to today?" he asked.

EIGHT

"Ah!" Mel put her hand over her heart. She wanted to make sure it hadn't stopped from fright. "That was totally uncool, Tucker."

He grinned at her. "You should see your face."

"No, you should see your face when it kisses my knuckles," Angie said.

Tucker gave her a wide-eyed look. "Still have the DeLaura temper, I see."

Angie blew out a breath. She closed her eyes for a second and her face became serene. Slowly she opened her eyes and said, "Well, I'm a Harper now, so I guess it's more of a Harper temper these days."

She tossed her hair with her left hand, letting her diamond wedding band sparkle in the sunlight. Tucker let out a low whistle. "So, it's true what they say about Harper. He's a money machine."

"Partly," Angie said. "Mel is the creative talent, I am the labor, and Tate is the financial genius."

"I always knew you outcasts were going to return victorious," Tucker said.

"Sure you did," Mel said. She didn't have a beef with Tucker but she knew his high school years had been spent chasing after Cassidy, and she didn't think Cassidy's death could be sitting this easily for him. The question was, what did he want from them?

"What do you want from us?" Angie asked. Always the direct one.

"Nothing." He shrugged. "I just saw you sitting here in the old lady hats and wondered what was up. You know as far as disguises go, those are pretty lame."

Angie flipped down the car sun visor. She studied her reflection. "I thought they were pretty good for before coffee."

"Yeah, no," Tucker said. "So, are you two going in or what?"

"Oh, hell, no. Dwight Pickard would make a scene, you know he would," Mel said. "We're just watching."

"For what?" he asked.

"Not what, who," Angie said.

"Sorry," he said. He rolled his eyes. "Who are you looking for?"

"Cassidy's murderer," Mel said.

"What?" Tucker's eyes went wide behind

his wire-framed glasses.

"Yeah, we think Cassidy was murdered," Angie said. "And we think it was someone at the reunion."

"Whoa." Tucker shoved his fingers into his short cropped curls as if trying to keep his brain from exploding. "I can't. Why would you even think this?"

"Because according to Danny, Cassidy didn't have anything physically wrong with her," Mel said. "But she sure had a lot of enemies."

"Like you," Tucker returned.

"What are you saying there, Tucker?" Angie asked. She flexed her fingers before balling them into a fist.

"Hey, now," he said. He raised his hands in innocence. "I'm just saying what everyone knows to be true. If anyone had a grudge against Cassidy, it was you, Mel. She hated you; like, really, really hated you."

Mel blew out a breath. "I know. What I never understood was why. What did I ever do to Cassidy?"

"You were the embodiment of everything she was afraid to be," he said.

"Fat?" Mel asked.

Tucker shook his head. "Invisible."

Mel stared at him. "I was hardly invisible. Believe me, I tried. But whenever I hid in the shadows, Cassidy invariably pulled me out and made a mockery of me. My god, she made my life hell."

"She did that because she resented you for not needing to be in the spotlight," he said. "She was like a sunflower, incapable of surviving without the sun shining directly upon her all the time, twenty-four-seven. But you, you were happy with just two good friends, old movies, quiet weekends spent doing whatever you wanted. She hated you for being content, for not needing the adulation of many like she did."

Mel stared at him for a moment. Could that be true? Had Cassidy hated her because she'd been okay with herself? Nah. "It really was my weight, wasn't it?"

Tucker shook his head at her and then stared her right in the eye and asked, "So, did you kill her?"

"No!" Mel insisted. "Why would I be sitting here trying to figure out who killed her if it was me?"

"Because you're trying to find someone else to blame it on," he said.

"Someone like you?" Angie asked. "We all know how in love you were with Cassidy in high school. Maybe seeing her married to Danny Griffin was more than you could take and in a fit of rage last night you murdered her."

"Fit of rage?" he asked. "Do I really look the type to lose it over a girl from fifteen years ago? I don't know if you know this or not but I'm ecstatically happy with my life in California. I'm successful, I have a huge house on the water, and a girlfriend, Kayla, whom I love very much. Plus, have you *seen* Kayla? There is no reason for me to pine for someone who never paid any attention to me and there's certainly no reason for me to murder her. Mostly, seeing Cassidy again made me feel . . . well, sorry for her."

"But you still care about her," Mel said. "I saw you trying to mediate the altercation between her and Danny."

"Of course I care. You never get over your first crush," Tucker said. "But that's all she was. That's all she could ever be. Cassidy didn't have enough love in her to give it to anyone else, and that included Dan."

Mel and Angie exchanged a look. "What do you know, Tucker?"

"Nothing specific," he said. "Just that it wasn't a happy marriage, which was pretty obvious last night at the reunion. You want to know who I think had a motive to murder Cassidy? Well, as the police always say, it's usually the person closest to the victim, like the spouse."

"Danny?" Angie asked. She wrinkled her nose as if the mere idea of their all-star being a murderer left a bad smell.

"Who had the most to gain?" Tucker asked. "Danny would have gotten his freedom and since you know how vicious Cassidy can be, you can imagine he might have done anything to get away from her."

"How do you know the marriage wasn't happy?" Mel asked.

"When it came time to plan the reunion, Cassidy called together everyone in the area to her house," he said.

"But you're in California," Angie said.

"Yes, but I have business in Phoenix," he said. "I come through town a couple times a month. It makes my mom happy."

"So, even though we're local, we weren't invited," Angie said.

"Duh," Tucker said. "Cassidy hates . . . hated Mel."

"This is so crazy," Mel said. "Even after fifteen years she still hated me. It's just ridiculous and such a waste of time and energy."

"She didn't really have a lot on her plate, being a sportscaster's housewife," Tucker said. "She was very lonely and miserable."

"Why not just divorce Dan?" Angie asked. "She could have found someone she was actually happy with."

"No." Tucker shook his head. "She was the child of divorce, and she really hated her parents for it. She viewed divorce as a failure. She told Dan when they got married that the only way he was getting out of the marriage was in a box."

"Harsh," Angie said.

Mel could see it, though. In her mind, she could see Cassidy's overly plumped lips with her particular shade of bright pink lipstick over her artificially white teeth, forming the sentence, *You'll only get out of this marriage in a box.* It sent a shiver down her spine and she had a sudden pang of pity for Danny. No wonder he was happy to be on the road and away from his wife. But it also begged the question: Was Tucker right? Was Dan so desperate to escape his marriage that he murdered his wife?

"Listen, since we obviously can't go in there, you need to do reunion recon for us," Angie said.

"Why would I do that?" Tucker asked. "I mean, for all I know you two killed her."

"We didn't," Mel said. She met his gaze full on. "You know we didn't."

Tucker heaved a huge sigh. "But what if the person who did kill her finds out I'm helping you? I could become a target."

"Don't worry," Angie said. "They'll come for us first. Besides, you're just stopping by the bakery later to pick up some cupcakes for your mom and to visit with old friends, right?"

"She's lactose intolerant," Tucker said.

"I have cupcakes for that," Mel said.

"Fine," he said. "But I better not get into trouble over this. Isn't your fiancé a county prosecutor?"

"Yes, and my uncle is a police detective," Mel said. "So look at it as doing your civic duty."

"And keeping yourself on my good side," Angie said. She cracked her knuckles.

Tucker swallowed and then nodded. "Well, when you put it like that, I'm happy to help."

"Great!" Angie beamed at him. "See you around two?"

"I'll be there." Tucker glanced out of the car to see that the street was clear. Then he gave them a tiny wave and hopped out of the car, slamming the door behind him. He looked both ways and then jogged across the street to Danny's house.

They watched until he went inside and then Mel said, "Let's hope Tucker finds something out."

"Yeah, your freedom might depend upon it."

■ ■ ■ ■

The bakery was buzzing. Marty was working the front counter with Angie while Mel and Oz cranked out cupcakes in the back. After a scuffle over the music, Mel won and they were listening to "Finesse" by Bruno Mars and Cardi B. When Mel looked like she was going to rap with Cardi B, Oz shook his head and gave her his disapproving face.

"Oh, come on," Mel said. "I could bust a rhyme. I have great flow."

"Lord no," he said.

Mel laughed. "Be nice or I'll put on 'Seek and Destroy' by Metallica."

"I'd be okay with that," Oz said.

"I thought you were all about the rap," she said.

"I'm nineteen," Oz said. "I'm all about rebellion."

"Ah," Mel said. Then it hit her that Oz had been four years old when she graduated from high school. Suddenly, she felt so old. What had she been doing with her life? She glanced at the table in front of her and noted it was covered in cupcakes. This. This was what she'd been doing. And suddenly the absurdity of it hit her. Cupcakes. She spent her life making cupcakes. How crazy was that? And the really crazy thing was, she wouldn't have it any other way.

"Why are you smiling?" Oz asked. He looked suspicious. "You're not going to start playing Adele or something are you?"

"Adele is the bomb, but no," Mel said. "I was just thinking that I'm so freaking lucky in my life. I work with people I enjoy, doing what I love; how lucky is that?"

"Pretty lucky," Oz said. "But you've worked hard for it."

"We all have," she said. "Speaking of which, I was thinking about you the other day. What's your plan? Do you want a bakery of your own? Or a franchise of one of ours one day?"

"Whoa," Oz said. "That came out of left field."

"Not really," she said. "You're almost done with culinary school. You're at the top of your class. You could get snapped up by a restaurant or work at a resort, but just so you know we'll finance you if you want to open your own place."

"Are you having a freak-out?" Oz asked. He put his pastry bag down and shoved his bangs aside so he could meet her gaze. "Because you are totally freaking me out!"

"No," Mel said. "Er . . . maybe?"

"Listen, I have no plan," Oz said. "Except

to stay here and bake cupcakes with you all until I have a plan and whenever that is you'll be the first to know. Okay?"

"Okay," Mel agreed. Then she smiled. "Can I hug you?"

"If you must," he said.

Mel circled the table and reached up to hug him. Despite his bellyaching, he hugged her back and his voice was gruff. "In case I haven't told you enough, I really appreciate you giving me this job. I'm not sure what would have happened to me if I hadn't ended up here but I don't think it would have been good."

Mel squeezed him tight one more time and then let him go, forcing the lump in her throat to move down by swallowing repeatedly.

"One of my two best hiring decisions for sure," she said.

They smiled at each other and Mel picked up her pastry bag, and so did Oz, just as the doors to the kitchen slammed open and Angie burst into the room. She gave Mel a stern look and said, "We've got company."

"Tucker?"

"Yup."

"I'll be right there." Mel put down her pastry bag and glanced at Oz. "You've got this?"

"Natch," he said.

Mel went to the sink to wash her hands and wiped them dry with a paper towel. She untied her apron and hung it on a hook beside the door before she pushed through the doors to join Angie back out in the bakery.

And there was Tucker seated in one of the booths with cupcakes in front of him and Angie seated across from him, looking like she was getting ready to hit him with a million questions.

Mel slid into the booth beside Angie. She was dying to know what had happened at the wake. Who had looked genuinely sad? Had anyone? How had Danny seemed? Was he grief-struck? What about Megan? How was she holding up? Instead, Mel knew that the best way to get on anyone's good side was through the magic of baked goods.

She pushed the plate of cupcakes toward Tucker and smiled. She felt Angie stir restlessly beside her and reached under the table to pinch her.

"Ow," Angie said and whipped her head in Mel's direction.

"Sorry, did I nudge you?" Mel asked. She tried to give Angie a meaningful look. "Let's let Tucker gather himself for a moment, and then we can ask him about the wake."

She looked from the cupcakes to Tucker and back and watched the light in Angie's eye brighten.

"Of course," Angie said. She turned to Tucker. "It must have been a very emotional day. Take your time, enjoy the cupcakes. Mel has some put aside for your mom, too. We're here to help you through this."

"You know," Tucker said as he picked up his fork and stabbed one of Mel's meringue hi-top frosted cupcakes, "you two are so full of bull, I'm surprised you don't moo. Honestly, if you think that I believe you care even a little about me —" He shoved a forkful of the cupcake into his mouth. He chewed twice and then like the sun exploding over the horizon on a glorious spring day, his face lightened up, his eyes sparkled, and his entire demeanor became one of bliss.

"You were saying?" Mel prompted him.

"This." He pointed at the cupcake with his fork. "This is the most amazing thing I've ever tasted. Seriously, wow."

Mel turned her head and winked at Angie, who was trying not to smile. They waited while Tucker plowed through that cupcake and got halfway through the second before he slowed down.

"You two are the nicest girls from our

graduating class, did you know that?" he asked.

Mel studied his face. He looked almost as if he was drunk. He wore a silly smile; his eyes were glazed. She glanced down at the cupcakes. They were her standard chocolate cupcake with hi-top meringue frosting dipped in chocolate. She knew they were amazeballs but she'd never seen this sort of reaction before.

"Um, I'm getting a little worried," Angie said.

"Same," Mel agreed.

She reached across the table to pull the plate away from Tucker. He wrapped his arm around it, blocking her and looking like he was going to hiss and spit at her if she tried to take the cupcake away.

"If he says 'My precious,' I am so out of here," Angie said.

"*Lord of the Rings,*" Mel piped up. Angie looked at Mel in exasperation.

"We're not playing right now," Angie said.

"Sorry, force of habit," Mel said. She turned back to Tucker. "Hey, buddy, how long has it been since you've had a cupcake?"

"Years," Tucker said. "I've been on a raw diet since I moved to Cali. Nothing impure in my system." He was licking a piece of

140

chocolate off his fork.

"And you thought today would be a great day to change that?" Angie asked.

"I'm in pain," Tucker said. "The grief is too much. It doesn't matter that she was a mean, selfish, vapid fluff head of a person, for some reason, I crushed on Cassidy hard all through high school. Seriously, I thought she was the embodiment of everything a woman was supposed to be —"

Angie made a retching noise.

"Yeah, I know, what was I thinking?" Tucker said. He shoved another bite of cupcake into his mouth and it seemed to help. "And now she's gone."

Mel figured this was as good a time as any to ask, "How was Danny doing this morning?"

Tucker's head snapped up. "Given that every female in our graduating class, minus you two, was there to hug and comfort him, I'd say he's holding up just fine."

Mel noted the bitterness in his voice. She remembered Tucker had been on the school newspaper and yearbook. He'd been the one viewing every event through a camera lens or with his recorder out, interviewing whomever about whatever was happening at the moment.

It occurred to her that while he was always

there, he was also an outlier, always on the outside looking in. She wondered if that's why he disliked Danny Griffin so much. Danny was always at the center and even now that his athletic career had crumbled, he was still the good-looking guy with the slow smile and the quick wit in front of the camera, making everyone feel as if he knew them personally and that he cared. There was no faking that sort of charisma.

"What about your girlfriend?" Angie asked. "Did she go with you today?"

"No," Tucker said. "Kayla was supposed to but then she goofed up her mascara or something and it led to a whole existential crisis, so she's resting poolside at the Phoenician Resort."

"Did you want to bring her some cup-cakes?" Mel asked.

Tucker gave her a horrified look. "She would stab me with the first sharp object she could find. She's on a raw diet, too. Sugar freaks her out, even coconut sugar, which is like the healthiest sugar you can eat."

"So, not our people?" Angie said. Tucker made a face at her and she shrugged.

"I hope she gets over her . . . crisis," Mel said. She wasn't really sure if that was cor-rect but Tucker nodded, so she figured it was good. "If you could tell us more about the wake today. What happened? What were people saying? Did anyone act suspicious?"

"You mean other than Danny?" he asked.

"Dude," Angie said. "You've got to let it go. You may not like that Cassidy married him, and his life might seem like an impossible dream to the rest of us, but your bias against him is not helping us process potential suspects."

"You're right," Tucker said. "You're totally right. I mean he's not even a bad guy. Always pleasant and friendly, but I swear — has a drop of rain ever even fallen on his charmed life?"

"Um, yeah, his wife was just murdered," Mel said. "I think that qualifies."

"Sorry," Tucker said. He shoved the last of the cupcake in his mouth. Once he swallowed he said, "You're right, but I forget because I feel like it's an outcome that's advantageous to him, so again, does he ever suffer?"

Angie made a rolling motion with her hands and said, "Explain."

"Okay, okay." Tucker wiped his mouth with his napkin and slumped back in his seat. He turned and looked at Mel. "You're not going to like it."

She felt her stomach drop to her feet.

"They blame me, don't they?"

"If by 'they' you mean Dwight Pickard, then yes. He showed up and was going on and on about the poison cupcakes," Tucker said. "He was getting everyone riled. Honestly, if I were you I'd have the cops watch the place in case someone decides to torch it in the night."

"What?" Angie cried. "That's insane. We don't even know if there was something wrong with the cupcake she ate. It could be totally unrelated."

Tucker lifted his hands as if to say *What can you do?* "It might have helped if you had shown up to represent yourself. Not only would it have put Dwight in his place but Danny asked about you. I think he was looking for some moral support from someone he considers a friend."

"Me? He asked for me?" Mel felt a sudden pang of guilt that she had let Danny down by not showing up at the wake that morning. She hadn't thought he'd notice but now she felt horrible for not being there for what was likely the worst time of his life.

"You," Tucker confirmed. "Well, until Dwight started going on and on about how you weren't there because you were probably the killer."

"Dwight!" Mel spat his name. "That walking rock has been torturing me since middle school. Why? What did I ever do to him?"

"You'd have to ask him that," Tucker said. "But he was telling everyone who would listen that he was certain you killed Cassidy to try and win Dan."

"But I'm engaged to Joe DeLaura," Mel said.

"Lianne pointed that out but Dwight said Joe was a poor second to Danny," Tucker said. "Although I gotta say the shiner he was sporting didn't make Joe seem second to anyone."

"Oh, for the love of buttercream," Mel said. "That's the dumbest thing I've ever heard. Clearly, Joe is the superior man. My god, he's kind, and funny, and sweet, and smart, so smart, and he's freaking gorgeous. Danny Griffin isn't even in the same league."

Angie grinned at her. "You're so in love with my brother."

Mel felt her face get hot. She couldn't believe she had just gushed like that, but really, there was no competition there.

"Yes, I am, but that's not the point," she said. "The point is why does Dwight feel compelled to blame me? I mean, how do we even know she ate the cupcake?"

"Dwight didn't seem to care about that

detail," Tucker said. "He was too busy making you out to be the villain. Megan did say that Cassidy was known to comfort eat and it wouldn't have surprised her if Cassidy had grabbed a cupcake before they were being served and hid in the bathroom to eat it. She was pretty weird about eating in front of people, like she wanted everyone to think she existed solely on lettuce leaves and almonds. According to Megan, Cassidy was really struggling with Dan being the most popular person at the reunion. His enjoyment of his return home as the conquering hero and celebrity sportscaster really bugged her since he seemed intent on spending time with everyone but her."

Tucker rolled his eyes, letting them know what he thought of Dan's return.

"You know, there were a lot of guys who worshiped Danny in high school. Do you think one of them had something to do with Cassidy's death, maybe in some misguided attempt to help Danny, and let Mel take the blame?" Angie asked.

"No idea," Tucker said.

"Ugh," Mel grunted. "I hate this." She looked at Tucker. "Did you get any other information?"

"Just the usual," Tucker sighed. "Brittany inserted herself as Danny's hostess, which

146

was weird because Megan actually brought food and was helping in a meaningful way. But you know Brittany, she was oblivious. Go Devils!"

Mel and Angie both nodded. Mel remembered Brittany's scene outside the bathroom when Dan arrived. She had apologized to Dan. At the time, Mel had thought it was because a tragedy for Dan had occurred, but maybe it was more. Maybe she was apologizing because she felt guilty about something.

"You guys don't think Brittany —" Mel said and then paused. Both Tucker and Angie seemed to consider it for a moment and then shook their heads. "Yeah, you're right. Crazy thought. The captain of the pep squad a murderer? Not likely."

"How did Megan seem?" Angie asked. "I never really understood her friendship with Cassidy, because Megan is nice and Cassidy —"

"Not as much," Mel supplied.

"You'll get no argument from me," Tucker said. "I always liked Megan. She was kind and beautiful, not my type, but still really pretty. I always wondered why she never married either of her fiancés. I mean, I understand getting engaged to the wrong guy once, but twice? They can't have been that bad, right?"

"Maybe they're the ones who ditched her," Mel said. "Maybe she doesn't want kids and they're looking for a baby mama."

"Or she might be super high-maintenance or something," Angie said. "She's a real estate mogul, so her expectations in a partner may have been pretty high. Perhaps they just didn't live up to it."

"It had to be something," Tucker agreed. He glanced at Mel and Angie. "So, what's your next move?"

"I have no idea," Mel said. "Wait and see, I guess."

"Wouldn't it be nuts if Cassidy actually died of natural causes?" Angie asked.

"Yes, because how does a woman in her early thirties with no known health issues just drop dead?" Mel asked. "She doesn't. Somebody murdered Cassidy. I'm sure of it."

NINE

"Mel, you need to come back here," Oz called from the kitchen door.

She turned her head to see if there was smoke billowing out from the kitchen. There wasn't, but the look on Oz's face was still one of mild panic.

"Excuse me," she said. "Tucker, thanks for stopping by. I have a box of cupcakes for your mom ready to go. They're behind the counter with your name on them."

"Thanks, Mel," he said. "It's been great seeing you, you know, in spite of everything."

"You, too, Tucker. I'm glad you're doing well." She left Angie to get his cupcakes for him as she hurried to the kitchen to see what was up.

Marty was chatting up a couple of elderly ladies at the counter and Mel saw him wink at one of them. Despite living with his girlfriend now, Marty knew how to charm the ladies and she wondered what he'd been like in high school. She suspected he'd been a wild one.

She pushed through the swinging doors into the kitchen. Standing in the middle of the room, eating one of Oz's newly decorated cupcakes, was her uncle Stan. Beside him, wearing an ill-fitting uniform and carrying what looked like a large toolbox was a tall skinny man she hadn't met before, but whose type she recognized. Crime scene specialist. Crud.

"What gives, Uncle Stan?"

"What? No hug?" he asked.

Mel narrowed her eyes and then stepped forward for one of the patented Cooper men hugs. It was a big old bear hug, the sort that let you know everything was going to be okay even though the ship was going down and the sharks were circling. She took what comfort she could get.

"Better?" Uncle Stan asked when he released her.

"Yeah, but —" she began but he interrupted her.

"This is Kyle Plummer," Uncle Stan said. "He's here to check out the bakery and I know you'll be happy to cooperate."

Mel heard the warning in his words. He was trying to tell her something, but this was her sanctuary and she did not want a crime scene tech in here, touching her stuff.

"Of course." She faked a smile at Kyle, who flinched, so she figured it came out as more of a baring of teeth. Oh, well, she'd tried. She turned to Stan and said, "But it would help if I knew what you were looking for."

"I can't tell you that," he said at the same time Kyle said, "Poison."

Mel gasped. "So, Cassidy was poisoned."

"No," Uncle Stan said at the same time Kyle said, "Yes."

Uncle Stan put his palm over his forehead. "Kyle, what have we talked about?"

"Me not talking," Kyle said.

"And when are you not supposed to talk?" Uncle Stan asked.

"Whenever we leave the police station," Kyle said.

"Look around you," Stan commanded. "Are we in the police station?"

"No."

"Then?"

"No talking," Kyle said. "Got it. I'll stop. Now."

"Thank you," Uncle Stan said.

Kyle looked at the room and then at Uncle Stan. He made a gesture with his hands and Uncle Stan tipped his head to the side as if trying to figure out what he was doing. Kyle made a few more gestures and Uncle Stan just stared at him as if bewildered by the man.

"I think he's asking if he can get started," Mel said.

"Oh, well why didn't you say so?" Uncle Stan asked. He waved his hand in a shooing gestures at Kyle. "Get to work."

Kyle rolled his eyes but didn't say a word. Mel watched as he moved to the far counter under the window and opened his kit. She turned back to Uncle Stan, who shook his head.

"No, I can't tell you anything."

"Do I need a lawyer?" Mel asked. "Can you tell me that?"

"No."

"But you're searching my kitchen," she said. "Does that mean Cassidy was poisoned by a cupcake and, if so, how can I not need a lawyer?"

"Well, it doesn't appear to have been a cupcake that poisoned her," Uncle Stan said.

"Oh. So, you're just ruling me out?" she asked.

"Something like that," he said.

"And what kind of poison was it?"

"Not telling you that," he said. He reached

for another cupcake and Oz slapped his hand.

"No cupcakes until I'm sure you're not going to contaminate my kitchen," he said.

"I would never," Uncle Stan protested.

"We'll just see, won't we?" Oz asked.

The two men stared at each other and Mel felt like clunking their heads together. She wanted information. Who cared about her kitchen? Wait. She cared. She cared a lot.

"Now, hold up," she said. She turned to her Uncle Stan and said, "You can't just come in here and search for a poison. What if word gets out? It could damage my business."

Uncle Stan gave her his *you're trying my patience* look. Mel didn't care. Cassidy had been poisoned. Her bakery was being inspected. Something had to give.

Uncle Stan jerked his head in the direction of her office. She gathered what he had to say was private. Fine. So long as she got to the bottom of this.

She led the way to her office. She looked at Oz on her way and said, "Don't let him near any of the perishables, or the baking supplies, or anything else."

Kyle opened his mouth and then closed his mouth and stood there, looking as if he didn't know what to do. Uncle Stan sighed.

"Check the surfaces, Kyle," he said.

Kyle nodded and turned back to his tool-box.

"Wipe down anything he touches," Mel said to Oz.

"Got it." Oz stared at Kyle as if he was a fly in the kitchen that he was preparing to swat. Kyle swallowed audibly.

Mel led Stan into her tiny office. It was formerly a closet but she'd managed to wedge in a desk and a file cabinet and a potted philodendron whose long trailing vines looked like they were reaching for the exit in a doomed escape attempt.

There was one hardback chair and Stan took it while Mel turned sideways so she could get around her desk. She sat and folded her hands on the surface, trying to look like the enterprising young woman she was and not the pigtailed, scabbed-knee niece that she was sure Uncle Stan always saw her as.

"So, what gives with Kyle the talker?" she asked.

Stan rolled his eyes. "Listen, I know this seems like a huge pain."

"Seems?"

Stan gave her a look and Mel piped down.

"But here's the thing: There are certain people on the force who would like to see you brought in for questioning and want this place turned upside down, looking for evidence. What I am doing here is a preemptive strike to keep those persons happy and keep you out of jail."

"Tara, right?" Mel asked. "The person you're talking about is Detective Martinez."

"Maybe," Stan said.

"Please, I know she has a thing for Joe and I know she has it in for me," Mel said. "Man, what is it about me that seems to bring out the worst in people?"

"That's not entirely true," Stan said. "Her beef with you is also because you chose Joe over her cousin Manny, and then he moved to Las Vegas."

"Where he's very happy," Mel said. "I think I should get points for facilitating that happiness."

"He was my partner," Stan said. He looked unhappy. "He was a good partner."

"So, you're mad at me, too?"

"Nah, but I am saddled with his cousin now and, frankly, she's a bit of a handful," he said. "Plus, she does have a thing for your man, so I don't see her forgiving you any time soon."

"Why is humanity so exhausting?" Mel asked.

"I don't know, but it keeps me employed,"

Stan said.

"All right, putting aside the fact that you're here disrupting my kitchen, tell me what you're looking for," Mel said. "I was at the reunion. I might be able to help you."

"Kyle is looking for traces of the poison used to kill Cassidy," he said. "You'll be pleased to know that there were no traces of the poison found in the cupcake she was holding."

"And what was this poison?"

"I'm not telling you that," he said.

"Why not?" Mel threw up her hands. She hated not having all of the information.

"Because you need to stay away from this," he said. "In fact, stay away from all of your old classmates and that includes Danny Griffin."

"Why? Do you think he did it?"

"I don't know, but we always look pretty closely at the spouse, you know that," he said.

"What about Dwight Pickard?" Mel asked. "Have you questioned him? He's awfully angry. Maybe some time spent in jail would be good for him."

One eyebrow on Stan's head lifted higher than the other. "Dwight Pickard? Why does that name sound familiar?"

"No reason," Mel said. She didn't want to

have to admit that the man had bullied her for years and still did whenever he got the chance.

"Is he an old boyfriend of yours?"

"Gack," Mel gagged. "God, no."

"So just someone you'd like to see made uncomfortable then?" Stan looked at her in a way that made her feel small.

"He's a bully," Mel said. "He bullied me at school and he bullies me now whenever our paths cross. I have no idea why, but he hates me."

"Did you reject him or something? Sometimes a guy takes that hard and never lets it go."

"No," Mel said. "I was mostly just the butt of all his jokes." She glanced away and then looked back. "You know, Angie talked me into going to the reunion. I didn't want to because of people like Dwight and Cassidy and, true to form, they tried to make me feel less than at the reunion. But you know who didn't? Danny Griffin. He danced with me and he made me realize that I was always okay. Danny didn't kill his wife. I'd stake all that I have on it."

Uncle Stan nodded. He considered her for a moment before he said, "I'm glad Griffin was a stand-up guy at the reunion, I am, but that doesn't mean he didn't kill his wife."

"I know you have to see it that way, but I don't," Mel said. "And I'm not going to stay away from him."

Uncle Stan began to protest but Mel held up her hand. "No, I'm not going to seek him out, either, but I will go to Cassidy's funeral and I won't let anyone stop me from being there for a friend. I already ducked out once by not going to the wake. I can't do it again."

Stan reached into his pocket for an antacid tablet. He looked unhappy but Mel wouldn't be moved. She felt bad that she'd been intimidated from showing up at Danny's house to offer him her support. Danny didn't have to dance with her at the reunion, but he did, and he'd put to rest so many of her own demons, she owed him her loyalty for that if nothing else.

"Fine, but you'll tell me when you go anywhere near him," Stan said. "You'll check in and you'll be careful. No eating or drinking anything in his presence, am I clear?"

Mel smiled. "Yes, I got it. Do you want me to wear a wire, too?"

"Funny," he said. "Watch yourself or I'll have to call your fiancé and tell him you're being difficult."

"Joe would expect nothing less of me," Mel said.

"You're just like your mother, you know that?" Stan said. "You Cooper women are a crafty bunch. She's got me eating healthy and working out. Gah, I don't even recognize myself."

Mel grinned at his mock upset. "You look happy, Uncle Stan, and I'm glad."

"Yeah, well, there's that," he said. He smiled and then jerked his thumb at the door. "I'd better go. Kyle is a bit of a basket case."

"So I noticed," she said. "If you find anything you'll tell me, won't you, Uncle Stan?"

"Sure," he said. "If I think it's relevant."

Which Mel knew was his way of saying, *No way in hell.* She supposed she couldn't fault him for trying to keep her safe even if it was super annoying. He disappeared back into the kitchen with a wave and Mel sat at her desk, mulling over what she knew for sure. Number one, Cassidy was poisoned, which was sort of what she had figured, and number two, poison meant murder. Someone at the reunion had murdered Cassidy and Mel knew that as far as people like Dwight Pickard were concerned, she was the prime suspect. Skipping the funeral was not an option.

She felt her anxiety spike at the mere idea of facing down a graduating class of people who believed her to be a murderer. It made her stomach cramp and she almost went after Stan to mooch one of his antacid tablets, but she refrained. She had to remember that she had done nothing, absolutely nothing, wrong and she wasn't going to cower and hide as if she had.

She opened up her laptop and read the latest news reports about Cassidy's death. There wasn't much to it except that she had been found dead at the reunion and her husband had no comment at this time. The local press loved Danny because he was the hometown hero, winning the high school state championship no less than four times, and because when his knee blew out and his pro career was over, he found a new career in front of the camera, and the camera loved him — as did most of the women in the Valley of the Sun. It did not surprise Mel to see that none of the local media was listing Danny as a suspect, not even hinting at it, which actually made her feel better. Perhaps they could both get out of this without going to jail.

■ ■ ■ ■

After Uncle Stan left, Mel called Tate, who was overseeing their local franchise in downtown Phoenix. He was on his way back to Scottsdale and when she told him about Uncle Stan and Kyle, he seemed unsurprised.

"Wait, did Uncle Stan call you first?" she asked.

"Yeah . . . no . . . maybe," Tate said.

"Did you want to commit to one of those answers?" she asked. Silence greeted her question. "Fine, as soon as you get back here, we need to have a meeting. You, me, and Angie."

"I'm parking in the back lot right now," he said. "Do we have coffee?"

"It'll be under way when you walk through the door," she said.

Sure enough, Tate banged through the back door as Mel hit the switch on the kitchen coffeepot.

"I'm guessing you want to go to the funeral," Tate said. He moved to stand by the coffeemaker as if his looming presence would make it brew faster.

"How did you — Wait, we need Angie," Mel said. She strode to the kitchen door

161

and stuck her head out. "Ange, I need you back here."

Angie was helping Marty work the counter. There were only three people in line, so Mel didn't feel bad about calling her back. She glanced across the bakery and noticed that Tucker was still sitting in the booth. He was staring at his phone and she wondered if he was working or just watching videos. It was hard to tell these days.

He glanced up and saw Mel and waved. "I like your place so much I decided to stay here and do some work."

"Great," Mel said.

Tate peeked out behind her and saw Tucker. "Hey, Tucker, how're you doing?"

"Kicking butt and taking names," Tucker said.

Mel rolled her eyes. From what she knew about Tucker's business, he developed webpages that he then sold for oodles of money. It wasn't like he was a brain surgeon.

"Good to hear," Tate said. "We were about to talk about the reunion, care to join us?"

Tucker perked up like a kid who'd been sitting on the bench his whole life and was just invited to play. "Sure."

Mel gave Tate an irritated look. She had been hoping to keep this convo just to the three of them.

"What?" Tate asked. "He's more in the know than the rest of us. It'll be good to have him weigh in on whether it's advisable for you to go to the funeral or not."

"I suppose," Mel said. She was going either way but she couldn't argue Tate's point. Tucker was more in the loop than the rest of them.

Tucker slid out of the booth and walked across the bakery. When he went to step behind the counter, Marty blocked his way, giving him a fierce once-over with one gray eyebrow lowered menacingly, as if he could read a person's soul at fifty paces.

"Easy, killer," Angie said. "He's one of us."

Marty stepped slowly out of the way. Tucker gave Mel a nervous look.

"Don't worry, he's never bitten anyone," she teased.

"Not yet anyway," Marty said.

"Great," Tucker said. He moved swiftly past Marty and followed Mel, Angie, and Tate into the kitchen.

Tate poured them each a cup of coffee, putting the sugar bowl and a small jug of milk in the middle of the steel table where they could all reach it.

"What's up?" Angie asked.

"Uncle Stan said that Cassidy was poisoned," Mel said. "He wouldn't say what the poison was in or what type it was but it must have been given to her at the reunion, don't you think?"

"That would make it a fast-acting poison," Tate said. "Arsenic, maybe, or cyanide."

"Who has access to stuff like that?" Angie asked. She blew on her coffee, trying to cool it. "And why Cassidy? I mean, I know she was annoying in high school but our class hasn't been together in fifteen years. Who could carry a grudge that long?"

"You're skipping over the obvious," Tucker said. "This confirms my suspicion that it's Danny. He would have had access to her food and drink, plus he could have poisoned her before the reunion even started, hoping it would be blamed on someone like Mel, someone with a hostile history with Cassidy."

"That'd be half of our graduating class," Angie said. "I mean, that girl had more enemies than I'll ever have in a lifetime."

"True," Tucker conceded. "But why did Danny make a point of dancing with Mel?"

"Because we're friends," Mel said. She didn't like where this was going.

"Are you?" Tucker asked. "You've stayed in touch over the past fifteen years?"

"Well, no, but . . ."

"He asked you so that Cassidy would lose her temper, reminding everyone of how much she hates you," Tucker said. "Making you the prime suspect."

Mel felt her heart sink. Had Danny done that to her? Had he used her like that? She didn't want to believe it.

"That's one theory," Tate said. "But there was also Brittany, who believes Danny should be her husband, and Kristie, who got cheated out of being the homecoming queen. Mel was Cassidy's target for bullying, for sure, but there were a lot of people who might have taken the reunion as their opportunity to get even."

"Thanks for including me in the suspect lineup," Mel said. "Really, I can't thank you enough."

"I'm not including you," he said. "I'm just pointing out —"

"My motive to kill her?" she asked.

Tate gave her a dark look and then took a long sip of his coffee. "I can't talk to you when you're defensive like this."

"Sorry, but 'most likely to kill the homecoming queen' wasn't really what I was going for in the yearbook," Mel said.

"Now, you two, take it easy," Angie said. "We're all on the same team here."

"She's right," Tucker said. "The only way

to find out what happened to Cassidy is to trace her steps at the reunion. You know, who she spoke to, what she ate, drank, inhaled, if she was partaking of anyone's vape."

"Did Cassidy vape?" Mel asked. "I have a hard time picturing that."

Tucker shrugged. "I'm just passing through. I really didn't know the old gang that well anymore."

"He brings up a good point, though," Tate said. "With prescription drugs being so readily available, she could have been an addict for all we know. Maybe the reunion was too much for her and when she went to self-medicate she overdid it."

Angie set her mug down and tapped her forefinger on her chin. "I suppose it's possible. Usually, an opioid addiction happens after a surgery or an injury when the person is prescribed a medication that they become addicted to. Do we know if she's had anything like that?"

"Not that I know of," Tucker said. "But Dan probably did when he blew out his knee a few years ago. Could she have started helping herself to his pain meds back then?"

"Who would know?" Tate asked.

"Her best friend, Megan, would," Mel said. "I'm pretty sure."

"Then we need to talk to Megan," Tate said. "Should we try at the funeral?"

"I'll do it," Mel said. "I could tell Megan that Joe and I are looking for a new house and that I was hoping she could help us. Then it's more of a work thing for her and she might loosen up a bit."

"That's a solid plan," Angie said. She glanced around the table. "It goes without saying that we have to be careful. Someone in our graduating class is a murderer and if they think we're looking into it, that puts a target on all of our backs."

"I gotta say this was not how I pictured this reunion going," Tucker said.

"That makes four of us," Tate agreed.

Ten

"This dress is itchy," Mel said. She was wearing a plain black shift. She wasn't sure if it was the fabric or the seams but she felt as if her skin was having an allergic reaction to the dress.

"It's nerves," Angie said, turning in the front passenger seat — Tate was driving — to look at Mel in the back. "At least you don't appear rashy."

"Thanks?" Mel said.

"You don't have to go, you know," Angie said. "Tate and I could go to the funeral and talk to Megan."

"It's more than talking to Megan," Mel said. "I feel like my reputation is on the line. If I hide, it's like admitting that I could have murdered Cassidy. You know, sort of like if you don't call out bad behavior when you see it, you're complicit."

"I think you'd get a pass, given that Cassidy was so cruel to you all through high school, but Angie and I will have your back in there the entire time. Promise," Tate said. He met Mel's gaze in the rearview mirror. "If anyone comes after you, we'll take care of it."

"You know Dwight will," Mel said. "And I really don't want a fistfight at the funeral, so let's just try to avoid him, agreed?"

"I'll take point on our mission," Angie said. "I'm short enough to blend."

"See? We got this," Tate said. "Still itchy?"

Mel stopped scratching her neckline. "Nope. I'm fine. Really."

In truth, she was dreading this encounter with her former classmates. She knew there was going to be a lot of whispering and possibly a confrontation or two. But she did consider Danny her friend and she wanted to be there for him and for herself. She hadn't hurt Cassidy and she wasn't going to hide and let the whispers get worse. She would call out the haters, or at least make them say their hateful words to her face.

She slumped back against the seat. Adulting was hard. Joe had offered to take off from work to come with her, but Mel knew he was working on a case with Child Protective Services and she didn't want to take him away from advocating for a child caught in a horribly abusive situation. She could handle this. She would handle this. It would be fine, and if it wasn't, well, at least she had chosen to be brave. That felt pretty good.

Cassidy Havers-Griffin's funeral was to be held at a mortuary on the outskirts of Old Town. Mel supposed they could have walked as it wasn't that far from the bakery, but it was nice to have a getaway car parked nearby if needed.

Tate found a spot at the back of the lot. Mel took a deep breath before she got out of the car. There were several people around them, also dressed in somber funeral attire, but she didn't see any familiar faces. Her shoulders dropped a bit and she exhaled. It was going to be okay.

Tate put his arm around Angie's waist and held out his other hand to Mel. She wasn't too proud to take it. Staying close to Tate's side, the three of them made their way to the doors. When they entered, Angie signed the guestbook for their party and a woman in a pale blue suit who worked at the mortuary handed them a program. It had a dazzling headshot of Cassidy on the front and beneath that, a poem by Helen Lowrie Marshall called "Afterglow." It was lovely and Mel wondered if Danny had chosen it specifically for his wife.

When they entered the main room, Mel scanned the space looking for Danny. He was seated beside the casket. He looked older and more haggard, as if he'd aged years, instead of just days, since Cassidy's death. Mel felt bad for him. She wanted to go and give him a hug but Tate led them to some vacant seats in the back corner of the room. There'd be time to talk to Dan later.

The seats filled up until it was standing room only. Mel hadn't heard anyone say her name but even in the corner she felt exposed and desperately wished it was the custom in the States to wear hats. She'd recently met some milliners from London, and both she and Angie thought it was a shame that the hat thing wasn't as big in the States as it was in Europe. She could really use a wide brim to hide behind right now. She tipped her chin up, knowing she was going to have to bluff her way through it.

A nondenominational minister stood at the narrow podium at the front of the room. While he spoke, an older woman beside Danny began to weep. She had the same red hair as Cassidy. Mel assumed she was Cassidy's mother. No matter how Mel felt about Cassidy, she had to feel for this woman who had lost her child. Suddenly, she wondered if she should be here. Because while she felt awful that Cassidy was dead, possibly murdered, she didn't grieve her loss, not as she should. She squirmed in her seat. She was debating getting up and leaving, when she saw a flash of yellow. Yellow at a funeral?

She turned her head and glanced from the dress to the woman wearing it. It was Kristie Hill. Her long dark hair was loose and her makeup perfect. She looked like she was at a party, not a funeral; it was almost as if she was reveling in her rival's demise. Mel elbowed Angie and tipped her head in Kristie's direction.

"Wow, that's a statement," Angie whispered.

"Who? Where?" Tate asked.

Mel and Angie hushed him together.

"Over there, in yellow," Angie said.

"Oh," Tate whispered. "Looks like someone is not hiding how she feels about Cassidy's death."

"Maybe she's just fashion impaired," Mel said. "There are other people here in colors besides black, blue, and gray."

"But nothing quite so bold as that," Tate said.

"I agree," Angie said. "Besides, she works in retail. I think she's making a statement.

172

Very bad form."

"So, Kristie moves up on the suspect list," Mel said. "Anyone else look like they're gloating?"

"I can't tell from here," Angie said. "We'll know more after. They're having a tea in the reception hall."

"Shh." A woman in front of them shushed them, and Mel and Angie stopped talking.

After the minister spoke, Megan Mareez rose from her seat on the other side of Cassidy's mom. She approached the podium with a notecard in her hand. She looked out across the packed room and promptly dissolved into tears. No one moved. No one said a word. She stood in front of them with her grief on full display. Mel reached over and took Angie's hand. She couldn't imagine how Megan must be feeling at the loss of her best friend.

After a few moments, it was clear that Megan wasn't going to be able to pull it together. Danny rose from his seat and hugged her. Mel heard him reassure her that it was okay and then he helped her to her seat. He approached the podium himself and cleared his throat.

"Today we honor the memory of Cassidy Ann Havers-Griffin," he said. His voice was gruff and Mel could see he was struggling to maintain his composure. He talked about the first time he saw Cassidy, and her best feature, her smile. He talked about how he couldn't have gotten through his darkest days post injury without her, and that for such a short life, Cassidy had had an incredible impact on everyone she met.

Mel knew that to be true. She glanced around at the assembled group. Aside from Megan and Cassidy's mother, no one else was crying. Not Tucker, who had crushed on Cassidy all through school, not Kristie or the other women who had made up the homecoming court. No one. In a room of more than a hundred people, the absence of grief was more palpable than anything else. It was more than a little unnerving.

Mel could see on the faces of the people around her that they were here not because they felt any real emotion, but because the social order expected them to be here and, probably, because they were curious. Would something happen at the funeral? Would they bear witness to a scene or a scandal? The whole sordid thing made Mel want to take a shower.

When Dan finished speaking, Lori Bird rose and joined the pianist at the front of the room. She took up the mic and began to sing. Short, with dark skin, long flowing hair, and a curvy figure, Lori had been the best singer in their class. Mel hadn't seen her in forever, but had heard that she had gone pro and sang backup with some national acts and had a standing gig at the local casino.

The notes from her mouth were so pure and clear that Mel felt the hair on the back of her neck stand on end. Lori sang "My Heart Will Go On" and it was breathtakingly beautiful. It no longer mattered that Cassidy had been so unlovable. She had been taken too soon and any redemption she may have found in life had been denied her. Mel felt a tear slide down her cheek. She glanced and saw that Angie, too, was overcome by the song. They exchanged a look and Mel knew that Angie was feeling the same thing she was.

Mel looked around the room and noticed a flurry of tissues had appeared. It seemed to hit them all at once that Cassidy, their homecoming queen, the woman who had ruled their high school hallways with such malicious glee, was gone. Mel couldn't believe that she was feeling grief but there it was. Not grief for the person who was gone, perhaps, but definitely grief for the person Cassidy could have been. The opportunity of a life wasted in vitriol and anger, and for what? It was such a sad legacy to leave behind. Mel grieved that for sure.

When the song ended, they rose from their seats. It was time to pass by the casket and give Cassidy's loved ones their condolences. Mel wasn't sure how to finesse this. She wasn't positive she could stomach looking down at Cassidy in her casket. It would feel hypocritical at best and ghoulish at worst. There was no help for it. Maybe if she, Angie, and Tate went together, it wouldn't be so weird.

The line moved slowly and since they were at the back, it was even slower. She tried to keep her head down but being above average in height did not make it easy. She stared at the program in her hand, at the picture of Cassidy, and when that got to be too much she flipped it over and read the verses printed on the back.

The line was finally moving and, as if by silent consensus, Angie took the lead and Tate stood behind Mel as if they could offer her a buffer from anyone who might take offense at her presence. It seemed to work. No one said a word to her although she could feel people staring.

They inched their way toward the front of the room. They were just stepping into the main aisle when Mel heard the distinctive voice of Dwight Pickard.

"What are you doing here?" he demanded.

Mel didn't need to turn around to know that he was addressing her. This was exactly what she had hoped to avoid. How had they missed him? She realized he had just come through a side door, so he hadn't been in the room before. Great, what were the odds?

"Leave her alone, Dwight," Tate said. His voice was firm. It was his corporate *I will destroy you and take every cent you have to your name* voice. It did not faze Dwight in the least.

"Make me," he said.

Tate whipped around so that they were nose to nose. "You want to go outside, Dwight? I'd be happy to serve you a dirt sandwich."

Dwight threw back his head in a bitter laugh, with no mirth. It was a mocking, derisive guffaw, as if Tate were too pathetic for words. Big mistake. Mel glanced at Angie, who was coming in hot.

"Easy," Mel said. She looped her arm through Angie's and anchored her to her side. "This is a funeral. Let's act like it."

"Oh, I'll act like it," Angie said. "I'm going to punch him in his big, blocky head."

"Okay, see, punching is bad form at a funeral. Besides, he still has a shiner from

177

where Joe socked him the other day," Mel said. She glanced around, hoping for an ally. There was none to be found. Grumbles and harsh words started to swell as if Dwight had a lit a powder keg of hostility in the center of the room, until one voice rose above the rest.

"You were never good enough for her." Tucker was standing in front of Danny. He was red in the face and looked as if he'd been crying. Clearly, Lori's singing had gotten to him, too. "She deserved so much better than you."

The room went dead quiet. Dan looked at Tucker, standing before him, obviously distraught. He could have tossed him out, or had him tossed — heck, he could have punched him in the mouth for saying such a nasty thing at his wife's funeral. Dan didn't. Instead, he opened his arms and he hugged Tucker. A real hug, a big old bear hug, then he thumped him on the back twice and let him go.

He looked Tucker right in the eye and said, "You're right. She deserved better than me. I wasn't a good enough husband to her and I'll have to live with that for the rest of my life."

And just like that, the hostility went out of the room. Tucker nodded and rubbed his eyes with a fist before moving over to the casket to look down upon Cassidy one last time. It was heartbreaking and Mel felt a lump form in her throat.

The scene snapped the tension between Tate and Dwight, who looked less likely to brawl now. Lianne and Brittany each took ahold of Dwight and led him to the back of the room. It was an obvious attempt to keep him away from Mel, for which she would be ever grateful.

At the front of the line, Mel expressed her sympathy to Cassidy's mom. The woman had no idea who she was, so that was a blessing. She then hugged Megan, who looked pale and exhausted, and told her how sorry she was. Megan nodded, but didn't look like she had any words to offer. Mel understood and squeezed Megan's hands one more time before moving on to Dan.

"I'm so sorry," she said.

That was all she got out before Dan folded her into a hug.

"Me, too," he said. "Thanks for coming. I know, well, I'm sure it couldn't have been easy, but I appreciate it. It's good to see a genuinely friendly face in the crowd."

"If you need anything . . ." Mel let her offer trail off.

"Thanks, but I'm doing all right. I'm sorry about Dwight," he said. "If he bothers you at all, let me know. He has no business coming after you like that."

"Thanks, but I'm fine," she said. "This is about you, not me. You handled Tucker really well."

"He was right," Dan said. He took Mel's arm and pulled her away from the others. "I wasn't a very good husband to her. We wanted different things — I wanted a family and she didn't — and we were making each other miserable. She deserved better than that. We both did."

Mel put her hand on his arm. "I really am sorry."

"Thanks, Mel," he said. "I know you're getting married soon. Make sure that guy is worthy of you." Mel nodded, even though it was Joe she was marrying and she was already absolutely positive.

The woman in blue who had been handing out programs approached to talk to Dan.

Mel glanced behind her, hoping for Tate to join her but he was still talking to Cassidy's mother. Mel had no choice but to move forward. Next stop: the casket. Her stomach cramped. She could feel the stares of everyone in the room on her as she made her way to the big white, glossy, flower-covered casket. It was an open casket, of which she was not a fan. She glanced around for Angie and found her in conversation with Lori, the singer. There was no help for her. She was going to have to look down at Cassidy alone. Oh, man.

Mel wiped her palms on her dress. Was she supposed to pray? Say something? Gaze at Cassidy's body with deep sadness? What? She'd never had to deal with an open casket for a person she didn't get along with before.

She decided that bowing her head was the way to go. Still, she walked slowly, hoping that either Tate or Angie would catch up to her. No such luck. Even dragging her heels, she ended up beside the casket by herself.

Cassidy looked peaceful. Her hair and makeup were on point. She was even wearing the only shade of lipstick she'd ever worn, that particularly bright shade of pink. The same one she used to write Mel's name . . . nope, Mel wasn't going to go there right now.

She would never know what Cassidy had been about to write in the bathroom. Mel knew it most likely would have hurt her feelings. That's what Cassidy did. But no more. It was strange to have her childhood tormentor silenced. It was not something Mel had ever really thought about before. This was the woman who had made her life a misery and now she was gone. Despite her moment at the reunion the other night, there was so much more Mel wanted to say to her arch enemy and now she'd never have the chance.

Mel glanced at Cassidy and realized that this was her lone opportunity to let her have it. She could say anything she wanted and get it off her chest once and for all. She could call the other woman out for making her life so bloody miserable. She could even call her all of the names she'd thought of over the years or hit her with all of the zingers she'd wanted to zap her with, the comebacks that had always come to her hours after Cassidy had humiliated her. She opened her mouth to let it out but instead, what came out surprised her.

"I wish things could have been different for both of us," Mel said. Her voice was a gruff whisper and she was filled with sadness. Not for Cassidy as much as for what could have been. They both could have been different. Their lives could have been different or at least not as difficult.

Feeling overly emotional, Mel headed for a side door. She needed to get it together, to regroup, to stop crying. She wound up in the kitchen. It wasn't very large, but it had all of the necessary implements to make coffee, tea, or to heat up a casserole or a cake. She wanted cake right now. Or at the very least a sustaining shot of frosting. A nice gob of buttercream would get her through until she could drown her sorrows in a cupcake or two at the bakery.

Maybe there was some canned frosting around here. Yes, it was against everything she believed in but, hey, beggars couldn't be choosers. She began to forage through the kitchen. There was nothing to satisfy except a box of very hard sugar cubes. She had never been a straight sugar sort of gal. She liked the smooth texture of frosting. The granules of sugar just wouldn't do it. Plus, she had to consider, what the hell was she doing?

She was in a mortuary at the funeral of her lifelong nemesis and she was foraging through the kitchen like a raccoon sifting through a garbage can. She needed help. Seriously, like an emergency therapy session or, yeah, a cupcake.

She glanced out the side door. There was a small meditation garden out there. She would text Angie and Tate to meet her when they were done, because there was no way she could go back into that room and face their old classmates again. She was done.

Mel pushed through the door and stepped outside. It was a beautiful sunny day in central Arizona. The air was cool, the sun warm, the rose bushes were getting ready to burst into bloom. She figured if she wandered to the far corner of the garden, she could sit under the pergola until her friends collected her.

She could just make out the top of the structure over the tall bushes on either side of the path. It reminded her of the highly manicured gardens she had seen when she'd traveled in Europe. The paths were enclosed in foliage, offering privacy and shade.

She was texting Angie and Tate to meet her, when she heard the low murmur of voices. She was about to turn around and go back, not wanting to run into anyone, most especially Dwight, when she recognized Dan's voice. Mel paused. She should turn around. She knew that and yet she didn't.

She stepped around a thick rose bush and there, standing under the pergola she'd been planning to escape to, were Danny and Megan. They were embracing, and it wasn't a friendly embrace, either. This was a full-on, making-out, spit-swapping lover's clinch. Mel felt her face heat up in embarrassment and she slid back behind the shrubbery. She was mortified that she'd caught them, but then remembered that they were at the funeral for *his* wife and *her* best friend. The scandal!

ELEVEN

Mel raised her phone and quietly snapped a picture. These two had some explaining to do and she was betting Uncle Stan would be more than a little interested to see this picture. She heard the door behind her open. Someone else was coming. What to do? Did she let them get caught by someone else? She thought about Danny, the boy she had tutored, and Megan, who had never been cruel to her, not really. Both had been caught in Cassidy's web. Was it any wonder that they were seeking solace in each other?

She coughed, loudly, and then strode back the way she had come. This was the best she could do to help them; now they were on their own. She hurried back to the building. Thankfully, the people who had come out to the garden were not people that she knew, so she could smile and nod and keep going. She needed to get out of here. Pronto.

Tate and Angie were coming out the door

as soon as she entered it. She jerked her head in the direction of the garden gate and said, "Let's go. As in, now."

"What happened?" Tate asked.

"I'll tell you in the car," Mel said.

"Was it Dwight?" he asked. His jaw jutted out. "I am more than willing to go back and give him the beating he deserves."

"That's my man," Angie said.

"No, no, no," Mel said. "We just need to leave. Quickly."

"All right," Tate said. "But you're killing me here."

"Bad choice of words," Mel said.

"Sorry," he said.

He hustled them out of the garden and down the side path toward the parking lot. Before they got to the car, he unlocked the doors and they all jumped in as if they were fleeing the scene of a crime. As they were getting ready to pull out, they heard a shout. Mel glanced back and there was Tucker. He was waving.

Mel knew he was trying to wave them down but she pretended he was waving good-bye and raised her hand and waved in return.

"Do not stop, do not slow down," she said. "I need to talk to you two and it has to be just the three of us."

"Whoa, okay," Angie said. She raised her arm and waved at Tucker, too.

Tate merely nodded and kept driving. It was a short drive to the bakery and Mel didn't want to talk about what she'd learned in public so she made quick work of it in the car. She told them about going to the garden to get some air and then turning the corner and seeing Danny and Megan in an embrace.

"No way," Angie said. "Are you sure?"

"Yes."

"Maybe he was just comforting her and it looked weird," Tate said. "Maybe it was just the angle."

"It wasn't the angle," Mel said. "There is no angle where mouths accidentally open and hands grab butts."

"You're positive?" Tate asked.

"I have a picture," Mel said.

Both Tate and Angie were silent, taking in this shocking bit of news. It was just as well. They had reached the bakery and they had to go back to work with their game faces on.

"What are you going to do?" Angie asked.

"I'm going to give the picture to Uncle Stan," Mel said. Because she knew this was the right and proper thing to do. "After I talk to Megan."

"What?" Tate asked. "Are you crazy? If she and Danny murdered Cassidy, you are going to be next on their hit list."

"He's right," Angie said. "Joe will freak out when he hears about this."

"No, he won't," Mel said. "I'm going to bring him into the loop and I'm sure he'll back me up on this. I don't really believe that Danny and Megan are capable of killing Cassidy. I need to give Megan the opportunity to explain this before I go to the police."

"Well, you're not going alone," Tate said. He glanced at his wife. "And you're not going with her. It's my turn."

"What do you mean?" Angie huffed.

"You always get to ride shotgun. I'm going to be the backup this time," Tate said.

"Well, that's totally uncool," Angie said. "You know just because you're my husband doesn't mean you get to boss me around."

"I would never," Tate said. He glanced at Angie meaningfully. Then he reached across the seat and rested his palm against her abdomen. "Remember it's not just about you anymore."

Mel went bug-eyed. She rocketed forward, sticking her head in between them. "Are you — ? No way! And you didn't tell me — ? Angie, a baby!"

"Hold up there, I'm not," Angie said. "At least I don't think I am, but I might be, because —"

"We're trying," Tate said. "So, Angie is not doing anything risky because there could be a lot more at stake if she gets hurt."

"As soon as you know, you have to tell me," Mel said. "Promise?"

"I promise," Angie said. She put one hand up. "I swear."

Mel spent the rest of the day thinking about her best friends becoming parents. She was so excited she could barely stand it. They were in their thirties, however, and she knew it might take them a little bit longer to get pregnant. She wondered if she and Joe should start trying as soon as they were married. She hadn't really gotten on top of the wedding plans as yet. And they were still adjusting to having a cat and a dog.

Captain Jack and Peanut had come a long way in cohabiting but there were moments when they acted up, like when Captain Jack opened the kitchen cupboards and Peanut went to town on her baking supplies, getting flour all over her kitchen. Joe had said it was clearly an accident but when Mel looked at Captain Jack, he had a mischievous twinkle in his eye and a sassy swish to his tail and she couldn't help thinking he had tried to get Peanut in trouble.

The other problem was her personal case of wedding post-traumatic stress disorder. She felt as if they'd tried to get this thing done so many times that perhaps less planning would be better. She hadn't told Joe yet, but she was thinking maybe they could just go to city hall and tie the knot and then throw the church wedding and the big party. She thought the wedding might be less stressful and less likely to be jinxed if they were officially married before they attempted to get married. Of course, there was her mother to deal with and Joe's parents, who wouldn't consider them married if it wasn't in the family church. And, of course, she had to find a dress and pick flowers, a first dance song, bridesmaid dresses — okay, and now she was done. Her brain was shutting down, so she pictured Angie with a baby in her arms and her peace was restored. For the moment.

Mel called Megan early the next morning and scheduled an appointment to see her at her office. Megan sounded tired, which Mel supposed could be from the grief of losing her childhood friend — or maybe the guilt from murdering her. Either way, she fully intended to badger it out of Megan when she stopped by her office.

She tried to dress more the part of a businesswoman than an old high school acquaintance. It was important to be on even footing with Megan during the interview. When she emerged from her closet-sized office, dressed in a suit jacket and skirt, both Tate and Oz stopped what they were doing to stare at her.

"What?" she asked. She ran her hands over her narrow pale blue skirt and then checked that her white blouse was neatly tucked in and not showing too much cleavage. A strappy pair of low-heeled silver sandals and a matching silver bangle bracelet on her wrist completed the outfit. She had even upped her game and put on makeup, but having them stare at her was not helping the fact that she felt like an imposter. "Seriously, what? Am I untucked? Is a tag hanging out? What?"

"No," Oz said. He frowned. "You look like a grown-up."

"Oh." Mel blinked. She looked at Tate. "That's good, right?"

"Yeah, just unexpected," he said.

"I was thinking that if I'm going to lull Megan into trusting me, then I need to look like someone in her world," Mel said. "You know, build a rapport, that sort of thing."

"Well done," Tate said. He glanced down at his own Ramones T-shirt and cargo shorts. "Since I'm just waiting in the car, I did not dress up."

"Good thing," Oz said. "You don't have the legs for skirts."

Tate gave him an outraged look and Oz shrugged.

"Come on," Mel said. She gave Tate a gentle push toward the door. "I have to be there in ten minutes."

"Fine," he said. They headed to the door and he said over his shoulder, "I have better legs than *some* people for skirts."

"Yeah, not really something you want to bicker about," Mel said. "Besides, anyone can see Oz has better legs than you."

"What?"

"He's younger than you and he skate-boards," Mel said. "What do you do?"

"I . . . I'm . . . You know what? That's age-ist," he declared. The door banged shut behind them and Mel was pretty sure she could hear Oz laughing.

"It is not ageist," Mel said. "He's more than ten years younger than you; of course he's more fit and has better legs. Besides, what do you care? You're going to be a dad soon, and then it's sympathy cravings and

193

weight gain."

Tate hugged his belly and looked at his reflection in the car window. He turned from side to side. "I think I'd be cute with a little pudge."

Mel rolled her eyes. "Whenever you're ready."

He unlocked the car and opened the door for her. Mel climbed in and they headed to the building where Megan's office was located. It was just north of Old Town, in a swanky new building that had been made to look mid-century modern, with loads of glass and edges, and accent colors of lime green and cobalt blue.

When they got there, Tate parked around back and then took out his phone. "Okay, how do you and Angie do this?"

"I call you, you answer the call, but don't hang up," Mel said. "You'll be able to listen in on the conversation and if I get into trouble you can charge in and rescue me or call the police. Did you download that recorder app? If you turn that on and put your phone on speaker, maybe we could get a recording of the conversation, too."

"You're scary clever," Tate said.

"Well, I am Stan Cooper's niece," Mel said.

"Did you ever think about being a cop?"

Tate asked. "You have a real knack for outing bad guys."

"Nah," Mel said. "There are too many rules on the force. Plus, I'd miss baking. Besides, I don't think Joe is marrying me for my investigative skills."

Tate laughed. "Yeah, he's definitely marrying you for your cupcakes."

"Was that an innuendo?" Mel asked. "Because it sounded like double speak."

Tate blinked at her, the picture of innocence. Mel shook her head.

"I'm calling you now," she said. She hit his name in the contacts and when his phone rang he answered the call. Mel turned down the volume on her phone so that if Tate made any noise, Megan wouldn't hear it come from her phone.

"One question," Tate said. "If the call drops, what do I do? Should I go charging in there or call the cops?"

"Use your best judgment," Mel said. "If it sounds like she's going to kill me, call the cops. But if she's cooperating and we're getting along then maybe just bide your time."

"I'm actually nervous," Tate said. "Is that normal?"

"Yes." Mel checked her hair and makeup in the mirror. So far so good. "All right, I'm going in. Wish me luck."

"Good luck," he said. "Get a confession."

Mel paused. "I really hope she's innocent, you know?"

Tate sobered. "I know. Danny, too."

"Yeah."

Mel climbed out and shut the door behind her. She crossed the small lot, checking that her phone was still in contact with Tate's. It was. She wondered if she was doing the right thing. She knew she could have texted the picture she took to Uncle Stan and let him run with it, but there was a part of her that wanted to give Megan and Danny the benefit of the doubt. She didn't want them to be guilty of murdering Cassidy. And so here she was.

Maybe it was because of the crush she'd had on Danny all those years ago, or perhaps it was because, out of all the mean girls, Megan was the only one who had shown her kindness. It was a memory buried deep, but she remembered a particularly rough day when Tate and Angie were both out sick and she was forced to navigate high school alone. She was coming out of her homeroom and slammed into Cassidy and her entourage.

Cassidy staggered back, exaggerating how hard the impact had been by careening across the hall and slamming herself up against the metal lockers. She struck a dramatic pose and exclaimed that slamming into Mel was like running headfirst into a bouncy house. All of her friends had laughed and Mel had wanted to die from the shame. Tears blurred her vision, so when Cassidy came back and slapped her textbook out of her arms, she didn't see her coming. Her book slid across the floor, papers scattering like leaves in a strong wind.

Cassidy cackled and strutted away with her minions following, all except one. Megan stayed behind. She dropped to her knees and helped Mel pick up her papers, every single one. She handed them to Mel without a word and then she held out her hand and helped Mel to her feet.

"I'm sorry," she said. Then she turned and ran after Cassidy and her pack of mean girls, leaving Mel alone in the hallway with her books clutched to her chest and her tears drying on her face.

Mel had never known why Megan helped her that day. She hadn't noticed before that Megan didn't laugh when Cassidy went after her targets, but she did notice thereafter that Megan looked uncomfortable and ill at ease, as if she'd rather be anywhere but there. It made Mel wonder again why

Megan was friends with Cassidy when she clearly didn't enjoy the other girl's cruel streak. It was what made Mel give her the benefit of the doubt right now.

She just couldn't believe that Megan would be embroiled in a plan to murder Cassidy. She didn't want to believe it of her or Danny and so here she was, confronting a woman who had been making out with her best friend's husband in the garden of the funeral home where they had just had a service for the aforementioned wife/best friend. Mel paused with her hand on the doorknob. Should she stay or should she go?

She stepped back, rethinking this whole idea. Movement behind the window caught her attention. It was Megan, waving as she approached the doors to greet her. She was wearing a loose peasant blouse over a flirty knee-length skirt, and she was smiling. There was no backing out now.

"Mel, come in." Megan pushed the door open and waved her hand, ushering Mel into the building.

"Hi," Mel said. It sounded like a squeak. She cleared her throat and tried again. "Hi, how are you?"

Megan shrugged. "Processing, you know? I mean, I just can't believe it."

"I know what you mean," Mel said. "When I agreed to go to the reunion, I could never have imagined anything like that would happen."

Megan stared at her hard for a moment and Mel got the feeling she was trying to determine if Mel was telling the truth. What the heck? Mel hadn't been the one making out with the deceased's husband!

"I know what you mean," Megan said. "Come on, I'll take you back to my office."

"Your office?" Mel repeated her, hoping that Tate could hear her on the phone. "Sounds great."

Megan frowned at her and Mel knew she was being weird, but she wanted Tate to know where she was. She tried to make her expression bland and had the feeling Megan was going to think she was an idiot, but whatever, it couldn't be helped.

Stepping out of the foyer, they entered a small reception area. There was a woman sitting at a large glass desk with a laptop. She was talking on the phone but nodded at them when they passed. A large potted palm was beside her desk and Mel thought it looked a little lonely. There was no art on the stark concrete walls and no seats in the waiting area. Clearly, loitering was discouraged.

Mel followed Megan through a door behind the reception desk. They strolled down a narrow hallway, too narrow for them to walk side-by-side. Mel took note of the small conference rooms they passed. They were all empty. They took a right turn and walked by several large and very plush offices. These had people in them, some on computers, some talking on the phone, one with clients sitting in the guest chairs. No one paid any attention to the women walking down the hall. Finally, they reached the back corner and Megan pushed open the door.

It had been a long time since Mel had been corporate but she remembered well how hard a person had to work to achieve corner office placement. Megan's office was modern but with warmth from several large desert landscapes done in vibrant shades of purple and orange. A glass display shelf housed a collection of Native American pottery that looked delicate and intricate in detail.

Floor-to-ceiling windows looked out over a xeriscaped yard that boasted barrel cactus and hesperaloe, as well as perfectly manicured palo verde trees. It was lovely. Mel knew appearances could be deceiving, but judging by their surroundings, she was betting that Megan was very successful at her real estate career.

Megan gestured for her to sit and Mel took the seat on the visitor's side of the desk, while Megan walked around and sat in her own chair. Mel noticed immediately that they were sitting at the same height. So there were no power-play shenanigans happening where Megan made her seat higher in order to intimidate whomever she was dealing with. Mel liked that; it made her think that the girl who had helped her pick up her papers was still in there.

"Your message said you were looking for some real estate?" Megan asked. "Are you and Joe looking to buy a new home now that you're getting married?"

"Sure," Mel said. Megan gave her a look and Mel knew she was flubbing this. "I mean, I was really more interested in what you might have that we could pick up for the cupcake bakery. You know we've started franchising, so we're always looking for a good deal."

Megan pursed her lips. "I'm sorry. I'm not a commercial real estate agent. I'm more luxury residences in Paradise Valley and Scottsdale. My colleague Richard does commercial properties; would you like me to connect you two? He's a great guy and super easy to work with."

"Actually," Mel sighed. "I lied. I'm not here about real estate. I wanted to talk to you about Cassidy."

Megan didn't look surprised. Instead, she nodded as if she understood. "I figured it was something like that." Mel raised her eyebrows and Megan explained, "I did a search on the tax assessor's website after you called. You and Joe just bought your house in Arcadia. It's a great neighborhood, big houses, big yards, and good schools. You don't want to move, so what exactly did you want to know, Mel?"

TWELVE

"Who do you think killed Cassidy?" Mel asked.

Megan blew out a breath. "That is blunt, isn't it? The police asked me the same question and the truth is, I have no idea."

Mel couldn't tell if she was lying. She decided to press harder.

"Were you still close to Cassidy?" she asked.

"Not as close as we were in high school," Megan said. She looked uncomfortable. Mel thought about her rendezvous with Danny. Small wonder.

"Why were you friends with her in high school?" Mel asked. It hadn't been her plan to ask that — it just flew out of her mouth — but it had been something she'd wondered about for years.

Megan blinked. Clearly, she hadn't expected the question any more than Mel had planned to ask it; still, Mel didn't retract the question. She wanted to know. What sort of hold had Cassidy had over Megan?

"We met when I moved to town in middle school. Cassidy lived next door. She was literally the first person I met in Scottsdale. I suppose I got swept up in having a friend because I was very insecure and terrified of being the new kid.

"Then as we got older and she made herself the arbiter of what was cool and what wasn't, I was in too deep to get out. Truthfully, I didn't like her most of the time, and I didn't like being her friend, but I didn't know how to get out of the relationship without making my life a living hell."

Mel nodded. She could see that. Cassidy would have taken it as betrayal if Megan had tried to leave her clique.

"I used to watch you and Tate and Angie," Megan said. "And I envied you. The three of you were always together, always laughing, and I wanted that. I wanted that so much."

Mel felt her jaw drop. "Really?"

"Oh, yeah, it was no picnic being one of Cassidy's entourage," Megan said. "It was constant catfights and drama and jockeying for position. That's why I went to college on the east coast; I wanted to get as far away as humanly possible. Three thousand miles seemed about right."

"Did you stay in touch?"

"At first," Megan said. "But I came home less and less and she was busy with her own life. When I moved back to take care of my folks we reconnected, but I tried to keep healthy boundaries and not get sucked back into her world."

"Because you really didn't like her?" Mel asked. She felt like she was zeroing in on her target. She didn't want to make a false move but she was going to have to call Megan out on her relationship with Dan at some point. However, she wanted to establish her feelings for Cassidy first.

"Listen, I'm really uncomfortable talking about Cassidy. I know that you have your own issues with her, but I don't want to talk poorly of the dead," Megan said. "It's not polite."

"Neither is making out with the deceased's husband at her funeral, but that didn't stop you," Mel said. She lifted her phone and turned the display around so that Megan could see the picture that clearly showed her kissing Danny.

Mel watched the color drain from Megan's face as her eyes widened. "How did you . . . that was you?"

"I'm the one who coughed, giving you a

205

heads-up that someone was coming," Mel said. "But, yes, I was there and took this picture."

"Give me that!" Megan tried to snatch the phone.

"It won't help you to take my phone," Mel said. "I have it saved to my cloud drive. You can delete it from here and it's still saved."

Megan slumped back in her seat. "You don't understand."

"Really?" Mel made a show of looking at the phone's screen and then back at Megan. "You're kissing your best friend's husband at her funeral, when it appears that her death was the result of a poisoning. Where am I getting it wrong?"

"You can't say anything," Megan said. She was shaking. Her eyes were huge. She looked desperate. "It would destroy Danny's career."

"Is that why you hooked up with him? Because of his celebrity?"

"No, god, no," Megan said. She spun in her chair and rose to her feet.

Mel braced herself for an attack. There was none. Instead, Megan strode over to a small cabinet in the corner. It was actually a small refrigerator. She took two bottles of water out and handed one to Mel. Mel gave her a dubious look.

"It's sealed," she said. "Do you honestly think I'd poison you?"

"Well . . ."

"I didn't poison Cassidy," Megan insisted. "I swear it."

Mel knew she was taking a huge gamble. After all, she hadn't seen Megan in years; maybe her acting skills were greater than Mel realized. Still, she said, "I believe you."

Megan relaxed bit at that. "Thank you."

"But someone killed Cassidy. If it wasn't you, then you have to consider that it might have been Da—"

"No, he would never," she said. "We're both so conflicted, but we're also in love. You know what that feels like. I know you do. I've seen you with Joe."

Mel nodded. She did love Joe very much.

"You know that feeling of wanting to be with someone so bad that it hurts?" Megan said. "They're all you can think about, all you care about, and nothing else matters."

Mel knew exactly what she was talking about. She did feel all of that with Joe. The problem was that what Megan was saying only made the possibility of one of them being a murderer that much more likely.

"Megan, I want to help you, I do, but there's just no getting around the fact that Dan had the best access to Cassidy to slip poison into her food or drink, and by having an affair with you, he also has the best motive," she said.

Megan waved a dismissive hand at this, then looked at Mel and said, "If either Dan or I were going to murder Cassidy, we would have done it years ago, most likely at their wedding."

Her tone was ripe with bitterness and Mel knew there was much more to the story than she had believed. "Go on," she said.

Megan paced the length of the room once more as if trying to decide what to do. Then she slumped back into her chair and fastened her gaze on Mel. "I don't suppose it's a secret, not really."

Feeling impatient, Mel wanted to reach across the desk and shake her. She didn't. Instead she glanced down at her phone and noticed her call to Tate was still connected. Thankfully, Megan hadn't noticed when she showed her the picture.

"About seven years ago, I was working a local charity event for the real estate company I worked for at the time," she said. "It was an exclusive event and a lot of local celebrities were trotted through to help squeeze money out of the wealthy."

Mel nodded. She had catered plenty of those events.

"Well, Danny was at this event. We hadn't seen each other since graduation and it was great to catch up as adults in our professional lives, without our group of friends around to make things awkward or weird. We really hit it off. We were both single at the time. I'd been dating a guy in California but broke it off because the long distance wasn't working and he wasn't the right fit for me. Dan and Cassidy had broken up after graduation and he'd been dating a supermodel but things ended between them for much the same reason. It was like the universe had pushed us together, you know?"

Mel did know. The universe had pushed her and Joe together and then tore them apart and then pushed them together repeatedly. In fact, she realized that she'd better get to planning her wedding so the universe didn't get any funny ideas in the meantime.

"Then what happened?" she asked, as Megan seemed to mentally relive the moment that she and Dan had met again.

Megan shook her head and her expression went dark. She glanced out the window. Her voice was tight when she said, "Stupidly, when Dan and I met, we didn't exchange numbers. We should have, but I think we were both wary. A few days after the event, Dan asked his mother to ask around among her friends to see if anyone had my number. Dan's mother asked Cassidy's mother, who asked Cassidy. When Cassidy asked why, her mother said that Dan was interested in asking me out. Well, Cassidy, who had been pining for Dan since they broke up, lied and told her mother, who told Dan's mother, that my number wouldn't do him any good since I was in a very serious relationship. Then Cassidy made a play for Dan, and when he blew out his knee, she made sure she was there every day to help him back on his feet."

"Ooh," Mel gasped. "That's low even for Cassidy."

"It gets worse." Megan looked miserable. "Guess when I found out what she'd done?"

"Um . . ." Mel shook her head. She had no idea.

"At the rehearsal dinner for their wedding," Megan said. "There I was as maid of honor, and one of the other bridesmaids, her cousin Sara, stood up and gave a drunken speech where she told everyone exactly what Cassidy had done to snatch Dan away from me. Then they high-fived each other like it was the greatest thing ever.

"I remember Dan and I looking at each

other and seeing the same devastation on his face that I felt. He was trapped. There was no backing out then. I remember feeling like I'd been gutted by a rusty spoon. How could one friend do that to another?"

"Cassidy was no one's friend," Mel said. They were both quiet, absorbing the truth of this statement. "When did you start having an affair with Dan?"

"A little over a year ago," Megan said. "I was in Los Angeles at a conference and he was there covering the Suns. We bumped into each other at the hotel bar and the next thing I knew we had spent the entire night talking, just talking, and it was amazing. When we got back to Scottsdale, I promised myself I would stay away. But he started to call me when he was on the road and we became friends, really close friends. And then I was in Seattle for business and he was there, too, and one thing led to another and I knew I should stop it, but I just couldn't walk away."

There was a bleak despair in her voice and Mel knew that Megan didn't want to love Dan, she didn't want to be having an affair, but her heart was refusing to be denied. It wasn't for Mel to approve or disapprove. Their lives had been ruined by one woman's lie.

Mel couldn't imagine a world where Angie would do something like that to her. Real friends just didn't do that sort of harm. She wondered how Megan had managed to get through the wedding or maintain any sort of friendship with Cassidy afterwards. Mel knew she would never have been able to do it.

"You do realize that this story doesn't help you at all," Mel said. "The affair is bad but the background is even worse. It gives both you and Dan a real motive for revenge. Cassidy ruined your chance at happiness, she stole the guy who was interested in you; I mean, it's bad. And Dan's being stuck in a loveless marriage doesn't help, either. Having you on the side makes it seem even more likely that he might kill to get out of his unhappy marriage."

"He didn't," Megan said. She put her hand over her belly in a protective gesture. "He would never put his family at risk."

Mel felt her jaw drop. "You're having his child?"

"Yes," Megan said. "But you can't tell anyone. It's still very early yet, but neither of us would ever do anything that would take us away from our baby. He'd been working on asking Cassidy for a divorce. He was trying to convince her that it was best for both of them, but she wasn't having it."

"Did she know about you or the baby?" Mel asked.

"No," Megan said. "She treated me just as she always had. I don't think she was a good enough actress to pretend she didn't know about our affair if she'd actually known about it."

"What are you and Dan going to do?" Mel asked. "You can't just hook up, and with a baby on the way, or everyone will know."

"We're hoping the police can figure out what happened to Cassidy," Megan said. "That's our primary concern, to see that justice is done. Yes, Cassidy did an awful thing by keeping us apart, but we're together now and we have the rest of our lives to be together. But someone took Cassidy's life away from her and I don't think Dan and I can move forward until we know who did it and why."

"I can understand that," Mel said. "I feel like the fact that Cassidy died at the reunion is critical. I really think it had to be someone who was angry with her. I know because of the bullying, I'm the obvious suspect, but it wasn't me."

"I never thought it could be you," Megan said. "Dan doesn't, either. We agree that you're far too nice and fair-minded to hang on to an old grudge and commit murder."

"Thanks," Mel said. "I'd like to think so. The question is if not us, then who? Brittany, who thinks she should have been dating Dan because she was captain of the pep squad and he was the school's MVP, or Kristie, who lost her shot at being our homecoming queen when the envelopes 'got switched' that night?"

"And that's just two of many people who had issues with Cassidy in high school," Megan said. "There was also Terry Gardner, who had the audacity to buy the dress that Cassidy had her eye on for our junior prom. Do you remember what happened?"

"No, I didn't go to prom," Mel said. She hoped it didn't come out sounding as pitiful as she feared.

"Cassidy 'accidentally' spilled her cup of red punch all over Terry's dress," Megan said. "Such a beautiful dress and it was ruined."

Mel shook her head. Wow, just wow.

"And then, of course, there's Dwight," Megan said.

"Dwight?" Mel asked. "He was always her sidekick in bullying. I can't believe he'd want to hurt her. He seemed to follow her lead."

"That's because he was hoping she'd

notice him," Megan said. "He was desperately in love with her. That's why he was so vicious to everyone. He wanted her to think of him as her protector."

"More like her enforcer," Mel said.

"Agreed."

"I don't understand what these guys saw in her," Mel said. "Danny, Dwight, Tucker, and the other men who seemed to flock around her. I mean, she was pretty but not stunning. She wasn't funny, smart, or kind, so really, what was the draw?"

"Dan and I have talked about it," Megan said. "We both felt as if we were held hostage by her. She was a master manipulator. She reeled you in by making you think you were so important to her and then once she got her hooks in you, it was impossible to escape. She didn't really befriend you so much as study up on your weaknesses so she could use them against you. I'd be willing to bet she did the same thing to all of the guys who hovered around her."

"What were your weaknesses?" Mel asked. "How did she keep a hold on you?"

"Being the new kid, I was petrified that if I lost her friendship, I wouldn't have any friends at all," Megan said. "Looking back, no friends would have been the better choice."

"And Dan?" Mel asked. "How did she reel him in?"

"In high school, she was the perfect arm candy," Megan said. "And then when they met later in life, she pretended that she wanted everything he did. Marriage, kids, camping trips out on the desert, beach vacations, all of that suburban domestic stuff."

"And she didn't."

"None of it," Megan said. "She wanted to be a celebrity's wife and be invited to all the biggest events, with all of the beautiful people, but she didn't want to have to go alone."

"So she got admittance into the elite by marrying him, but then because he was on the road, she had to go alone anyway," Mel said.

"Yes, and the reality was, she had nothing to offer anyone but access to her husband and that was limited since he was always traveling," Megan said. "She found out pretty quickly that because she did nothing, she had little to no value to anyone. It was a bitter pill."

Mel didn't need to work too hard to imagine how poorly that would have gone over with Cassidy. It was important to her to have people bow and scrape before her and without that, Mel could only imagine how impossible she had become. Impossible or desperate?

"Megan, you don't think — and I know I am reaching here — but you don't think Cassidy could have taken her own life, do you?"

Thirteen

"No, absolutely not," Megan said. She was vehement and Mel wondered how she could be so sure. "I mean, yes, she was unhappy in her life, but to take her life — that's not how Cassidy responded to adversity. She was a fighter."

Mel thought about the Cassidy she had known and felt like this was a fair assessment, but they had gotten older, and maybe she had gotten depressed and miserable as she tried to navigate a life that wasn't what she had expected. Maybe she felt as if there was no way out. Mel didn't say it, but she wondered if Cassidy had found out about Megan and Dan. Maybe that had broken her spirit. Either way, she needed to get to Uncle Stan and tell him what she knew.

"Mel, promise me you won't say anything to anyone," Megan said. "About me and Dan."

Mel winced. She'd been hoping Megan

wouldn't ask her that. "I don't know if I can do that. I mean, someone murdered Cassidy and it really doesn't look good for you and Dan."

"But if the media finds out about us, it could destroy his career," Megan said. Mel stared at her and she had the grace to look embarrassed. "I know, it's incredibly selfish of me to be worried about that when there's a killer among our classmates, but I want to have a family and a life with Danny and if we start under a cloud of suspicion, well, I'm just worried that we won't be able to salvage us." She gave Mel a desperate look. "After all we've been through, after everything Cassidy did to keep us apart, I feel like we deserve this chance. Please help us, Mel, please."

Mel felt like she was the chewy, gooey center of a taffy pull. The right thing to do would be to show the picture of Megan and Danny to Uncle Stan. There was no question about that. He needed to know that the spouse of the murder victim was having an affair. But she couldn't help but remember the girl who had helped her in that hallway all those years ago. She didn't believe Megan was a killer and she didn't think Dan was, either. She was willing to give them some time.

"I can't promise that I won't share what I know with the police eventually," she said. "Especially if I find reason to believe that you or Dan are involved with the murder. But I will wait and give the police a chance to investigate first. That's the best I can do."

"Thank you, Mel," Megan said. She looked so relieved that Mel got the feeling that she believed it was just a matter of time before the killer was caught. "You won't regret it. Dan and I are innocent. You'll see."

Mel arrived back at the car. She opened the door and slid in, collapsing against the seat.

"What's your damage?" Tate asked.

"Heathers," Mel said.

"No, I was being serious," Tate said. He fired up the car and drove away from the building. "I heard everything she said. Even after seeing the picture, I can't believe they were having an affair, I really can't believe she's having Dan's kid, and I'm shocked she asked you not to say anything. You're absolutely going to say something, right?"

"I don't know," Mel said. "I'm torn. On the one hand I believe her and on the other Cassidy is dead and, wow, they really have a lot of motives for her to be dead by their hands."

"Truly, which is why it probably wasn't

them who killed her," Tate said. "It's way too obvious, right? Isn't that a rule?"

"I think the rules got tossed out the window on this one," Mel said.

"Agreed," he said. "So, back to the bakery to call Joe or Uncle Stan?"

"Yes, but we need to make one stop first," she said.

"No." Tate shook his head.

"We have to," Mel said. "I have to hear his side of it."

"Danny is the prime suspect," Tate said. "It's too dangerous for you to approach him."

"Good thing I have you with me then," she said.

When Tate sighed like someone had taken the last of his favorite cupcakes, she knew he was on board.

Unlike the day that Mel and Angie had staked out the wake, Danny's house looked vacant. Mel wondered if he was even home. Maybe Megan had called and warned him that Mel was asking questions. She couldn't really blame Megan but it would be annoying.

As they approached the house, Tate moved so that he was standing in front of Mel. She wasn't sure if he was expecting a brawl or if he was just being protective, but she moved him aside. When he gave her a blast of stink eye, she shook her head at him.

"Dan barely knows you," she said. "I was his English tutor. He'll open the door to me. Maybe."

As if he'd been waiting for them, the front door opened. Dan stood there, holding his phone to his ear. He gave them an unsurprised look and said, "Yes, she's here. I'll call you later. You, too. Bye."

"Megan?" Mel asked.

"She said she had a feeling you'd be dropping by," Danny said. He stepped back and gestured for them to come in. "I don't think I can tell you any more than Megan has."

His house was huge. Stairs at the end of the foyer led up to a massive living room, which had a white leather sectional, a large-screen TV, and a fireplace. Windows on the far side gave a floor-to-ceiling view of Camelback Mountain rising above them. It was impressive and a little intimidating.

Dan gestured for them to sit. Mel sat in the middle, Tate sat beside her, and Danny settled on the other side of the L-shaped couch, keeping the glass coffee table between them. A basketball game was on the big-screen TV and he switched it off, turning his attention to Mel.

He met her gaze and said, "I know what you're thinking, but I didn't kill Cassidy."

"What makes you believe that I think you killed her?" Mel asked. She felt Tate stiffen beside her.

"Because I have the most to gain by her death," Danny said. "I can't deny that, just like I can't deny that I wanted out of the marriage."

"Did she know that?" Tate asked.

"Yes, I asked her for a divorce a few weeks ago," he said. "She said no. When I said I was going forward with it anyway, she begged me to wait until after the reunion."

"And you agreed?" Mel asked.

Dan rose to his feet and began to pace. He was wearing basketball shorts and a tank top. It occurred to Mel that he had likely been shooting baskets on the court by the side of his house. His hair was mussed and his face was pink, as if he'd been out in the sun earlier.

"She cried," he said.

Mel looked at Tate and he nodded. "That's legit. When a woman cries, it's pretty impossible to say no."

"It was more than the tears," Dan said. "I felt guilty because I was leaving her for her best friend and she didn't know. I felt bad that we were going to have to untangle our lives from each other and on the way there were going to be casualties, because there always are in breakups."

"Did she know there was someone else?" Mel asked. "Do you think she suspected?"

"She accused me of it, a couple of times, rather dramatically," he said. "But I denied it. I knew I didn't want to become a bad episode of *Real Housewives* and I really wanted to leave Megan out of it."

"Don't you think she could have had you followed?" Tate asked. "I mean, how careful were you?"

Dan gave him a worried look. "I thought we were extremely careful. I mean, she never said anything to Megan. She even had her helping to plan the reunion."

"That must have been awkward," Mel said.

"Megan struggled with it, and there were a couple of times that I think she wanted to tell Cassidy, but she didn't. We both felt that the news of our relationship had to come from me," Dan said. "Megan was afraid that Cassidy would use it to destroy my career."

"Do you think she would have?" Mel asked. Personally, she had no doubt that Cassidy would have destroyed both Megan and Dan without hesitation if she knew that they were having an affair, but she didn't say so.

"Yes," he said. "Cassidy could be ruthless and she wasn't one to hold in her anger. I really think if she'd known about me and Megan, she would have done everything in her power to destroy us."

"Wow," Mel said. "That's fairly terrifying."

"Yeah," Dan said. "What's really crazy is I didn't care. I'd have left it all behind, given her the house, the cars, alimony, my career, all of it, just to be free to be with the woman I love."

"Okay, you may want to keep that to yourself," Tate said. "You sound like a man who was close to desperate. The police don't know Cassidy like we do, and they won't understand if you talk like that to them."

"I know." Dan turned and looked at Mel. "I'm sorry."

Mel frowned. She studied Dan's face. He looked weary, like all-the-way-down-to-his-bones exhausted, but she couldn't imagine why he'd apologize to her.

"What for?" she asked.

"Cassidy picked on you unmercifully when we were in high school," he said. "I knew, but I never did anything about it. I was so caught up in playing basketball and getting my scholarship that I didn't think about anyone else. You were my tutor. You're the only reason they even kept me on the team and, still, I never defended you from Cassidy."

"That wasn't your job," Mel said. She didn't want to talk about this. She didn't want to think about how miserable Cassidy had made her feel back in high school.

"No, it wasn't," Dan agreed. "But it should have been. I ignored all of her nastiness because it didn't impact me directly, but I shouldn't have. She was a bully and a mean girl and someone should have called her out. I was dating her. It should have been me."

"Thanks," Mel said. "I appreciate the thought but we were just kids back then. We were all trying to survive adolescence the best way we could, even Cassidy."

Dan gave her a dubious look and Mel smiled. Despite the horrible events that had brought them together, it was good to see Danny again. She did a gut check and felt positive that he was telling the truth. She doubted he had anything to do with Cassidy's death. But if not Dan and Megan, both of whom had excellent reasons to poison Cassidy, then who?

"Do you know of someone who had a

recent grudge against Cassidy?" Tate asked. "Maybe it didn't have anything to do with the reunion, maybe it was someone else in her life."

"Cassidy didn't have a life," Dan said. "The only thing she cared about over the past few months was the reunion. She was dieting, working out, having planning meetings; it became an obsession for her. Especially the thought of being crowned homecoming queen again. She repeatedly told me that she couldn't wait to take the stage and wear her crown again. She even ordered a specially made tiara for the event."

Mel felt her jaw drop. High school may not have been her favorite years but suddenly she was one hundred percent okay with that. When she thought about the life she had carved out for herself since then, well, it had been a heck of a ride and she had enjoyed every bit of it. But Cassidy hadn't had that. Her life had remained centered around her glory days. It made Mel feel badly for her but it also took away the likelihood that Cassidy had harmed herself, especially on a night that had been so important to her.

"So, you don't think there's any way she would have taken poison on her own?" Tate asked. He must have reached the same conclusion that Mel had.

"Oh, hell no," Dan said. "She was living for the moment she got to strut her stuff in front of our class. Nothing short of murder would have caused her to miss it."

"You said she was having a lot of planning meetings," Mel said. "But I was under the impression that Brittany Nilsson was in charge of the reunion since she was the president of the pep squad."

Dan nodded. "Yeah, that didn't go over well." He shook his head and then his face took on an *aha* expression. "You know, it actually got pretty ugly between them."

Mel and Tate exchanged a look. "In what way?" she asked.

"Brittany told Cassidy that she didn't think we should have a queen at the reunion," Danny said. His eyes grew wide and he said, "They fought about it and it got rather nasty with Cassidy showing up at Brittany's workplace to ream her out."

"Really?" Mel said. She thought about how Brittany had arrived with Lianne right after Mel had left the bathroom. Had that been a coincidence or had Brittany planned it after she killed Cassidy?

"Yes. Cassidy called me in a rage after Brittany had her escorted off of the premises of the hospital because Cassidy was be-

228

ing verbally abusive," Dan said. "I called Brittany and smoothed things over. I even agreed to be crowned king again, which I definitely did not want to do, so that I could rein Cassidy in. Brittany said she had plans for the crowning ceremony. I assumed she was going to let Cassidy be crowned queen, but maybe . . ."

"How did Megan feel about the two of you being king and queen?" Mel asked.

"Neither of us were thrilled but we both felt it was the last thing I could do for Cassidy before I filed for divorce," he said. "Honestly, we had just found out that Megan was pregnant, so we were pretty preoccupied with our own happiness. Cassidy and all of her petty nonsense couldn't really touch us."

"Until she was murdered," Tate said.

"Yeah," Dan said. "I feel like I'm going crazy. The police have been here every day asking questions and I know it's only a matter of time before they find out about me and Megan." He gave Mel a hard stare. "I know I have no right to ask, but —"

"I won't tell," Mel said. She glanced at Tate. "Neither of us will."

Tate nodded and then considered Dan. "Unless I find out you're lying to us, and then all bets are off."

"Fair enough," Dan said. He held out his hand. Tate shook it and they all stood.

"What will you do now?" Mel asked Dan as he walked them to the door.

"I'm on leave from work, so I'll wait it out," he said. He shrugged. "Someone killed Cassidy. I don't know who and I don't know why, but I owe it to Cassidy to do everything I can to catch whoever did this. The only thing I can think of is that she must have made someone really angry, because you don't just poison someone on a whim."

"No, poisoning requires premeditation," Mel said. "You'd need access to the poison, you'd have to know the dose, you'd need to be able to slip it to the person you're planning to poison undetected. This was a cold, calculated murder."

"Most definitely not a crime of passion," Tate agreed. "So the person who is angry could have been angry for a very long time, say, fifteen years at least."

"Meaning it probably is someone from high school who's just been waiting," Mel said. She glanced at Dan. "Megan told us how Cassidy interfered when you were interested in her. That had to have been infuriating when you found out."

"It was," he said. "But it was also at our wedding rehearsal, so I didn't feel like I could call it off, and I convinced myself that she did it because she loved me so much."

"She didn't?" Tate asked.

Dan looked rueful. "I don't know that love is an emotion that Cassidy had more than a passing acquaintance with, and then it was more in regards to things, like, 'I love this ring, house, car, etcetera.' "

They walked down the stairs and stood in the foyer. Mel had just one more question. She felt bad even asking it, but she knew it was important.

"Dan, I have to ask," she said. "Given that you were away from home and on the road while starting a relationship with someone else, do you think Cassidy could have done the same?"

"Meaning?" he asked.

"Do you think Cassidy might have been involved with someone else?" Mel asked. "Romantically."

Dan's eyebrows went up as he considered the question. "No, wait, I don't know. Maybe?"

Mel nodded. It was clear the thought hadn't occurred to him before.

"You'd better hope she was," Tate said. "Because that would sure take the heat off you."

"Yeah," Dan said. "I suppose it would."

Mel noticed he didn't look relieved by the possibility and when he closed the door behind them, he looked thoughtful and a little sad. She had no idea what to make of that.

FOURTEEN

"Do you believe them?" Angie asked when Mel and Tate had returned to the bakery. "I mean, they're having an affair and she's pregnant; that's not exactly operating from a super honest place."

The three of them were in the kitchen. Oz and Marty were working out front while Angie decorated a batch of Cinnamon Sinner Cupcakes with cinnamon sticks.

Mel and Tate exchanged a look. They had talked about it on the ride home and they both agreed that Danny and Megan seemed to be telling the truth, but was there any way to know for sure? Mel believed that they were committed to each other and to the family that they were starting, but it also made her think that maybe one of them had decided to get rid of the only obstacle standing in their way — Cassidy.

"I believe them," Tate said. "Mostly."

"Me, too," Mel agreed. "Pretty much."

"But there's no way to be sure," Angie said. "And given that Cassidy was vicious to you, Mel, you still look like suspect number one unless, of course, you tell Uncle Stan about their affair and the baby."

"I promised them I wouldn't," Mel said.

Angie rolled her eyes. "Why? Why would you do that?"

"It seemed like the right thing to do at the time," Mel said. She glanced at Tate. "Back me up."

"It was pretty awkward, grilling them about Cassidy's murder," he said. "And they do seem genuinely in love and distraught about Cassidy's death."

Angie shook her head at the two of them and said, " 'He was elegance walking arm in arm with a lie.' "

"*Velvet Goldmine,*" Tate said. "And may I say I'm impressed?"

"You may." Angie smiled. Then she glanced at Mel. "What's our next play?"

"Brittany," Mel said. "I have to talk to Brittany. I think I'll catch her at work so it's most definitely neutral territory."

"I have a meeting with our franchise attorney about the Portland shop," Tate said. "I can't go with you."

"I'll go," Angie said.

"No. We talked about this. You can't put

yourself in harm's way."

"We're going to be at the hospital. You can't get much safer than that."

Tate frowned. Finally, he said, "Yes, you can."

Mel and Angie exchanged a look but Tate ignored them, opening up his phone and furiously typing a text with his thumbs.

"Oh, no," Mel said. "Whichever DeLaura brother you are thinking of sending with me, you can forget it. I'd rather go alone."

Tate glanced up at her and opened his mouth as if to argue. His phone chimed and he held up a finger, indicating she should hold that thought. Mel sighed as he read the incoming text.

"Alone is not an option," he said. "Joe will be here in twenty minutes."

Mel and Joe arrived at the hospital, parking in the garage adjacent to the main building. As they crossed the lot into the main entrance, Mel tried to figure out what she was going to say to Brittany.

"Remind me again why we need to talk to Brittany Nilsson," Joe said.

"Huh?" Mel wasn't listening. She had almost crafted the perfect excuse to talk to Brittany, but then she got distracted, wondering how she could tell Uncle Stan what she had learned without telling him what she had learned. She didn't want to go back on her promise to Dan and Megan but their affair and her pregnancy were a very big deal, and Mel didn't want to be the one to withhold important information from an investigation. She debated telling Joe about Dan and Megan but figured it might be best if she waited until after they talked to Brittany.

"Brittany?" Joe asked. "Why do we need to talk to her?"

"Oh, right," Mel said. "Tate didn't tell you?"

"No."

Mel turned to look at her fiancé as they strode through the sliding glass doors into the building. The temperature dropped into the sub zeros like it always did in hospitals.

"We need to talk to her about cupcakes and stuff."

"And stuff," Joe said. The look he gave her told her that he knew "and stuff" wasn't just about frosting flavors.

"Yeah, you know, like did she murder Cassidy and stuff," she said.

"Mel," Joe's voice held a warning note. She ignored it.

She approached the board to the right of the information desk. The administrative offices were listed by department head's name. She scanned until she saw Brittany Nilsson. Her office was listed as number three-twenty-two. Mel knew from her own time in the hospital a few years ago that the three hundred meant the third floor.

"Cupcake, you can't just barge in there —"

"May I help you?" a woman at the information desk asked.

"Yes, please," Mel said. She turned away from Joe to face the desk. "We're here to visit a friend."

"Of course. You'll need to sign in," the woman said. Her name tag read *Alice*. She was older with tightly curled gray hair and kind blue eyes, and she was slightly built. Mel got the impression that she was the sort of person who liked to keep busy.

"What was the patient's name?" Alice asked.

Mel looked at her in alarm. If she didn't come up with the name of someone who was actually in the hospital, she had no doubt Alice would kick their butts right out.

"Actually, we're here to do some research in the library," Mel said. She glanced at Joe, daring him to contradict her. He sighed.

"It's his gallbladder," Mel said, pointing at Joe. "It makes him irritable."

He raised his eyebrows and said, "Really? I thought it was your skin disorder we were researching."

"See?" Mel asked Alice. "Irritable."

Alice looked at both of them and said, "I see you two have your work cut out for you. The library is on the third floor. When you step off the elevator follow the yellow line all the way to the end. Sign in here, please."

She gave them a clipboard and when they had both signed in, she handed them visitor badges to clip to their shirts.

"Thank you, Alice," Mel said and Joe added, "You've been very helpful."

"You're welcome." Alice waved as they walked away and called after them, "I hope your skin and your gallbladder are feeling better soon."

As they turned the corner, Mel glowered. "Skin condition? Really?"

"It was the first thing that leapt to mind," he said.

"I gave you a sad gallbladder, totally not something people can see," Mel said. "And now I'm itchy."

"It's just the power of suggestion," Joe said. "It'll pass."

Mel scratched her upper arm, then looked at her skin. "That's a rash. Wait. It's flaky. What if the irony is that I actually have a skin disease?"

"You don't have skin disease," Joe said. He pulled out his phone and began to text Tate.

"What are you doing?" Mel asked.

"Texting Tate," Joe said. "The next time you come up with a plan like this, he needs to talk you out of it, not drag me into it."

"Aw, but this is our first investigation together," she said. "Consider it a bonding moment."

"I'm an officer of the court, Mel," Joe said. "I shouldn't be talking about a pending investigation with anyone. Plus, I'm pretty sure that Brittany woman hates me."

"Because she was so mean at the reunion when she was guarding the bathroom door?" Mel asked. "That's just her personality."

"Oh, goody, so this should go well."

"Come on," Mel said. "According to the board downstairs, the offices are going to close for the day soon and I don't want to miss her."

They followed the yellow line down the hall until they were in the thick of administration. Then they veered right to the receptionist's desk. The receptionist was young, with long brown hair and a wide, warm smile. Her name tag read *Judi*.

"Hi, we're looking for Brittany Nilsson's

office," Mel said.

"Great! Is she expecting you?" Judi blinked at them from behind impossibly long lashes. She was super perky. Contrary to its intent, it was a tad off-putting.

"Yes," Mel said at the same time Joe said, "No."

Judi's eyelashes fluttered in confusion.

"What we meant to say is that we're old friends so she's always expecting us," Mel said. "You know, how old friends turn up unexpectedly and all."

Judi tipped her head to the side as if not quite following.

"But we don't have an official appointment with her, no," Joe said.

"Great! I'll just call her." Perky Judi turned away from them and picked up her desk phone.

While she waited for the call to go through, Joe said, "Great!" in a spot-on impression of Judi that made Mel look away so she didn't burst out laughing.

As Judi spoke quietly into the phone, Joe glanced at Mel and said, "Try to keep the conversation with Brittany short and to the point."

"Promise," Mel said.

"Great!" Judi said into the phone. Then she hung up and turned to them. "She said to send you on down." Judi rose from her desk chair and pointed to indicate the hallway in the middle. "Ms. Nilsson's office is halfway down on your right. You can't miss it."

"Gre—" Mel stopped herself from saying "great," fearing Judi might think she was making fun of her. "Thank you, Judi," she said. "You've been very helpful."

When they were out of earshot, Mel asked. "How old do you think Judi was, twelve?"

"Pretty close," Joe said. "Maybe a little older, possibly twenty-two? Twenty-three?"

"I feel old," Mel said.

"You're not old," he said. "We're not even middle-aged yet."

"Only a man would think mid-thirties is not old," she said. "Men age more slowly than women."

"How do you figure?"

"A woman is only born with a finite number of eggs, whereas a man makes sperm right up until he dies," she said. "You could actually father a child when you're eighty."

Joe frowned at her. "Just because you can doesn't mean you should. Why are you freaking out about your age?"

"Because I've just realized that at my next

reunion I'll be almost forty," Mel said. "And that seems really old."

"Well, it's not," Joe said. Then he looked at her in surprise. "Are you really planning on going to your next reunion?"

"No." Mel shook her head. She paused in front of Brittany's office door.

"Well then, problem solved." He smiled at her and Mel felt it all the way to her core. Only Joe could do that to her.

Mel rapped her knuckles on the wooden door. A nameplate was fastened to the door that said *B. Nilsson*. The walls of the office were glass but they were thickly frosted and she couldn't see through.

"Come in," Brittany called.

Mel pushed the door open and she and Joe strode into the room.

Brittany stood up behind her desk and Mel didn't think she was imagining the way Brittany was assessing Joe, as if he was here as anything more than Mel's escort. The thought irritated her.

The office was as meticulous as Brittany. No dust, no piles of papers, no random paperclips scattered on the desktop. There was a goldfish bowl with a blue betta fish in it, happily swimming around the stalks of several lucky bamboo shoots. It was oddly whimsical in the austere office.

"I like your fish," Mel said.

"Thank you," Brittany said. "Do you want him?"

"No," Mel said.

Brittany sighed. "He won't die."

"Isn't that usually a good thing?" Joe asked.

Brittany shrugged. "He's from an ex-boyfriend. He has officially outlived the relationship five times over. I feel like he should have gone with my ex when we broke up but my ex wouldn't take him. Isn't that just like a man, weighing a woman down with unwanted stuff?"

"It could have been worse," Mel said.

"And it could have been a lot better," Brittany countered. She gestured to the two seats opposite her desk. "But enough about that; what can I do for you?"

"We just want to ask you —" Joe began but Mel cut him off.

"How the bakery could be of service to you for hospital functions," Mel said. "Staff parties, retirements, stuff like that."

Joe gave her a look and Mel could tell he was impressed. She had to admit this sounded almost plausible.

"Yeah, no," Brittany said. She looked at Mel. "Your Uncle Stan was here earlier and he told me you might be stopping by.

Something about being terminally nosey. I didn't expect you to bring the big guns with you."

She gave Joe an admiring glance and he shifted in his seat. "I'm just her driver."

"Dang that Uncle Stan, he's always one step ahead," Mel said.

"Yeah, it's almost like he's a homicide detective or something," Joe said. His voice was dry and Mel gave him a flat stare before turning back to Brittany.

"Okay, fine, full disclosure. We're here to talk about Cassidy and who might have had a reason to murder her."

"I would think it would be obvious," Brittany said.

"Given that the police haven't made an arrest, no, not that obvious," Mel said.

Brittany gave her an impatient look and then said, "Listen, we all know you are the prime suspect because Cassidy was writing your name in the bathroom when she died."

"It could just as easily be you," Mel countered. "You were right there when we found out she was dead, which was awfully convenient. Also, you work here. How hard would it be for you to get poison?"

"Are you kidding me?" Brittany asked. "I'd have an easier time getting a kidney. You have to sign your life away on medications. There is a protocol. Trust me, there's no way I could just raid the dispensary and help myself. Besides, do you even know what poison killed her?"

"Details." Mel shrugged but it sounded lame even to her.

"Pretty important details if you ask me," Brittany said. "Besides, why would I kill her? Because she was annoying about the reunion? Big deal. I knew it would end eventually, and I wouldn't have to talk to her for another five years. And I have an alibi. I was with Lianne the entire time. There's no way I could have poisoned her."

"That's a fair point," Joe said. Mel scowled at him.

"Well, if it's not me and it's not you, and I don't think it was Danny," Mel said, "then who else wanted Cassidy dead?"

"I still say Danny had the most to gain, but if not him, then I'd guess the same person who wanted to murder her fifteen years ago," Brittany said. "Kristie Hill."

"Her homecoming runner-up?" Mel asked. "That seems a bit extreme so many years later."

"Did you see what she wore to the funeral?" Brittany asked. "Yellow — like sunshine, buttercup, daisy yellow. She was making a statement."

"Which, if she killed Cassidy, also seems pretty odd," Mel said. "Wouldn't she have been better served to wear gray and blend?"

"She probably couldn't contain her joy," Brittany said.

"Did you say the same thing to my uncle?" Mel asked.

"Oh, yeah," Brittany said. "He didn't confirm it, but I got the feeling he was on his way over there next."

"Can you think of anyone else who had a grudge against Cassidy?" Mel asked.

Brittany waved her hand as if frustrated with Mel. "It'd be easier to list who didn't have beef with her. She was the original mean girl, you know that."

Mel rolled her hands to indicate she did and that Brittany should continue. Brittany glanced away. She picked up a small container of fish food and dropped a few nibbles into the tank. The betta attacked as if he was afraid the food might get away.

"Barring the obvious, you, Danny, and Kristie," Brittany said, "I guess I'd have to say Dwight Pickard."

"What?" Mel asked. "Dwight? But he's like her goliath minion."

"And why do you think he was so devoted to her?" Brittany asked.

"Because they both hated me," Mel said.

"What's that old expression? The enemy of my enemy is my friend, or something like that?"

"Dwight didn't hate you," Brittany said.

Mel closed one eye and squinted at her. Brittany must have fried her brain over the reunion, because now she wasn't even making sense.

"He didn't," Brittany insisted.

"Did you see him at the reunion or the funeral?" Mel asked. "He went right after me. Heck, he even tried to turn the crowd against me."

"Old habits die hard, I guess," Brittany said. "The truth of it is, Dwight was in love with Cassidy and has been since we were in elementary school together."

"Dwight loved Cassidy; I knew it," Mel said. "But why weren't they ever a couple?"

"Weren't they?" Brittany asked. "I don't have any proof that there was more going on, but who do you think she spent all of her time with when Danny was on the road?"

"Is that why Dwight's been single all these years?" Mel asked. "He's just been playing second-string to Danny his whole life."

"But if Dwight was in love with Cassidy, why would he have murdered her?" Joe asked.

"Maybe he couldn't stand being her bench warmer anymore," Brittany said. She looked sad. "There are things you don't know that I only learned when we were planning the reunion. Cassidy liked to drink during our meetings and sometimes she got chatty. One night, she told me about Dwight."

"That they were involved?" Mel asked.

"Not in those exact words but the message was clear," Brittany said. "She told me the only person she'd ever been able to count on was Dwight but that he didn't fit her image of what her husband would look like. That role was reserved for Danny. She did say that Dwight had a horrific home life with an abusive father and alcoholic mother. To Cassidy's credit, when we were kids, she always gave Dwight her lunch because she knew he didn't get fed at home. She was likely the only person in his life who cared about him."

Mel sighed. She felt bad for the little boy who'd had such a horrific upbringing. She did. But she could never forgive him for taking it out on her with the constant bullying and name calling. He had made school a living hell for her. If it hadn't been for Tate and Angie, she didn't know how she would have survived it.

"Again, if they were so close, what makes you think he would have harmed Cassidy?" Joe asked.

"Because at one of our meetings when Cassidy got plastered, Dwight came to pick her up and take her home," Brittany said. She made a distasteful moue before she continued. "He had to carry her out. On the way, I heard him tell her that he loved her and he'd always be there for her." Brittany glanced up and met Mel's gaze. "She laughed in his face. She asked him what a woman like her could ever see in a man like him. That he could never be the one for her. Not ever. It was . . . awful."

"Was he angry?" Joe asked. "Did he yell or rage? Did you get the feeling he would harm her?"

"Worse," Brittany said. "He looked heartbroken, like his entire reason for being had just died in his arms."

Fifteen

"What do you make of that?" Joe asked. They were driving back to the bakery and Mel felt as if her brain were on fire from all of the information Brittany had shared.

"I'd be happier if we'd just found proof that Brittany did it," Mel said. "She's pretty insufferable for having been captain of the pep squad."

"Agreed," Joe said. "But she has an alibi."

"Unless she and Lianne offed Cassidy together," Mel said.

"Lianne won the Nightingale Award for Excellence in Nursing," Joe said. "Not really a killer mentality there."

"Did she?"

"Yes, it was listed in the achievements section in your reunion booklet," Joe said. "You remember, that thing they handed us when we went in."

"Oh, right, that thing I threw in the trash." Mel frowned. "You actually read it?"

"Yes," Joe said. "Since my girl's fabulous cupcake empire was mentioned. I can't believe you didn't even look at it. You know, you really should be proud of all that you've accomplished since graduation."

"I am," Mel said. "It's just that the reunion was really not my thing and, honestly, if I hadn't gone, I wouldn't be in this mess right now."

"But, cupcake, didn't you have a moment of victory at the reunion?"

"Victory?" Mel asked. "I don't know, it's all overshadowed by Cassidy's murder. I guess for a second there, yeah, I did get to walk in there on my incredibly handsome fiancé's arm and feel as if all of the crap that happened in high school didn't matter anymore, but it wasn't because anyone's opinion of me had changed, it was because my opinion of me changed. I realized I didn't need anyone's approval but my own."

"Exactly." Joe grinned and asked, "So, it was worth it?"

Mel rolled her eyes. She parked her Mini Cooper in its usual spot.

"Okay, fine, yes. That was a pretty cool takeaway," she said. "But I could have lived with not going and being considered a suspect in a murder and I'd be okay with that, too."

"Spoilsport."

"Totally."

As she climbed out of her car, Mel tried not to feel defeated, but she was running out of possible suspects if she didn't want to lay the blame on Megan and Danny, who were looking guiltier by the minute. She most definitely did not want to confront Dwight Pickard. Just the thought of it gave her the sweats, but what else could she do? She was going to have to question him, too. She needed a cupcake or three to fortify.

Joe had to get back to his office before he called it a day so he gave her a quick kiss and promised to meet her at home for dinner. Mel waved good-bye, wishing they could just go home now and ignore work, and Cassidy's murder, and Mel's position as a person of interest. Most especially that last part.

She entered the bakery through the back door to find the kitchen empty. This was odd. Usually at this time of day, Oz was baking while Marty manned the front counter. Mel pushed her way through the kitchen door into the bakery to see what was happening.

Chaos! Complete and total chaos!

Marty was halfway over the counter with Oz and Angie holding him back by the ties of his navy blue apron. Marty's bald head was red and he looked like he was about to take a swing at the behemoth who stood on the other side of the counter.

"Don't ever talk like that about Mel again or I'll knock that big blocky head right off your body!" Marty yelled.

"Yeah, you big bully," Angie snapped. She let go of Marty's apron and was halfway over the counter when Oz grabbed the back of her shirt

"What's going on here?" Mel demanded. They all glanced her way, surprised to see her.

"A little help here, boss," Oz called as he planted his feet on the floor and used his full body weight to keep Angie and Marty from launching themselves at the glowering giant on the other side of the counter.

Mel glanced over the counter and her gaze met Dwight Pickard's. Well, it didn't look like she was going to have to go find him after all.

Marty flailed against Oz's hold. He reached back and grabbed a cupcake off of the counter. Mel knew exactly what he was thinking and she had no doubt that Dwight would snap Marty in half if he smashed that cupcake on him. She raced forward.

"Stop! Stop it!" Mel reached up and

grabbed the cupcake out of Marty's hand. "This will not solve anything."

"Maybe not, but a little frosting might sweeten his disposition," Marty said.

"Listen, old man —" Dwight leaned forward until he and Marty were practically nose-to-nose.

"Who are you calling old?" Marty jutted his chin forward.

"That's it!" Mel said. "Oz, get Marty out of here."

"Easy for you to say." Oz let go of Angie and Mel pushed her way between Angie and the counter. Oz bodily hefted Marty off of the counter and carried him into the kitchen.

"Put me down!" Marty howled. "I could take him. One knuckle to the eyeball and he'd drop like a bad habit."

"Simmer down," Oz said. "You know your daughters will freak out if you're in a brawl, and I am not protecting you from Olivia, either."

The door swung shut behind them.

"What do you want, Dwight?" Angie demanded. She was breathing hard and she'd made a fist with her right hand that Mel knew was going to pop him in his fading shiner if he said the wrong thing.

"I came to talk to her, not you, short

stack." Dwight pointed at Mel and she tried not to notice how enormous his hands were, like he could crush three cupcakes in one squeeze, she was pretty sure. Oh, dear.

"Listen, Thanos, if you want to talk to Mel, you can call and make an appointment," Angie said. "You know, so we can have the cops here."

"Cops?" Dwight barked out a laugh. "Good idea, then they'll be here to arrest her when I beat a confession out of her."

Mel stared at him. He really thought he could scare her by threatening to hit her? Okay, so it worked a little, but she'd rather eat a raw egg than admit it to him.

She glared at him and said, "Put one finger on me, and I'll make sure you are put away for life."

"It'd be your word against mine," he said. He crossed his arms over his massive chest and looked smug.

"And mine," Angie said.

Dwight swiveled his head in her direction. "You don't matter, pip-squeak. People will think you lied for her."

"Maybe, but *that* matters and it doesn't lie," Mel said. She pointed to the corner of the room where the red light of their security camera was visible. "You're under surveillance even now. And most likely, my staff has hit the panic button we keep in the kitchen and the authorities are on their way." The panic button part was a lie, but he didn't know that. She raised her hands and waved him in with a bravado that was so fake it almost made her smile. "You want to go? Come on."

Dwight shook his head at her. "You really think you're so great now, don't you? But I see you, Melephant. You're the same insecure pathetic loser you were in high school."

"Yes, I am her," Mel said. She stepped forward, even though inside she was shaking and felt like throwing up. "And you know what? She's awesome. I never gave myself the credit I deserved for being a badass and showing up at school every day even though I had to deal with you and all the rest and your constant bullying. Now get out of my bakery and don't come back."

Dwight stepped forward. He leaned over Mel until she could feel his hot breath in her face. He sneered and said, "I know you killed Cassidy and I'm going to prove it."

"I didn't," Mel said. She heard the kitchen door swing open and she felt Oz and Marty join Angie behind her, silently having her back.

"She started to write your name," he said. "It was as good as identifying her killer."

"Ha!" Mel scoffed. "More likely, she was going to write something nasty about me — again," She looked Dwight up and down, letting her contempt show. "Some people never change."

"I saw the red lipstick," he said. "I saw what she started to write on the wall. She named you. Now, you might be able to charm that idiot Danny into thinking you're innocent, but you'll never fool me. You're a kill—"

"Wait! What did you say?" Mel interrupted. She felt her heart pound in her chest. Maybe he was wrong. Maybe he didn't see it right. Either way, she needed clarification on the significance of what he'd just said.

"You heard me, I said, 'You're a kill—' "

"No, not that," Mel snapped. "The lipstick. What did you say about the lipstick?"

Dwight reared back from her with a weird look, like he thought she was crazy. "I said I saw the red lipstick —"

"That's it!" Mel pointed at him with both hands. She whipped around and found Angie standing right behind her. "Did you hear that?"

"Yeah, but I'm not sure why we care, unless it means I get to punch him in the mouth," Angie said. She had one eyebrow up and was looking at Mel much the same way Dwight was.

"We care because Cassidy never wore *red* lipstick — ever," Mel said. "She always wore that distinctive shade of bright pink."

She glanced back at Dwight. "You were close to her. You've probably seen her more than anyone else; did she ever change her lipstick color from the one she wore in high school?"

Dwight's eyebrows went up. Then he looked at Mel as if he was meeting her for the first time. He looked surprised or a little impressed. "No, never, she always wore the pink. 'Pink Cashmere' was the name. She never wore anything else."

"Then why would she have had red lipstick in the ladies' room with her?" Mel asked. She stared at Dwight as if she could see inside his skull. "Are you absolutely positive it was red lipstick that you saw on the wall?"

"Yes." He nodded. "And it wasn't her pink. Not even close."

Mel clapped her hands together. Then she spun around to face the others. "We have to find out who was wearing red lipstick at the reunion." She looked at Dwight and added, "And we need you to identify the color. No one else here saw it."

Dwight nodded. He looked Mel up and down as if considering her from every angle before agreeing. Finally, he nodded. "Okay, I see where you're going here. I'm in."

"One problem," Angie said. "How do we get any pictures from the reunion?"

"There was a social media page," Dwight said. "Everyone loaded their pictures onto it."

"Oz, go grab my laptop, please," Mel said.

Oz stepped forward. He moved right in front of Dwight so they were mere inches apart, and said, "I'll be right back."

It took Mel aback to realize that he had a few inches and a few pounds on Dwight. It checked Dwight a bit, too, as he jutted out his jaw and said, "Don't worry, kid."

"Don't call me kid," Oz said. Then he blew aside his bangs and met Dwight's gaze with his own. Whatever Dwight saw, it convinced him not to antagonize the youth. He gave Oz one swift nod and Oz turned and headed back to Mel's office.

He was back in a moment and handed Mel her laptop. She took it over to one of the café tables and opened it up. She gestured for Dwight to sit and once she logged in, she turned the laptop to him.

"I need a cupcake; anyone?" she asked.

"Blonde Bombshell," Dwight said. Mel

and Angie stared at him. He must have sensed the silence because he looked up and added, "Please."

Angie put her hands on her hips and stared him down. "How did you know the name of it?"

Dwight looked flustered. He gave an impatient shrug and said, "I don't know. I read it on the sign."

"It's not on the sign today," Angie said. "Have you been here before?"

"You're crazy," Dwight said. "I would never."

Mel shook her head. "No, she's right. You've had our cupcakes before."

"Well, duh, they were at the reunion," he said.

"Not the Blonde Bombshells," Mel said. She crossed her arms over her chest. "Explain yourself."

"Fine," Dwight said. "If you're going to be weird about it. Cassidy liked your cupcakes so she used to have me pick them up from the franchise downtown or hit up the cupcake van if it was in the area."

"Cassidy liked our cupcakes?" Mel asked. She looked at Angie. "I'm not sure how I feel about that."

"What's to feel?" Dwight asked. "You make a good cupcake. I mean, it's not like it's brain surgery."

"And you were doing so well," Mel said. She shook her head and went into the kitchen to retrieve a tray of cupcakes from the cooler, including a couple of Blonde Bombshells for Dwight. If anyone had ever told her they'd be allies in the search for Cassidy's killer, she never would have believed it. She still loathed him but she could put up with him if it meant they found the killer.

When she came back, Marty was helping some customers while Oz assisted. Sort of. Mostly, he stood behind the counter glaring at Dwight. Mel would have told him to dial it back, but she liked having him there in case everything went south as it was prone to do when Dwight was involved.

She slid into a seat at the table. Dwight and Angie were paging through the pictures and Angie had a pad and pen, noting who in the crowd was wearing red lipstick.

"How goes it?" Mel asked.

"Needle in a haystack," Angie said. She tapped the monitor. "What about that one?"

"Wrong shade. That's too orange; it was a deep red," Dwight said. "Like blood."

Mel and Angie exchanged a look and they both shuddered. Dwight reached over the laptop and grabbed one of the almond cupcakes. He peeled off the wrapper and took a huge bite, getting crumbs all over Mel's keyboard.

"Dude!" she said. She grabbed a napkin out of the holder and swiped the crumbs off the laptop.

"What? We're on a mission here," he said.

He clicked through the pictures. All of them were from before Cassidy's body was discovered. It was weird. Mel saw her classmates, people she barely knew, smiling and laughing, enjoying being with one another once again. She hadn't felt any of that. Oh, sure, she was happy to see a few of them but mostly, she could have skipped the whole thing and then she wouldn't be sitting here with her mortal enemy going over pictures, which was so strange she might require a quick session of therapy to put it behind her.

She reached for a Red Velvet cupcake. She needed the bite of the cream cheese frosting to keep her grounded in reality. This brief step into Bizzaro World couldn't last that long and she needed to be prepared to come back to terra firma. Cream cheese frosting would certainly help.

"That one there," Angie said. She tapped the monitor. "Who is that?"

"Gina Findley," Dwight said. "She's a

redhead now."

"Oh, yeah," Angie said. "She sat next to me in Trig. She certainly came out of her shell."

Mel glanced at the picture. Gina was downing a shot of tequila with two other women. She didn't recognize any of them, not even Gina. Her hair was a vibrant cranberry and her lips were a flame red. They clashed spectacularly.

"That's not the right red," Dwight said.

"Are you sure?" Angie asked. "It might have looked different on a wall."

"I'm sure." Dwight polished off his cupcake and reached for another.

Angie flipped through the pictures. One of Mel dancing with Danny popped up and Mel felt herself stiffen. Was Dwight going to have an episode over this?

"He should have married someone like you," he said. "Everyone would have been better off."

"Not me," Mel said. "Joe DeLaura is the only guy for me."

Angie reached back and gave Mel a knuckle bump. The only person as happy about her upcoming marriage as she and Joe were was Angie. It was clear Angie felt like she was finally getting the sister she'd always wanted.

Dwight ignored them and nudged Angie's hand out of the way so he could take over the pace of the photos. He flipped through several that were of all men, then he paused on a few that showed groups of women. Mel wanted to believe he was scrutinizing their lipstick but she had the feeling he was checking out their bazooms.

After several more photos, they had only a handful of names written down and they were dubious about them as none of them had any connection to Cassidy — at least none that Dwight could think of.

Angie let out a big yawn and said, "Who needs coffee?"

Mel and Dwight both agreed. Mel slid into Angie's seat. Dwight ran a hand over his face and then gave her side eye.

"This is weird."

"Hunting for a lipstick?" Mel asked. "Yeah."

"No, doing it with you," he said. "I never would have thought . . . I feel like I owe you an . . ."

Mel waited. If he was going to choke out an apology, she wasn't going to make it easy for him.

"But it was your own fault," he said. "If you hadn't been so —"

"Fat?" Mel asked. "Seriously?"

"I was going to say lame, seriously; you never once stood up for yourself," he said. "But, yeah, Cassidy really hated that you were well liked and overweight."

"What business was it of hers?" Mel asked. "I mean, honestly, what the hell?"

"The hell was that she wasn't allowed to be overweight," he said. "Her father was a total bastard. He made her weigh in every single night and if she gained an ounce, he fat shamed her and withheld food."

"That's horrible," Mel said.

"You have no idea," Dwight said. "Some parents shouldn't be parents, know what I'm saying?"

"So, Cassidy hated me because I was overweight and she was taught to hate people who were chubby?" Mel asked. She was trying to process this new information. She supposed it should have made her feel less animosity toward Cassidy, but it didn't. Just because her home life sucked didn't mean it was okay for Cassidy to take it out on everyone else.

Dwight shrugged. "Probably. Also, you were super lame."

Mel looked at him. He was still the big, square-jawed thug who had made her check around corners before walking down a hallway or entering a classroom. No, he'd never physically harmed her, but the words, oh, the words, had cut her so deeply.

"You were such a jerk," she said. "Actually, you were worse than that, you were a complete ass —"

"Coffee's here," Angie interrupted. She gave Mel a look, and Mel tipped her chin up in defiance. She didn't care if they needed Dwight to identify the lipstick. He was a jerk and she wasn't sorry she had called him on it.

"You're right," Dwight said. He took the mug of coffee Angie held out to him. "I was an ass — worse than a jerk."

Mel took a mug, too, and tried to hide her surprise that Dwight was owning his bad behavior. She never would have believed it.

"I have no excuse, not really, but my home life wasn't good," he said. Thanks to Brittany, Mel knew this to be an understatement but she said nothing, letting him speak without interruption. "I know it doesn't sound like her, but Cassidy looked out for me. Her father had her on a diet from the time she was two, so her mother tried to make it up to her by packing her enormous lunches that he didn't know about. Cassidy was so freaked out and guilty about it that she gave them to me, and it was usually the only meal I got all day."

Mel thought of her own mother, Joyce, who showed her love through food. Mel had never known a day of hunger in her life. She couldn't even imagine being a little kid and dealing with that.

"Hunger makes you angry," Dwight said. "I think I spent my entire life in a rage until I signed up for the Marines. For the first time in my life, I had three squares and a safe place to sleep. The anger went away until I was deployed and then had to deal with people trying to kill me, and watching my buddies get shot and, in a few cases, die. Then the anger came back."

"That sounds rough," Angie said. She glanced at Mel and they exchanged a look of horror. Dwight had certainly lived a tougher life than most.

"It was, but guess who was there for me the entire time I was gone?" he asked.

"Cassidy," Mel said.

"Yeah," he said. "Letters, care packages, Skype talks when we could meet up online. She never went a week without contacting me one way or another. And now she's dead."

Mel felt her heart drop into her shoes. It was the first time she'd heard of Cassidy thinking of someone besides herself. It didn't jibe with what she knew about the other woman, but it had been years since Cassidy had been her nemesis; did she really know her anymore?

"I'm sorry," she said. "It sounds like you lost a very good friend."

Dwight took a loud sip of his coffee. His voice when he spoke was gruff. "Thank you."

Brittany had told Mel what Cassidy had said to Dwight when he told her he loved her, but Mel wondered if she'd only said that because she was drunk. Had there been more between them than that one moment? Could they have been having an affair, and if so, how did Dwight feel about Danny?

"Why didn't you and Cassidy ever . . . ?" Mel asked. Out of the corner of her eye, she saw Angie sit up straight.

"Hook up?" Dwight asked. "Yeah, that was never going to happen."

"Why not?" Mel asked. She wondered if he'd share the scene that Brittany had witnessed. If he did share such a humiliation, he was a stronger person than Mel was.

"Listen, I loved her. I was in love with her," Dwight said. He looked pained, raw even, and for the first time in her life Mel felt sympathy for the guy who had been nothing but a tormentor to her. "But she never felt that way about me. In Cassidy's eyes, I wasn't husband material. I wasn't rich or good-looking or famous. I was just — me."

"But Danny was husband material?" Mel asked.

"She thought he was," he said. "She said she loved him, but it was never real. He was too busy being famous and chasing his glory days to be the husband she deserved. Tucker had it right at the funeral. Danny didn't deserve her."

Mel and Angie looked at each other again. It was obvious Dwight had no idea about Dan and Megan. Mel was not going to be the one to enlighten him.

"Sounds like you and Tucker had a lot in common," Angie said.

"Not really," Dwight said. "He didn't know her, not like I did. I was here, ready to take care of her. He was off in LA, trying to prove himself. Idiot. She was never into him."

"He obviously moved on," Mel said. "I mean his girlfriend, Kayla, is a supermodel."

Dwight sipped his coffee and then shook his head. "You really are too stupid to live."

"Hey!" Angie snapped. "I thought we were all getting along here."

"My apologies, but that woman was not Tucker's girlfriend," Dwight said.

Sixteen

"But Tucker said —" Mel began. Dwight interrupted.

"He lied. That girl was bought and paid for and I'm betting she was not cheap."

"Whoa," Mel said. "That explains why she wasn't at Cassidy's funeral."

"Yeah, I'm pretty sure that would have cost double overtime," Dwight said.

"Hey, wait a minute," Angie looked down at her notepad. "I have Kayla on here as one of our red lipstick girls."

"Let's look at her again," Mel said. She began to scroll through the photos. "Dwight, see if it's the same shade."

It took a while but Mel finally got to the picture of Kayla and Tucker. It was snapped just as they'd been walking into the reunion. She was holding his arm and walking like she was a runway model with the sucked-in cheeks and pointed stare. Her lipstick was definitely red.

"Nah, that's not it," Dwight said.

"Are you sure?" Angie asked. "I mean, if she is a working girl and she sees Tucker as her sugar daddy, it could very well be that she decided to off her competition. And if she's a 'professional,' she might have connections who hooked her up with whatever poison killed Cassidy."

"Yes, I'm sure," he said. "That is a cherry red, the one I saw was darker."

"Dang it," Angie said. "I got excited there for a second."

"Hey, kids," Tate said as he walked through the front door. Mel could tell he was striving to look casual but his eyebrows were up so high they looked like they were high-fiving his hairline, which gave away the mild state of panic he was in.

"We were just doing some research," Mel said. "And Dwight here was helping us."

"Cool," Tate said. He and Dwight stared at each other but neither of them greeted the other. "How about we have a short convo in the kitchen, ladies . . . now."

"Keep looking," Mel said to Dwight. "We'll be right back."

"Roger that," he said. He reached for another cupcake.

Angie and Mel followed Tate around the service counter. Marty nodded as they

272

passed and said, "Don't worry, we'll keep an eye on him."

"I'm sure he'll be fine," Mel said.

Oz just crossed his arms over his chest and fixed his stare on Dwight.

"Good man," Tate said and clapped him on the back as they walked by. He pushed through the door and held it open for Mel and Angie. Once the door swung shut behind them, he turned on them and asked, "What is *that* doing in our bakery? Have you two lost your minds?"

"No," they answered together.

"Dwight and I have come to an understanding," Mel said.

"That he's a Neanderthal nut job and you're his target? Because we already knew that," Tate said. "What on earth would possess you —"

"He saw what Cassidy wrote in the bathroom," Mel said. "He saw it. I wasn't allowed anywhere near it, but he barged his way in and saw it."

"And?" Tate said. "We know what it said. Uncle Stan told us it was your name, or the first few letters of your name at any rate."

"It was written in red lipstick," Angie said. "Bloodred."

Tate shook his head. "Not seeing the point."

"The point is Cassidy has only worn one particular shade of lipstick her entire life, Pink Cashmere, which was confirmed by Dwight."

"Meaning what? She's not the one who started to write your name?" Tate asked. He glanced between them as this bit of news filtered in. "Oh, wow. Then whoever was wearing the red lipstick could be the killer, trying to make it look like it was you."

"Exactly," Mel said. "So the three of us are going through pictures from the reunion and looking at all of the lip colors, hoping Dwight can find a match."

"That's genius," Tate said.

"Thank you," Mel and Angie said together. Then they laughed.

Marty popped his head into the kitchen and said, "Hey, Mel, big, tall, and scary is asking for you."

"Thanks," she said. She gave her friends a closed-lip smile and said, "This could be it."

She pushed back into the shop, leaving Tate and Angie to follow. There were several customers at the counter and she smiled a greeting as she walked by. Oz was taking their order and she noticed he glanced at Dwight every few seconds as if to make sure the man didn't move.

She studied Dwight's face as she neared. He didn't have the happiest of countenances to begin with but at the moment, he looked positively menacing. Uh-oh.

"What did you find?" she asked.

"This," Dwight said.

He turned the laptop to face her and Mel could see it was zoomed in on Megan's face. She was standing next to Cassidy and her head was thrown back with her long dark hair falling behind her. Her mouth was open in laughter and her full lips were done in a deep bloodred.

"That's the lipstick I saw on the bathroom wall. I'm positive," he said.

"Megan?" Mel asked. She and Tate looked at each other and she knew he was thinking the same thing she was. If anyone had a reason to kill Cassidy, it was Megan.

Dwight looked as if he couldn't believe what he was seeing. Mel realized that he'd known Megan as Cassidy's best friend all through school, so to see her as the prime suspect in the murder didn't work for him.

"This doesn't make sense," he said. "Megan and Cassidy were, well, they hadn't been close lately but Megan was always there. I mean, she was Cassidy's maid of honor at her wedding."

"The same wedding where Megan found

out that Cassidy shotgunned her chance with Danny?" Angie asked.

Dwight frowned. "How did you hear about that?"

"Everyone knows about it," Mel said. At least she was pretty sure if they hadn't before, they would soon, probably when Megan was arrested for murder.

"It's not like it sounds," Dwight said. "Megan had no interest in Danny, so Cassidy was just doing her a favor to keep it from becoming awkward."

"And you called *me* too stupid to live?" Mel asked. "On what planet is a woman not interested in Danny Griffin?"

Dwight's lips puckered and twisted up to the side. "Are you telling me that the story was true, that Cassidy actually went after Danny knowing that he and Megan were interested in each other?"

"I don't think she bothered to find out if Megan was interested, but she knew Danny was," Mel said. "You could see where there might be some hurt feelings."

"Sure but not enough to murder someone," Dwight said. "No, I don't believe it. Megan wouldn't do that. Besides, there's more pictures to go through. There could be someone else with red lipstick. I haven't even seen Kristie Hill yet and she most definitely is holding a grudge."

"That's true," Angie said. "We shouldn't jump to conclusions."

"All right, but I'm still going to call Uncle Stan and see what he thinks about all of this," Mel said. "Maybe they've already checked out the red lipstick connection."

"See if you can get him to tell you what the poison was," Angie said. "That might help narrow it down, too."

"I'll do my best," Mel said. She ducked back into the kitchen to make the call in the privacy of her office. Partly because she didn't want to tell Uncle Stan what she knew in a public area, but also so that no one else heard him when he started yelling. Yeah, it was mostly because of the yelling.

"Mel, don't tell me, let me guess: You were at the car wash and found a dead body," Uncle Stan answered his phone.

"Funny," she said. "No. And hello to you, too."

"Coffee shop? Library? Post office?" he asked. "Seriously, there has to be a dead body somewhere."

"That's it. I am telling Mom to take you off the diet," she said. "You're turning into a crankypotamus."

"I haven't had a potato chip in weeks."

"It's for your own good."

"Or dessert!" Stan cried. "No dessert for weeks!"

"Oh, that is too far. That's positively abusive," Mel said. "I'll talk to her."

"Promise?" he said. "I need dessert. I mean what's the point of being alive if you can't have dessert?"

"If I bring you some cupcakes, would that help?" she asked.

"It would," he said. He sounded happy just at the suggestion. "Wait. What's your angle?"

"No angle," Mel said. She hoped she sounded sufficiently outraged.

"You want to know something, don't you?" he asked.

Mel sank back into her office chair. "So, if I bring you cupcakes, do you want the hi-top meringue frosting or the chocolate coconut ones, or something else?"

"Chocolate coconut? Your Moonlight Madness ones with the thick layer of coconut?" he asked.

"Just made a fresh batch this morning," she said.

"You're killing me," he said. "Okay, what do you want to know? I'll see if I can share."

"The lipstick Cassidy was holding, the one she used to write on the bathroom wall," Mel said. "Do we know whose it was?"

Stan was quiet for a moment. "How do you know it wasn't hers?"

"Cassidy has only ever worn the same bright pink lipstick," she said. "I could have told you the night of her murder if you had let me see the lipstick then."

"How do you know she never changed it?" Stan asked. "She might have. The lipstick could still be hers."

"It wasn't. She was wearing the same bright pink at the reunion," Mel said. "Also, I confirmed with a friend of hers that she never changed."

"Megan Mareez?" he asked. "Mel, you're supposed to stay away from this."

"We already had this fight," Mel said. "I told you I would be there for my friends and I am."

"Last I checked you weren't friends with Megan," he said.

"It so happens it's not Megan who confirmed her lipstick choice, it's Dwight Pickard."

"What?!" Mel held the phone away from her ear as the shouting began. When the volume got lower, she held it closer. He was in the home stretch. He said, "Why on earth would you have anything to do with a known sociopath?"

"Because he showed up here, looking for

me," Mel said. "Because he still thought it was me who poisoned Cassidy, but we had a chat and he realized that makes no sense. He's here right now, going through the reunion pictures with Angie."

"I'm on my way," Stan snapped. The call ended.

Mel held the phone away from her and said, "Good talk."

She knew Uncle Stan would come barreling through the backdoor in five minutes. His office was nearby, in the local police precinct. She figured she'd better get those Moonlight Madness cupcakes ready.

She unlocked the back door for him and then plated a few cupcakes and made a fresh pot of coffee. Oz was still in front, helping Marty and keeping an eye on Dwight. Mel took a deep breath and enjoyed the solitude of her kitchen for a moment. It didn't happen often these days that she got to be here alone. She soaked it all in. It didn't last.

"So, you're what, friends now?" Uncle Stan demanded as he banged through the back door of the bakery.

"No, never that," Mel said. She grabbed a mug and the coffeepot and gestured for Uncle Stan to sit. "But we have a mutual interest in finding out who murdered Cassidy. So, what can you tell me?"

"Nothing," he said. "We're still waiting for the toxicology report to confirm what was in her system."

"How about the delivery?" Mel asked. She handed him a fork. "Any idea how she was poisoned?"

Stan was quiet for a beat. "There were trace amounts of a toxic substance in her drink. But we have to wait to find out if it's what was in her system and whether it killed her. We are being very thorough."

"Her drink was poisoned?" Mel asked.

"Possibly," Stan said. "We are waiting on confirmation and that is all I'm saying." He then tucked into his cupcakes and didn't speak until he had scraped the last coconut flake up with his fork. Then he leaned back and sipped his coffee as if his reason for living had been restored.

"So, someone wrote *M-E-L* on the bathroom wall in red lipstick, probably trying to make it look like it was me, because everyone knew about our history," Mel said.

"I'd say that's a safe bet," Uncle Stan agreed.

"I think whoever did it used their own lipstick," Mel said. She peeked through the round window in the swinging door. Tate, Dwight, and Angie were hunkered over the laptop. "And I'm betting Dwight and Angie have a short list of names for us."

Stan rolled to his feet. He kept his coffee in one hand as he gestured for her to lead on with the other. Mel pushed through the door, hoping that Dwight had come up with someone more than Megan to give to Uncle Stan.

Marty and Oz were helping some customers and they both glanced up when Uncle Stan appeared. Mel noticed they both looked relieved to see him as they exchanged handshakes with their favorite detective.

" 'You've got to ask yourself one question: "Do I feel lucky?" Well, do ya, punk?' " Oz said.

Uncle Stan laughed.

"*Dirty Harry,*" Mel said, and then asked, "Are we done here?" The men nodded.

She led Uncle Stan to the table where Dwight sat with the others. Uncle Stan and Dwight eyed each other like predator and prey. She wasn't sure which was which, and she wondered who would strike first.

"So, cupcake bakeries have replaced donut shops for cop hangouts?" Dwight asked. "Good to know."

"Apparently, it's also the place for the chronically unemployed," Uncle Stan.

Tate hissed through his teeth. "Solid burn."

Dwight glared at him and then turned his sneer on Uncle Stan. "I have a job."

"Yeah, you've had several," Uncle Stan said. "Let's see, airport baggage guy, fired for your bad attitude; pool maintenance man, fired for anger issues; car salesman, fired for threatening a customer; house-painter, fired for foul language; hmm, am I missing anything?"

"At least I'm my own boss," Dwight said. He tipped his chin up in defiance.

"Yeah, you're the king of going nowhere," Uncle Stan said. "Good for you. You know we've asked for the fingerprints of anyone who was close to Cassidy Havers-Griffin on the night of the reunion. You were supposed to drop by the station for fingerprinting. Any reason why you haven't made it there yet?"

"I've been busy," Dwight said.

"Yeah, with all that employment," Uncle Stan retorted. "Let me be clear, you can come in voluntarily or we can *make* it happen."

Dwight looked like he was going to swear or take a swing at Uncle Stan, so Mel stepped forward and said, "Great, I see you two know each other, so let's move on." She turned to Angie and asked, "What did you find?"

"We looked at all of the women wearing red lipstick at the reunion and then narrowed it to the top ten who looked like they wore the right shade of red," Angie said. "Then we did a sweep to get rid of people we didn't recognize, spouses of classmates who wouldn't have any reason to harm Cassidy or to implicate you — that was Dwight's idea, by the way."

Mel looked at Stan, who glanced at Dwight and gave him a small nod. Dwight's sneer got deeper, as if he couldn't care less what Uncle Stan thought, which Mel didn't believe. Not anymore.

"So, who are we left with?" Mel asked.

"Megan Mareez, Lianne Marsten, and Kristie Hill," Dwight said. "There are a couple others who knew Cassidy but these three were the closest to her inner circle."

Angie had kept the pictures of the three women up on the computer and Uncle Stan leaned in to get a look at them. He nodded but didn't say a word.

"I think you can let the police handle it from here," he said.

"Make me," Dwight said. He rose to his feet and crossed his arms over his chest. His big lantern jaw was jutted out and he looked like he was hoping Uncle Stan would take a swing at him. Uh-oh.

SEVENTEEN

"Hey, gang, what's the haps?" a voice called from the front door. It was pushed open and Tucker strolled in, wearing his usual khaki pants and loafers with his shirt neatly tucked and his brown leather belt matched precisely to his shoes.

"Hey, Tucker," Tate said. He had moved ever so slightly so that he was in between Uncle Stan and Dwight. Mel was grateful but suspected if Dwight put his mind, or rather his fists, to it, there would be no stopping him. "What brings you here?"

"I'm on my way back to LA," Tucker said. He had his laptop bag over one shoulder and a blazer folded over his arm. "I just wanted to say good-bye."

"Bye," Dwight growled.

Tucker seemed to notice him for the first time. His eyebrows went up as he glanced from Dwight to Mel and back. He looked at her in alarm.

"Save it," Dwight said. "I can read your face like a bad hand of poker. Mel and I are working on a thing."

"Together?" Tucker asked. His voice went up an octave and he cleared his throat.

"Crazy, huh?" Mel asked. "By any chance have you loaded all of the pictures you took to the reunion website?"

"No, I didn't have the heart after, well, you know," he said. "Most of them are just in my photo file on my laptop."

Mel looked at Dwight. "There might be people we've missed."

"Can we see them?" Angie asked.

"I . . . uh . . . I have to catch my plane," Tucker said. "But I want to help, I do."

"Excellent," Uncle Stan said. "Go ahead and open up your laptop. Then you can re-book your flight."

Tucker let out a huge sigh. "But my girlfr—"

Dwight shook his head at him. "Pictures."

"Fine, but it'll take me a second to open up the files," he said.

"We'll wait," Uncle Stan said.

He sounded so reasonable. Mel knew this was his detective voice. He was very mild and unassuming and then when the suspect least expected it, he pounced.

"Can I at least ask what you're looking for

287

in the pictures?" Tucker asked.

Mel glanced at Uncle Stan. He was the professional, this was his call.

"The lipstick used in the bathroom to write on the wall," he said. "We're looking for any women who were wearing that shade."

"Why?" Tucker asked. "Clearly it was Cassidy's —"

"No," Mel said. "She never wore that shade. We need to know who did."

"We have a few people already but we want to make sure we didn't miss anyone," Angie said.

"Oh," Tucker said. "Wow, that is worth missing my flight for." He set to work opening the files on his computer while they waited.

"What will you do with the names we've found?" Mel asked Uncle Stan.

"Interview them again," he said. He looked at the pictures on Mel's laptop. "Or bring them in."

Mel knew he was looking at Megan Mareez. She supposed she needed to tell him about her affair with Danny. Why did it feel like such a betrayal? Because of the baby. She hated that she had to be the one to go back on her word and tell Uncle Stan about their relationship. She glanced up and found

Tate studying her. This was the best thing about lifelong friends. They frequently were thinking the same thing at the same time. Mel had told Megan *she* wouldn't say anything; she hadn't said that the person listening to their conversation wouldn't. She nodded at him.

"Can I talk to you for sec, Stan?" he asked.

Uncle Stan looked at Tate. His eyes narrowed and then he gave a curt nod. "Don't go through the pictures without me."

He and Tate moved across the bakery to the opposite side of the bubblegum-pink interior. They both leaned in and Mel knew Tate was whispering. At one point, Uncle Stan looked at her and Mel tried to make her face look as innocent as possible. Judging by his frown, he wasn't buying it.

"File's open," Tucker announced. Dwight reached around him and moved the laptop so it was in front of him.

"Hey!" Tucker protested.

"I'm the one who saw the lipstick," Dwight growled.

Tucker raised his hands in surrender, and Mel knew it must pain him to turn his laptop over to a thug like Dwight. They were living in weird times when Dwight was the leader and they were all working together. She had a feeling she'd be dreaming a

Hunger Games version of this moment when she went to bed that night.

Uncle Stan and Tate returned to the table. Dwight began scrolling through the pictures. Like the former high school reporter he was, Tucker had captured pictures of everyone. The most telling was one of Cassidy and Kristie Hill giving each other the cold stare. It didn't look like Kristie was going to forgive the hijack of her homecoming tiara anytime soon.

Mel glanced at Uncle Stan to see if he was getting this. His eyebrows were lowered into a V, meeting over the bridge of his nose like an accent mark of frustration.

They went through a few more pictures, and then there was a series of pictures of Cassidy. Mel wasn't sure about what she felt, seeing her old nemesis. She was a beautiful woman and the pictures caught her smiling and laughing. Mel probably would have thought they were lovely if she knew Cassidy wasn't laughing at the expense of someone else, but she probably was. It tainted the pictures for Mel. She glanced at Dwight and Tucker, the two men who'd adored Cassidy since high school. Their expressions were of grief and mourning. Mel tried to be empathetic; after all, no matter how vile Cassidy had been, she didn't deserve what had happened to her.

The next picture that popped up was one of Cassidy and Dan. They were standing close. It looked like an intimate moment between a husband and wife. What was interesting in the photo was that Cassidy and Dan were in the forefront and slightly out of focus and behind them in sharp focus was Megan. The shot of her face revealed an expression of pure fury and gave a close-up of her eyes and lips much better than the other picture of her. Mel caught her breath when she saw it.

"That's the lipstick I saw on the wall," Dwight said. He tapped Megan's face with his forefinger. "I'm sure of it."

Mel felt Uncle Stan straighten up beside her. He fished a business card out of his pocket and tossed it to Tucker. "Send that picture to my e-mail and any others like it. I have to go."

Mel followed him to the door while the others went back to viewing the pictures. "Uncle Stan, where are you going?"

"It's better if you stay out of this, Mel."

"You're going to arrest Megan, aren't you?" she asked.

"Just look for more pictures, okay?"

The door banged shut behind him. Mel leaned against it. If Megan had murdered

Cassidy she deserved to be arrested, but Mel couldn't help feeling horrible for Dan and the baby and, honestly, for Megan. If Cassidy hadn't interfered with Dan and Megan getting together, then Megan would have been with Dan from the start.

Mel knew that if someone had stopped her from being with Joe, oh, she'd be furious. But murder, there was never any excuse for that, no matter what the person had done. To take a life was just inexcusable. Even if Cassidy had refused to divorce Dan, there was no excuse for murdering her.

Dwight continued to search through all of Tucker's pictures, flagging the ones he saw that Uncle Stan would be interested in. Mel returned and sat beside him, taking notes on a pad she'd retrieved from her office. It occurred to her that establishing a timeline would be helpful and she had Dwight click on the pictures to see the time each photo was taken. She focused on the pictures of Megan and Cassidy, trying to see when Cassidy left for the ladies' room and where Megan was at the same time.

"What are you doing?" Dwight asked.

"Establishing a timeline for the murder," Mel said. "We know the poison was put in Cassidy's drink. I'm trying to figure out her whereabouts before she disappears into the bathroom, and I'm trying to track Megan, too."

"Huh," Dwight grunted. "Smart." His tone was grudging. Mel ignored him.

They continued combing through the photos. It was painstaking and at the end of an hour, she felt as if her eyes were glazing over. Between Tucker's pictures and the pictures posted on the class reunion's website, Megan's whereabouts were accounted for to the minute in the time after Cassidy disappeared from the pictures to go to the bathroom. One thing was certain, Megan never left the main room at the reunion. So she couldn't have been the one to write Mel's name on the bathroom wall. It had to have been someone else.

Mel leaned back in her chair, studying the timeline on her notepad. She glanced up at the others. "It may have been Megan's lipstick, but she wasn't the one who wrote on the bathroom wall. She's in pictures with everyone and there isn't more than a minute or two between the photos. I don't think she had time to get to the bathroom, write on the wall, and get back to the party. I think she's innocent."

Dwight frowned at her and she shrugged. "Sorry. But the timeline — it doesn't read that it was her."

"What about Dan?" he asked.

"He was with his basketball team, recounting their glory days at the bar," she said. "According to Tim Halloran, he and Dan were together after Dan and Cassidy had their argument right up until her body was found."

"You need to tell Stan," Tate said. "This opens the case back up. I mean, it could have been anyone if Cassidy was poisoned at the reunion. How many people were in our graduating class anyway?"

"Three hundred and forty-seven," Tucker answered. "But only two hundred and thirty-five came to the reunion with dates, giving us about five hundred people at the reunion at the time of . . . well, you know."

"Wow," Angie said. "Our class didn't seem that big at the time."

"That's because we didn't really hang out with anyone but each other," Tate said. He put his arm around Angie and hugged her close. "And I wouldn't have had it any other way."

"Me, too." She smiled up at him. Their newlywed glow was practically atomic.

Mel looked at Tucker and Dwight, who were still studying the computer monitor. Dwight had brought back the picture of Cassidy laughing. Both men looked pensive, but Tucker looked more indignant at the loss of her while Dwight appeared more touched by the loss, with indelible marks of grief deepening the lines around his eyes and mouth.

"Whoever did this," Dwight said, "I want them to pay."

"They will," Tucker said. "They will."

The two men had nothing in common except their affection for Cassidy. It occurred to Mel that they had the potential go vigilante on this whole thing, so she decided a distraction was in order.

"Whatever happened to Mr. Meehan?" she asked. "Did you all have him for Biology? He was a kick, wasn't he?"

"He's dead," Dwight said. "Cancer."

"Oh," Mel said. She felt the shock of it reverberate inside of her. Mr. (Howie) Meehan had been one of the few teachers who'd really taken the time to get to know her. He had always provided a safe haven from the bullies in his classroom even though it always reeked of formaldehyde. She sighed. The hits just kept coming.

Dwight rose out of his chair, pushing the seat back with a scraping noise against the floor. He looked restless, like he wanted to go do damage. He strode to the door, calling over his shoulder, "I gotta go."

"Dwight!" Mel called after him. He ignored her and pushed out the front door. Without overthinking it, she chased after him. "Hey, Dwight!"

Outside the day had turned hot, waves of heat rising up from the sidewalk as the desert sun beat down. Mel took a second to acclimate herself and looked around to see where Dwight was. He'd taken a right and was almost at the corner.

Old Town, where the bakery resided, was a kitschy collection of shops, galleries, bars, and restaurants. Housed in old western buildings complete with porches with railings and cobbled walkways, it fully embraced the love of cowboy culture from the fifties. Mel had loved it when she was a girl growing up in the neighborhood, so when it came time to open her shop, Old Town was the natural choice. Luckily, she'd been here long enough to know most of the other shop owners, so when she went running down the covered sidewalk, no one batted an eye.

"Dwight, wait!" she cried. He was almost at the crosswalk. Before he could step into the road, she grabbed his arm.

He looked down at her and Mel remembered the contempt and disdain he used to blast her with in school. There was none of that present. Instead, he looked agitated and helpless. Mel knew that feeling. She'd felt the kind of powerlessness he was suffering from, usually because of people like him when they went after her about her weight when she was younger, and now that she was a professional baker, she found the haters liked to go after her cupcakes.

Honestly, some people were so full of hate. She'd gotten only a handful of one-star reviews on the local business review sites, and she was always amazed at the outrage some people felt over the price of the cupcakes, or because they closed at eight, or they didn't like the look of her workers just because Oz had a few piercings and they were afraid of him. Little did they know, he was on his way to being one of the best pastry chefs in the country. Truly, it seemed some people just wanted to create outrage and then hurl it back out there at anyone who would listen. Such a waste.

If anything good had ever come out of being bullied, it was that she had developed a hide like a rhinoceros and it was practically impossible to hurt her feelings these days, because she had learned that the only opinion that truly mattered was her own.

"What?" Dwight asked. He glared at her hand on his arm and Mel removed it. "Did you chase me down just to stare at me?"

"Sorry, I got lost in thought," she said. In truth, she wasn't much of a runner and she needed a second to catch her breath.

"I have places to go," Dwight said.

"I just want to say that you can trust my uncle Stan on this. He's a great detective. One of the best. He'll find out who murdered Cassidy," she said.

"And what if he doesn't?" Dwight asked. "Or what if he does, but the golden boy who is responsible for Cassidy's murder gets off because nothing ever sticks to him?"

"You don't really think Danny had anything to do with this, do you?" she asked.

"I don't know, but you saw the picture," he said. "Your uncle saw it, too. Megan looked furious. Maybe she didn't kill Cassidy herself. Maybe she had someone do it for her."

"I find that hard to believe. There's still Kristie to consider, among others. The important thing is that you don't do anything you'll regret," Mel said. When he looked like he'd protest, she said, "Listen, if you do something rash like confront one of the suspects, you could damage the case the police are building. If you want justice for Cassidy, you have to let the police do their jobs."

"Just let me go, okay?" he asked.

"Dwight." She said his name just like she did her nephews' when they were kicking up a fuss. He shook his head at her and walked away, so, yeah, the tone worked about as well on grown-ups as it did on kids, which meant not at all.

Mel wondered if she should call her uncle. What could she say? Dwight was on the loose and he might go after Megan or Kristie? She knew exactly what Uncle Stan would say. Did she have any proof? She didn't. She just had a gut feeling that things were about to go sideways.

She jogged-walked, mostly walked, back to the bakery. Tucker was packing up his laptop and chatting with Angie and Tate while Marty manned the front counter. Oz was nowhere in sight so Mel figured he'd gone back to the kitchen now that Dwight was gone.

"What's with him?" Tate asked when she joined them.

"He's upset," Mel said. "Understandably. He thinks Megan had someone do her dirty work for her. I think it's just hard to believe one of our classmates could murder another."

"I can't believe it," Tucker said. "I mean Cassidy, like her or not, was a personality that was larger than life. It's weird to imagine the world without her."

Mel nodded. Although she didn't have the same affectionate memories of Cassidy, she had to agree that her world would be different knowing that the woman who had been her chief tormentor was gone. Mel supposed she should be glad, but she wasn't. Instead she felt oddly bereft, sort of like if she kept hitting her thumb with a hammer it would be a weird absence of pain when she stopped.

"Did you manage to rebook your flight?" she asked.

"Yes, in fact, I have to go or I'll miss it again," he said.

"Well, thanks for your help," Mel said. "I'm sure Uncle Stan is grateful, too."

"No prob," he said. He paused. "I'm glad your timeline proves it wasn't Megan who killed her. Nasty business to be murdered by your best friend. It's lousy, but it makes more sense when it's an enemy."

Mel looked at him. Everyone knew she and Cassidy had been at odds since grade school. Was he implying . . . ?

"Not that I think you did it," he said quickly, and Mel nodded. So long as they were clear on that. She had taken a polygraph after all.

Tucker was shorter than Mel by a few

inches, so she hunched down a bit to hug him. He then hugged Angie and shook hands with Tate. As he walked to the door, he called back, "Will you keep me in the loop? I want to know what's happening, you know, if they arrest anyone."

"Definitely," Angie said. "When we know, you'll know."

"Cool, well, see you in another five years," he said. He waved and the door swung shut behind him.

"See ya," Mel said. She turned to her friends. "So, today was bizarre."

"And how," Tate said. "I almost freaked out when I saw Dwight in here."

"Tell me about it," Mel said. "When he showed up, your wife was half over the counter ready to take him on."

"Ange, babe," Tate said. "We've talked about that. You have to be careful."

"I was careful," Angie said. "It was just a show of strength. I wouldn't have mixed it up with him or anything."

Tate hugged her close and said, "Let's go home."

Angie looked at Mel. "Are you good here?"

Mel glanced at the clock on the wall. "Yeah, I'm going to stay late tonight. I want to send the timeline to Uncle Stan and then

I have a wedding I want to start prepping since Oz has to leave for his evening class at cooking school."

"Can you and Marty handle it by yourselves?" Angie asked. "I'm happy to stay if you need me."

"Thanks, but you opened this morning," Mel said. "Don't worry. We've got this."

"If you say so." Angie untangled herself from Tate, pausing to kiss his cheek before she disappeared in back to take off her apron and grab her purse.

"Hey, I know you think the timeline lets Megan off the hook, but Dwight might be right to think someone else killed Cassidy for her," Tate said. He didn't name Danny specifically but Mel knew that's who he was thinking about. "Try not to get too invested in this."

"What makes you think I'm invested?"

"Because you care about her and Dan," he said. "Mel, she was wearing the lipstick, she was having an affair with Danny — heck, she's having his baby. There is no one more suspect than her in Cassidy's murder and just because she's pregnant does not mean she gets a pass."

"I know, I know," Mel said. "But I really didn't get the killer vibe off her."

"What is the 'killer vibe'?" he asked.

"You know, the feeling that someone could actually do something that heinous; she doesn't even have crazy eyes," Mel said.

"That doesn't mean she didn't do it," he said.

"She's going to have his child," Mel said. "They seem to have a life plan. I can't believe she'd jeopardize it all by poisoning his wife."

"The wife who interfered in her getting together with him to begin with," Tate said. "And who was refusing to divorce him. She might have been feeling desperate."

"You're right," Mel said. "I know you're right. I'm just having a hard time accepting it."

"Send the timeline to Stan and go work on your wedding cupcakes," he said. "You'll feel better."

Mel hugged him close and said, "Have I ever told you how glad I am you became my friend in middle school?"

"You might have mentioned it a few hundred times," Tate said. "And I feel the exact same way."

"I don't think I could have gotten through those years without you and Angie," she said.

"Same," he agreed. "Let's never break up the band."

Mel laughed. "Never."

Feeling better, Mel snapped a picture of her notes and sent it to Uncle Stan, then she went to her happy place, the kitchen, to work on an enormous batch of wedding cupcakes. The bride and groom had requested chocolate cupcakes with vanilla frosting, decorated with white fondant and pale pink flowers with edible pearls to look like a bride, and vanilla cupcakes with chocolate frosting and a fondant tuxedo jacket and bow tie to represent the groom. Mel liked making the fondant decorations as she found massaging the dye into the fondant to be very therapeutic.

She waved to Oz as he departed for the night and told Marty to come get her if the bakery got busy. Then she set to work, mixing the batter up in her industrial mixer. She made the chocolate cupcakes first. Her industrial convection oven was enormous and she used cupcake trays that baked thirty-six cupcakes at a time. While the chocolate ones were baking she set to work on the vanilla. She had just put all of the ingredients into the mixer when she heard a commotion coming from the front of the shop.

She paused the mixer and wiped her hands off on a dish towel, then she went to see what was happening. She pushed through the door to find Danny Griffin standing on the other side of the counter from Marty.

"What is it with you and angry men today?" Marty asked. His bald head was bright red and he was hunched over with his arms out, looking like he was getting ready to wrestle Danny to the ground.

"Stand down," Mel said. "He's a friend. Sort of."

"You!" Danny snapped. "How could you? They arrested her. Did you know that? They just arrested Megan for Cassidy's murder."

EIGHTEEN

"What? When?" Mel asked. She glanced at the clock. Uncle Stan had left a couple of hours ago, but he should have gotten her text by now.

"An hour ago," he said. "They won't let me see her. They have her in an interrogation room at the police station. What did you say to your uncle?"

"Nothing," Mel said. At least that part was true; it was Tate who had told Stan of the affair. "But Uncle Stan came by when Dwight was here this afternoon accusing me of being the one who harmed Cassidy."

"Why would Dwight do that?" Danny asked.

"Because Cassidy was poisoned and in his mind, I had motive and opportunity," Mel said. "But while we were talking, he said that he went into the bathroom at the reunion and saw the lipstick that Cassidy wrote what might have been my name with.

He said it was a red color, a deep, dark red."

"So?" Danny looked bewildered.

Mel blew out a breath. "Is there any way Megan might have . . . ?" She couldn't finish the sentence. Good thing Danny didn't need her to.

"No!" he cried. "Megan isn't like that. She would never. Even on the eve of my wedding when she found out that Cassidy hadn't told her about my interest in her, she still smiled through it all and wished us well. Tucker was there. He could tell you. Megan was so gracious, considering. Dwight was there, too, for that matter."

"Well, that just means she has her pride," Marty said. "Doesn't mean she wouldn't poison someone who stole her man."

"But Cassidy didn't steal me," Danny said. "I am . . . I was leaving her. Megan and I are together, we're a couple. She knows I was trying to get out of my marriage with the least amount of fuss. She's the one who told me to try and ease out of it when I would much rather have just packed a bag and left."

Mel frowned. "Is there any way Cassidy might have known about the two of you?"

"No," Dan said. "We were so careful. And you know her, there's no way she would have been able to hide how angry she'd be.

I mean, her husband hooking up with her best friend? That's why Megan and I were so careful. We both knew Cassidy would be psychotically angry."

"Psychotic enough to take her own life?" Mel asked. She'd thought this before and everyone said it was impossible, but she wondered. Cassidy was impulsive and might have done something to harm herself when she was already drunk and not thinking clearly.

"No, Cassidy would never," Danny said. "She'd have had to give up being the victim and torturing us for the rest of her life. She'd never pass that up."

"Harsh," Marty said.

"But true," Danny said. "I'm sorry, but that's the sort of woman she was."

Mel looked at Marty and nodded at him. "I'd say that's accurate. So, what are you going to do?" Mel asked. "For what it's worth, there were other women who were wearing that particular shade of red lipstick at the reunion."

"Kristie Hill?" Danny guessed. Mel's eyes went wide and he explained, "She was brought into the station while I was trying to see Megan."

Mel almost didn't want to know, but curiosity won out. "How was she?"

"Furious," Dan said. "She was yelling and taking badge numbers. She was promising that heads would roll."

"Oh," Mel said. "Well, judging by her temperament, they could have a solid contender there for a person angry enough to commit murder."

Danny's shoulders dropped a tiny bit.

"Listen," Mel said. "It doesn't sound like they arrested Megan. It sounds like they brought her in for questioning, which is a very different thing. You should go back to the station and wait for her. She's going to need you when it's all over."

"She says she doesn't want us to be seen together until Cassidy's murder is solved," Danny said.

"Given that the police know you two are a thing now, I don't really see the point," she said. She put her hand on his arm and gave it a squeeze. "Everything's going to be okay. Listen, I probably shouldn't tell you this, but when we were going through the reunion pictures, I made a timeline of Cassidy's and Megan's whereabouts during the reunion. From what I could tell, and I'm an amateur, there is no way Megan could have been anywhere near the restroom when Cassidy was in there. I sent it to Uncle Stan because I think it proves she couldn't have been the one to write my name in the bathroom, meaning she didn't try to frame me, which also means she likely didn't poison Cassidy. Someone else did."

"You did that?" Dan blinked.

"Yes," Mel said. She took a napkin out of a holder and grabbed a pen off of the counter. "Not that you'll need this, but this is an attorney friend of mine, Steve Wolfmeier. He's the best. He can make sure the system is treating you right. You'll see."

Danny pocketed the napkin, then he opened his arms and hugged Mel close. "Thanks," he said. "Sorry I yelled. You've been such a good friend."

Mel felt a twinge of guilt that she'd had Tate do her dirty work for her by having him tell Uncle Stan about the affair, and that it was likely their fault that Megan had been picked up. But then she reminded herself that if Megan or Danny were guilty, she'd done the right thing by alerting Uncle Stan to the red lipstick matchup. And at least she'd made the timeline, which should help. She hoped.

When Danny left, Mel locked the door after him and flipped the OPEN sign to CLOSED.

She looked at Marty and said, "That's it. I can't have another person come through that door and yell at me. I'm done."

"Seems reasonable to me," Marty said. Together they closed up the front of the bakery. When they were finished, Mel resumed her baking and Marty headed out the back door.

"Don't work too late," he said. "And lock up behind me."

"Of course," Mel said. She was just taking the vanilla cupcakes out of the oven before she started on the fondant.

She flipped on the radio, happily listening to Beyoncé singing about girls who run the world while she fired up her industrial KitchenAid mixer to produce a large batch of vanilla buttercream frosting. While that blended, she took several rolls of fondant out of the walk-in cooler. She put on gloves before she started to work the color in. Using a toothpick, she used just a tiny dab of pink gel-based color to massage into the fondant until it was the perfect pale pink for the flowers she wanted to create.

She bagged the colored fondant to save for use later. She spread the buttercream onto the cooled cupcakes, prepping them for when she would wrap them with a layer of white fondant, on which she would decorate the cupcakes with the pink flowers and pearls. She could see in her mind exactly how she wanted them to look.

Despite how horrible the day had been, she took solace in knowing that for this couple, she could make something delicious and beautiful. It made her world seem less horrible, as a good cupcake should. Much as she tried, however, she couldn't stop thinking about Dwight and how Cassidy had been there for him. She never would have expected that. She had only thought of Cassidy in terms of how awful she had been. It had never occurred to her to look deeper and see more. Of course, she was pretty sure Cassidy had never looked more deeply at her, either. And now she never would.

There was a feeling of loss that came with that realization that surprised Mel. She'd never wanted to be friends with Cassidy. She'd never wanted to be in her life. But now, any possibility between them for a better understanding of each other was gone. That was a loss.

Mel glanced at the worktable. She could tell already that she was going to be too tired to make the flowers. This would have to wait until tomorrow but she could get the white fondant on over the buttercream. She had done so many of these at this point in her career that she could pop them out pretty quickly.

She began to roll out the white fondant, when there was a knock on the back door. It was three sharp raps and she felt herself jump. If it was one of her people, they would have used their keys. She peered at the door.

"Mel, it's me, Tucker." Relief surged through her. "Sorry to bother you, but I think I left my sunglasses in the bakery. They're prescription, otherwise I'd let them go."

"Hang on, I'm coming," Mel called.

She stripped off her gloves and wiped her hands on her apron. She moved toward the door. Poor Tucker, he was having a hell of a night. He couldn't manage to leave the city and go home. She had her hand on the knob and the deadbolt. She was just turning the lock when she stopped.

Tucker. *Tucker was there. He could tell you.* Danny's words from earlier flitted into her mind. Tucker had been at the rehearsal dinner when everyone found out that Cassidy had manipulated Danny into marrying her instead of pursuing his interest in Megan. Tucker had been the one in high school, always with the camera, always on the fringe, always in love with Cassidy.

But it made no sense. Tucker didn't wear lipstick, red or otherwise. He didn't have anything to gain by killing Cassidy. And yet,

Mel couldn't deny that the hair on the back of her neck prickled. Something felt weird about this. She needed to stall him.

"Just a sec, Tucker," she said. "I forgot to deactivate the alarm. I'll be right back."

She heard him say something, but it was a mutter she couldn't decipher, and with her heart racing and the blood pounding in her ears, she could barely think, never mind listen. She needed to talk to her uncle Stan about Megan. She needed to know if it was her lipstick and whether she had been the one to write on the bathroom wall.

She hurried to her office to grab her phone and slid it into her pocket. She stepped back into the kitchen and saw Tucker's face peering through a window by the back door. His face was pinched as he squinted into the room.

Mel felt her adrenaline spike and she thought she might pass out. Every instinct inside of her was telling her to flee. She had to get out of there. She forced her lips to turn into a smile and she held up one finger. Then she gestured in a crazy pantomime that she was going into the front to deactivate the alarm, which was hilarious because while they had a security camera, they didn't have an alarm system, just like they didn't have a panic button — both of which she planned to rectify if she managed to survive this day. Tucker stared at her for a moment and then gave her a thumbs-up.

Mel swallowed. It went down hard and for a second she thought she was going to choke on her own spit. She hurried into the front of the shop and glanced at the table where they'd been sitting. There were no sunglasses there. She and Marty would have found them when they cleaned up. Her only way out was to slip out the front door while Tucker waited.

Mel thought about calling Joe for help, but she knew she needed to get out of there first. As soon as she was away from the bakery, she would call. She unlocked the front door with shaking fingers. She dashed outside, slamming right into the shorter form of Tucker Booth.

"Mel, really," he said. He grabbed her by the upper arm in a hold that hurt. "Where exactly do you think you're going? The alarm is inside, isn't it?"

"I thought I heard a noise out here," she lied. She glanced around the street. It was empty at this hour; the tourist shopping for the day was done and people were off eating and drinking. The nearest restaurant couldn't be seen from the patio of the bakery. Damn it.

"Don't lie to me!" Tucker shook her. He looked crazy mad and she would have broken his hold and run but in his other hand he had a gun. "Back inside."

Mel thought about resisting. He released the safety and held the handgun and pressed it right under her jaw.

"Don't even think it."

"Okay," Mel said. Her voice was tight because the gun forced her jaw into a weird angle. Tucker was digging the metal barrel into her flesh and she knew there would be bruises tomorrow, assuming she survived. He pushed her backwards over the doorjamb and into the bakery, where he kicked the door shut and let go of her arm only long enough to turn the lock.

"Sit down," he ordered.

Mel slid into a seat at one of the café tables. She tried to casually slide her hand into her pocket so she could do something with her phone. She was not casual enough.

"Keep your hands on the table," he snapped.

Mel put her hands flat on the surface. She was annoyed to see that they were shaking, that her breath was short, and that her heart was pounding so hard in her chest it felt like it was trying to punch its way out. She was pretty sure she was having an anxiety attack. She tried to slow her breathing. She had to be calm. She had to convince Tucker they were on the same side.

"Tucker, we're friends," she said.

"No, we're not," he spat. "You, your friends, you're all losers."

Mel blinked. The vitriol was a bit of a surprise. He sounded as if he hated all of them. It grounded her. He could say whatever he liked about her, but her friends were sacred. She took a steadying breath. She pushed down on the table, getting centered.

"Why are you here?" she asked. "What do you want from me?"

Tucker paced the shop. He looked behind the counter and peeked into the kitchen. Mel tried to calculate the distance to the door. He'd shoot her before she made it out. Then he'd likely make it look like a robbery.

He came back to the table and stared at her. "You ruined everything."

Mel frowned. "How?"

He just stared at her and Mel was certain she saw him thinking, plotting, planning. The lack of warmth in his eyes made her shiver. She knew in that moment that as far as Tucker Booth was concerned she was collateral damage.

Panic was trying to claw its way up her

throat. She swallowed it down. It went with a fight and she thought she might throw up. She pushed that down, too. If he was planning to harm her, she wasn't going to make it easy for him. She wasn't going to give up her life or all that it meant to her because of this jerk.

"You killed Cassidy," she said.

"I didn't!" he argued. "It was Megan. I would never harm Cassidy."

Mel looked at the gun. This made no sense. If it was Megan, then why was he holding a gun on her? Unless . . .

"It wasn't Megan," Mel said. "It was you, but Cassidy wasn't your target, was she? You knew about them."

He tipped his head to the side as if he didn't understand. He was a terrible actor. "What?"

"Megan and Dan," she said. "You knew they were having an affair."

His face, which had looked tight to begin with, became a mottled shade of red and Mel wondered if he was going to shoot her just for saying their names.

"Dan didn't deserve her," he said. "She was never happy with him and then he cheated on her with her best friend. Disgusting. I could have made Cassidy happy. She should have married me."

"How did you find out?" Mel asked.

"I saw them," he said. "Dan was in LA, doing his sportscaster thing, and I went to see him after the game to see if he wanted to grab a beer. Well, Megan was there. I saw them together. They were clearly a couple, and I knew it was going to break Cassidy's heart."

"So, you decided to kill Megan?" Mel asked. "To spare Cassidy's feelings?"

"No! I wanted to help Cassidy get out," he said. "I thought if I made it look like Megan committed suicide, because her lover wouldn't leave his wife for her, then Cassidy would finally reject Dan for cheating on her with her best friend, and then I could be there to give Cassidy the life she deserved."

It clicked with Mel then. Tucker wanted to be Cassidy's hero. And how could he be that? He could get rid of the woman who was going to cause the end of her marriage and then step in.

"You tried to poison Megan," Mel said. "But Cassidy got the poison by mistake, is that right?"

Tucker raised his free hand and grabbed a tuft of his own hair. He tugged on it as if he could release some of his frustration that way.

"Megan wasn't drinking," he said. "How was I supposed to know that? I slipped the cyanide into Megan's drink when no one was looking and then I left the group, so I wasn't with her when the poison hit, but Megan gave her drink to Cassidy. Why? Why would she do that?"

Mel knew why, because Megan was pregnant. She didn't say anything. If Tucker didn't know, that news would set him off and she didn't want to deal with the ramifications of that.

He looked distraught and Mel didn't know how to play it, whether to placate him about how it wasn't his fault or berate him for killing the woman he obviously still loved. She opted for silence and hoped he would keep talking. He did.

"When I found Cassidy in the ladies' room with the empty glass beside her and realized what had happened, I knew there was only one other way to punish Megan for her betrayal. I went back out to the party and took her lipstick. Then I ducked back into the women's room and wrote your name, or started to, and pressed the lipstick into Cassidy's hand," he said.

"But that made it look like *I* was the killer," Mel said, outraged. "How was that repaying Megan?"

"Because I knew the cops would figure out that the lipstick was Megan's and then they would deduce that she was trying to make it look like it was you when it was really her," he said. "I'd already taken the photo of her glaring at Dan and Cassidy. My original plan had been to use that photo to prove that Megan had taken her own life because she was so distraught that Dan and Cassidy were still married and Dan was never going to leave Cassidy for her. But she messed it all up, so I decided the best way to make Megan pay would be to see her charged with murder. It was perfect. You would be dragged through the mud but Megan would pay the ultimate price. Cassidy would have been so pleased."

A bittersweet smile twisted his lips and Mel felt the full force of his crazy eyes as they bore into hers. Her skin crawled. He was completely insane.

"Unfortunately, your uncle Stan asked for the fingerprints of anyone who'd been near Cassidy that night. I can only surmise that one of my fingerprints was left on the lipstick," he said. He began to pace, never taking his eyes off Mel. It was clear he'd thought and thought and thought about the case and it was making him paranoid. "In my haste to get out of the ladies' room, I didn't get to wipe it down before pressing it into Cassidy's hand."

Mel felt her heart sink. She had a feeling she knew where he was going with this.

"If and when they do identify the print, I'll simply say I saw the lipstick on our table and assumed it was Cassidy's and gave it to her," he said. "That will explain why she had a lipstick that wasn't hers when she went to the bathroom to write another ode to her longtime enemy."

Mel swallowed. She didn't want to hear the rest. She knew what he was planning. It was so obvious. He was going to make her look like the murderer. Oh, man, how did she get into these things and how was she going to get out?

"It's too bad you walked in on Cassidy writing mean things about you," he said. "Of course, you'd been planning all along to poison Cassidy at the reunion, but when you caught her in the bathroom you decided to do her in right then and there using her drink to poison her since putting it in her cupcake would lead the police right to you."

"No one is going to believe that I killed Cassidy," Mel said. "I already passed a lie detector test just to prove it."

Tucker stared at her. "Lie detectors aren't completely accurate. Besides, you're going to write a suicide note expressing your guilt right before you drink some of the same poison you gave Cassidy."

He held up a small glass vial filled with a pale blue powder. Then he smiled. It was the creepiest look Mel had ever seen and it made her skin crawl.

"Where did you get that?"

"I design webpages for corporations," he said. "One of my clients is a pharmaceutical company. They gave me access to all of their labs full of drugs while I was there to take pictures and shoot video. I knew this" — he shook the vial — "would come in handy one day."

"You can't make me take that," Mel said. "You're going to have to shoot me, because I will never confess to a crime I didn't commit."

NINETEEN

"Yes, you will," he said. "Because if you don't, I'll just shoot you and write the note myself, making it look like you used a gun to kill yourself instead."

Mel felt woozy. This could not be happening. Either way, she was going to die. She had no way out. If she didn't do as he said, he would shoot her, and if she did do as he said, she'd be participating in her own murder. Why had she decided to stay late tonight? Why?

"Get up," Tucker said. He pocketed the poison. "We'll stage this in your office."

She didn't move fast enough and he hauled Mel to her feet. She was so terrified she'd forgotten how to walk. A hard shove to her back got her moving. She staggered forward, wondering if she could fight him. If she hit him with a hard elbow to the throat, would that do it?

Crash!

The sound of bakeware being smashed in the kitchen made her stop short. Tucker plowed into her from behind and she felt the gun at the small of her back.

"What was that?" he demanded.

"I don't know."

"I thought you were here alone."

"I was." Mel felt suddenly queasy. If one of her friends had come back or if it was Joe visiting, she could not let them be harmed. "Please, don't hurt anyone else. I'll do whatever you want but, please, if someone is here, let them go."

"It's too late for that," Tucker snarled. "They're ruining my plan."

He lifted his gun and charged toward the kitchen, pulling Mel behind him by gripping her wrist with one hand. He raised his foot to kick the swinging door open but it slammed out at him, clipping his knee and knocking him off balance.

Tucker went down, pulling Mel with him. She yanked her wrist out of his grip and scurried away from him. Tucker rolled to his side and lifted his gun. He fired a shot at the man looming in the doorway. Dwight Pickard. Thankfully, Dwight was already in motion, and the shot missed him as he dove down to scoop up Mel while at the same time he threw a massive cupcake tin at

Tucker, clipping him in the face. It hit his temple with a *crunch* and a *clang,* cut his forehead, and blood spurted down over his eyes.

That was the last Mel saw of Tucker as Dwight hauled her through the kitchen and shoved her out the back door. He slammed it behind them just as a shot rang out. Dwight pushed Mel toward a waiting motorcycle.

"Get on! Now!" he ordered.

Mel didn't hesitate but jumped onto the bike at the same time Dwight did. He fired up the engine just as Tucker came running out of the back door. He was covered in blood but still brandishing his gun. Mel wrapped her arms around Dwight and closed her eyes, waiting for the bullets to rip into her flesh, but Dwight launched them out of the alley at top speed. If she hadn't been holding on, she'd have fallen off the back. As it was they bounced over the curb and slid onto their side with only Dwight's leg keeping them from dropping to the ground as he took the corner at a clip, rocketing them down another alley and out onto the street.

Dwight glanced back at her as they sped down the street, and shouted, "You okay?"

Mel nodded but he'd turned forward and

couldn't see her. She coughed and shouted, "Yeah, I'm okay." Then, because she couldn't believe she was saying those words, she promptly burst into tears and cried into his back while she held on.

The ride was short. Dwight parked his bike in front of the police precinct and helped Mel off. Then he grabbed her hand and ran inside, pulling her behind him.

Uniformed officer Octavia Flores was manning the front desk. She glanced up from her computer monitor and caught sight of Mel and her eyes went wide. She immediately grabbed the radio on her shoulder and said, "Detective Cooper, I need you up front. Now."

Then she hopped off her stool and circled the desk, grabbing a tissue out of the box on her way. She was a tall, athletic black woman who looked like she could take down a suspect with a diving tackle and never break a sweat. She handed the tissue to Mel and put a protective arm around her. Mel dabbed at her eyes and blew her nose.

"You okay, hon?" she asked. She glanced up at Dwight, her eyes narrowed in suspicion. "What happened?"

"A murderer shot at us when I was saving her stupid ass," he said.

That brought Mel up short. "Did you just

call me stupid?"

"Did you let a murderer into your bakery?"

"No, I was trying to escape and he caught me," she said. "I am not stupid. This was not my fault."

"Psh," he said.

"It wasn't," she said. "How did you get into my bakery anyway? The back door was locked."

Dwight shrugged. "I have skills."

"What were you even doing there?" she asked. "Not that I'm not grateful, but . . ."

"I was following that sycophantic little weasel," he said. "Didn't you think it was weird that he showed up at the bakery right when your uncle did? Clearly, he was following him to see —"

"If they identified his fingerprint on the lipstick," Mel finished his sentence. "Wait. Did you just use the word *sycophantic*?"

"Yeah, are you implying *I'm* stupid?" he retorted.

They stared at each other. Mel was pretty sure they still hated each other but now there was a level of respect mixed in that was weird. Plus, the man had just saved her life.

"What's going on?" Uncle Stan burst through the security door and looked from

Mel to Dwight and back.

"Tucker Booth murdered Cassidy Havers-Griffin," Mel said. "And he just tried to murder me, too. He wanted me to write a suicide note claiming I killed Cassidy and then he planned to make me drink the same poison he gave her. If Dwight hadn't shown up when he did . . ."

Uncle Stan took in her windblown hair and tear-streaked face. Mel could only imagine what she looked like and he pulled her into a bear hug that crushed. Mel felt the tears roll out of her eyes again but she knew they didn't have time for this. She hugged Uncle Stan back hard and then stepped back and said, "He's still out there. We have to get him. He was wearing the same thing he had on earlier. Khaki pants and a button-down shirt."

"He also has a huge gash on his forehead and should be covered in his own blood," Dwight added. The smile on his face was more a show of teeth than mirth.

Uncle Stan studied him for a second and then reached out and shook his hand. "Thanks."

"No problem," Dwight said.

"You have to hurry," Mel said. "We left him at the bakery with the back door wide open. He has a gun. Who knows who he'll go after next? He's looking to pin this murder on someone."

Uncle Stan nodded. "We've got this. Don't you worry." He spun around and began barking orders. Mel and Dwight stepped back to let the police do their thing. While they were leaning against the wall, she glanced at him.

"You didn't have to save me," she said. "You could have let him finish me off."

"Is that what you think of me?" he asked. He looked outraged. "That I'd let you be murdered because I don't like you?"

"Well, I'm not your favorite person," she said. "You certainly didn't have to put yourself in harm's way to save me."

"I can't stand you," he agreed. "But you do make a mean cupcake, and I hate him more."

"So, you saved me for my cupcakes?" she asked.

"And I hate him more, don't forget that part," he said. "But, yeah, the cupcakes definitely weighed in your favor and you seem to have grown a spine since we were kids. I respect that."

Mel started to laugh. She couldn't help it. Probably, it was an emotional fallout from almost being murdered, but still she laughed until her stomach cramped and the tears she shed were from humor instead of fear. When she pulled it together, it was to find Dwight staring at her like she was deranged.

"What is your problem?" he asked. "Do I need to call someone for you?"

" 'The problem is not the problem. The problem is your attitude about the problem,' " she said.

"Are you quoting *Pirates of the Caribbean* at me?" Dwight asked. He sidled away and Mel grinned.

"You got the quote right! Dwight, I think this is the beginning of a beautiful friendship," she said.

"Oh, god." He looked pained, which only made Mel laugh even harder. It might have been because she was just so damned grateful to be alive, but it also might have been the twinkle in his eye when he said it. Either way, she had a feeling Dwight Pickard was not going to be leaving her life anytime soon, and she was okay with that.

Mel and Dwight were led into an empty office, where they kicked back on the well-worn faux-leather chairs, waiting to hear what happened to Tucker. Some quick detective work at the airport verified that he'd never gotten on his plane and that he'd rented a car from one of the agencies near the airport. They had the make, model, and license plate of his car and an all-points bulletin had been put out on him.

When Joe arrived, he came straight at Mel with his arms wide. He hugged her close and kissed her quick once, twice, three times, as if he needed to reassure himself that she was okay. It made Mel feel like she was valued and precious and she loved him so much for that. His relief wrapped around her like a big, puffy coat and she could have stayed there all night.

Joe pulled back and looked at Dwight. He didn't say anything but extended his hand and Dwight shook it. The two men sized each other up for a moment, but Joe being Joe, the chief mediator of his six brothers, knew exactly what to say.

"I heard you clipped him with a cupcake tin," he said. He had a small smile on his lips when he added, "Quick thinking."

Dwight studied him for a moment and nodded. "I would have preferred it was a tire iron or even a chair, but you use what you have at hand. Am I right?"

"You are," Joe said. "You saved Mel's life and for that I can't thank you enough. I hear you're a veteran."

"Marine Corps," Dwight said.

"I happen to know we have some job

openings for quick thinkers who can handle themselves at the county prosecutor's office," he said. He reached into his pocket and took out his business card. "Call me if you're interested. I'll get you an interview."

Dwight stared at the card for a long moment. Mel wanted to yell at him to take the card, but she knew the decision had to be his. Finally, he took the card and slipped it into his pocket. "Thanks."

"You bet," Joe said. He turned to Mel. "All right, tell me everything that happened."

She recounted the story with some minor corrections from Dwight, including his insistence that they did not almost die while fleeing from Tucker on his motorcycle. When she finished, Joe's face was set in hard lines.

"I'm going to go see what the status is on Booth," he said.

"I'm coming, too," Mel said.

"Me, too," Dwight added.

Joe opened his mouth to protest but Mel shook her head and said, "We deserve to know."

He nodded. Mel could see that it pained him but he let them both join him as he tracked Stan down to the detective's office. It was chaos. Detective Tara Martinez,

Stan's partner, was on one phone while Stan was on the other. He saw Joe and Mel in the doorway and waved them in. He frowned at Dwight but he didn't kick him out, for which Mel was grateful.

They pressed up against the wall, trying to stay out of the way. As soon as Stan ended his call, Joe pounced.

"What's the status?" Joe asked.

"There was a sighting but Booth lost them in traffic," Stan said.

"He tried to kill Mel!" Joe snapped. "He needs to be caught."

"You don't say. Huh, did you hear that, Detective Martinez? Booth needs to be caught," Stan said. His sarcasm would have left a lesser man bleeding.

"I'm sorry," Joe said. He held his hands up in a placating gesture. "I'm a bit on edge."

"Welcome to the party," Stan said. His phone buzzed and he picked it up. "Cooper."

There was a pause. "Where?" His eyes lit up and he snapped his fingers at Detective Martinez. When she glanced at him, he pointed at her repeatedly and her eyes went wide when he said, "Five minutes out."

Tara began to bark orders into her phone while Stan said, "Stay on the line" to whomever he was talking to.

"What's going on?" Mel demanded. She couldn't take it anymore.

"Booth has been spotted five minutes away from Daniel Griffin's house, where he and Megan are holed up with a SWAT team," Stan said.

Mel glanced at Dwight. He looked as on edge as she did. Clearly, because Dwight had saved her, Tucker was redirecting his plan to harm Megan or Danny or both. He probably figured he had nothing to lose and this was his last grand gesture to the woman he had loved. Mel felt queasy. She didn't want to be responsible for anything happening to them.

Dwight met her gaze and shook his head. "This is not on us. It's on Tucker for being a deranged mental case."

"I know," she said.

"We have undercover officers on the scene," Stan said. "They'll be all right."

The room was quiet except for Tara, talking low into her phone. Mel had the feeling she was communicating with the undercovers, giving them instructions, listening to what they were seeing. She could hear the round industrial clock on the wall ticking. It made her edgy.

Just when she thought she would jump

out of her skin, the radio on the desk sounded off. Mel could hear yelling. There was a gunshot and a scream and then silence. Everyone stood completely still. Mel was certain they had collectively stopped breathing. Then an officer came on the air and said, "We got him."

Mel reached for Joe's hand. She was terrified that Tucker had shot Megan or Danny. She glanced at her uncle. He nodded and she heard him ask whomever he was speaking to on his phone if everyone was all right.

He nodded while he listened and Mel saw his posture relax. She took that as a good sign and squeezed Joe's hand, hoping that her guess proved true. Stan ended his call at the same time Tara ended hers.

"They're bringing him in," Tara said. "I'm going to meet them."

"Right behind you," Stan said. Then he turned to Mel and said, "No one was harmed. The gunshot we heard was Booth but he missed the officer he was aiming for and shot Griffin's garage instead."

"Thank goodness," Mel said. She sagged a bit, happy to have Joe to bolster her.

Stan looked at the three of them. "You are free to go. We have your statements and Booth has been arrested. You're safe now."

"Thanks," Dwight said. He held out his

hand and Uncle Stan shook it.

Mel stepped forward and gave her uncle a big hug. "Best detective ever."

Uncle Stan's ears turned red at the tips, and she knew she had embarrassed him. "Yeah, well, go home and stay out of trouble." He thumped Joe on the back as he walked by him. "You'd better put a tracking device on her when you marry her. You're going to need it."

Mel glanced at Joe and he had one eyebrow up as if he was considering it. She shook her head. "No."

He sighed. He looped an arm around her shoulders and kissed the top of her head. "Come on, cupcake, let's go raid the bakery. I need a Dreamsicle Cupcake in the worst possible way."

They headed for the door and Mel noticed Dwight wasn't moving. She turned back to him. "Well, come on. If anyone deserves a cupcake, it's you."

He stared at her for a second and then his lips tipped up in the corner. "All right," he said. "But just one and this doesn't mean we're friends."

Mel met his gaze and said, "Don't be stupid. Of course it does."

TWENTY

When they arrived at the bakery, everyone was there. Oz was cleaning while supervising Marty, Tate, and Angie. When they stepped through the back door, Angie grabbed Mel and hugged her hard.

"Don't ever scare me like that again," she said. Then she promptly burst into tears.

"Me, either," Tate said. He moved his wife aside so he could hug Mel, too.

"I can't believe it was Tucker," Angie said. She pressed the heels of her hands to her eyes to stop the tears. "I mean, he was here with us. He hung out with us. I thought he was one of us."

"Well, he wasn't," Mel said. "He made that perfectly clear."

"Why did he come after you?" Tate asked.

"Because he never meant to murder Cassidy," Mel said. "The poison that killed Cassidy was meant for Megan."

"Then how —" Tate looked confused.

"Tucker didn't know that Megan is pregnant so she isn't drinking. She gave her beverage to Cassidy," Dwight said. Mel looked at him and he shrugged. "I figured it out when I caught her and Dan in the garden at Cassidy's funeral. They were in the garden kissing, and then I saw him put his hand on her belly in that way expectant fathers do."

"Oh, you saw them, too?" she said. She studied him. "Weren't you mad?"

"Not really," he said. "They were meant to be together. Cassidy never should have kept them apart."

Mel met his gaze. It went without saying that Cassidy should have been with him. Dwight had clearly brought out the best in her but Cassidy had never seen it. Mel reached out and squeezed his arm, letting him know she understood. When she turned back, Angie was glancing between them as if she couldn't believe what she was seeing.

"Why did Tucker come after you?" Angie asked.

"He was afraid that Uncle Stan was going to figure out that it was him who wrote on the bathroom wall with the lipstick he stole from Megan, because there was a partial print on the lipstick and Uncle Stan was gathering fingerprints of anyone who'd been near Cassidy that night. Tucker thought he could pin Cassidy's murder on me if he made me write a confession, and then he planned to stage my suicide," Mel said.

Mel felt a little queasy at how close he had come to pulling it off. Joe gave her a quick squeeze, and she wasn't sure if he was reassuring her or himself that she was all right.

"That's totally mental," Oz said.

"Well, it would have worked if Dwight hadn't been following Tucker," Mel said. "He foiled the whole thing."

Angie turned and stood in front of Dwight, looking like she wanted to take a piece out of him. Instead, she leapt up and hugged him hard. Her voice was choked when she said, "Thanks for saving my best friend."

Dwight patted her back twice in what he obviously hoped was her quick-release button. It didn't work. Angie started sobbing and Tate had to step forward and peel his wife off. She immediately turned into him to finish her cry.

"Is she always this emotional?" Dwight asked. "I mean I get it, but that's a lot of tears for a happy ending."

Tate and Angie looked at each other. "You have been pretty emotional," Tate said. Their eyes went wide. They looked back at

Mel and Angie said, "We have to go."

Mel laughed. She knew right away what they were thinking. "Call me, you know, if there's anything to report."

Tate hustled his wife out the door, waving as they went.

"What's going on with them?" Oz asked.

"They're newlyweds," Marty said. "What do you think?"

"Oh . . . oh!" Oz turned bright red beneath the fringe that covered his eyes. He glanced at Mel and said, "You know, I had to throw out all of that fondant. I made more, but seriously, that was a ton of product wasted, not to mention if we hadn't come back tonight we could have had bugs, rats, and other vermin infesting our kitchen."

"So sorry," Mel said. "Next time I'm running for my life, I'll be sure to ask if I can just wrap up my baking supplies before I flee."

"Well, okay then," Oz said. "I'm just saying you need to respect the kitchen."

He turned away and Marty rolled his eyes as if he couldn't believe what he was hearing.

"Someone needs to get more comfortable with his feelings," Marty said. "Sheesh."

"Why are you all here anyway?" Mel asked. "I mean, how did you know what was happening?"

"Joe called us when he was on his way to the station. They had a couple of uniforms watching the place in case that lunatic came back, but once they caught him, they gave us the go-ahead to come in and clean up," Marty said. He hugged Mel and then turned to look at Dwight. "All right, hero, what's your poison?"

Dwight raised his hands. "I didn't poison anyone."

"I know that," Marty said. "What I meant was what flavor cupcake do you want?"

"Uh, I'd like . . . well, one of those raspberry-lemon ones," Dwight said.

Marty looked him up and down as if trying to match the flavor to the man. "One Tinkerbell, coming up."

"He just had to call it that, didn't he?" Dwight asked. He looked so put-upon that Mel laughed.

"Well, that is the name," she said.

"You could give it a manlier name," Dwight said. "You know, like the Lumberjack."

"Or the Shark," Joe said.

"I am not naming a cupcake after a fish or a tree cutter," Mel said.

"How about the Danger Zone?" Marty said.

The other two nodded in approval. "No," Mel said. "Oz, back me up."

"Nope, you know, I think they might be onto something," Oz said. He tapped his chin and then snapped his fingers. "How about the Diesel?"

"That's what I'm talking about," Dwight said. He pointed at Oz. "He gets it."

"No!" Mel squawked. "I am not naming a cupcake after truck fuel."

Marty returned with a plate of cupcakes. Dwight opened his mouth, looking like he was going to continue arguing, and Mel held up one hand in a stop gesture. "No, enjoy your Tinkerbell."

He grumbled but she noticed he chose the raspberry-lemon confection anyway. Mel chose a Peaches and Cream Cupcake. As soon as she unwrapped it and took her first bite, she felt the sugar hit her bloodstream and suddenly her world made sense again. Tucker Booth had been caught. He wasn't going to harm anyone ever again. They were all safe and — she glanced at Dwight — she'd made peace with her past and gained a new friend.

It was going to be okay, better than okay in fact, because cupcakes always made everything better.

RECIPES

PINEAPPLE UPSIDE-DOWN CUPCAKES

A rich, buttery pineapple cake topped with a caramelized pineapple ring and maraschino cherry.

1/2 cup butter (1 stick), softened
3/4 cup sugar
2 eggs
1 teaspoon vanilla extract
1 2/3 cups all-purpose flour
1 teaspoon baking powder
1/2 teaspoon salt
1 can crushed pineapple, undrained

Topping:
12 pineapple rings
12 maraschino cherries
Brown sugar

Preheat oven to 350 degrees. Line cupcake

pan with paper liners. In a large mixing bowl, cream together butter and sugar until light and fluffy. Add the eggs and the vanilla. In a medium bowl, sift together the flour, baking powder, and salt. Alternately add the flour mixture and the crushed pineapple to the large bowl, mixing until the batter is smooth. Fill paper liners until two-thirds full. Place one pineapple ring and one cherry on top of each cupcake. Bake for 17 to 22 minutes until golden brown. After cupcakes cool, sprinkle brown sugar on top of the pineapple ring and use a kitchen torch to caramelize the sugar and pineapple. Makes 12.

Leave plain or top with vanilla buttercream.

CINNAMON SINNERS CUPCAKES

A moist cinnamon cupcake with cinnamon cream cheese frosting.

1/2 cup butter, melted
1 cup sugar
4 eggs
1 teaspoon vanilla extract
1 1/2 cups flour
1 teaspoon baking powder
1 teaspoon cinnamon

1/2 teaspoon salt
3/4 cup buttermilk

Preheat oven to 350 degrees. Line cupcake pan with paper liners. In a large mixing bowl, cream together butter and sugar until light and fluffy. Add the eggs and the vanilla. In a medium bowl, sift together the flour, baking powder, cinnamon, and salt. Alternately add the flour mixture and the buttermilk to the large bowl, mixing until the batter is smooth. Fill paper liners until two-thirds full. Bake for 17 to 22 minutes until golden brown. Makes 12.

Cinnamon Cream Cheese Frosting with Cinnamon Stick Garnish

8 ounces cream cheese, softened
1 stick unsalted butter, softened
1/2 teaspoon vanilla extract
1/2 teaspoon cinnamon
3 1/2 cups powdered sugar
1/4 cup sugar
1/8 teaspoon cinnamon
Cinnamon sticks

Beat cream cheese, butter, vanilla, and cinnamon in a large bowl until well blended. Gradually add powdered sugar and beat until frosting is smooth. Put frosting in a pastry bag and pipe onto cupcakes in thick swirls, using an open tip.

Mix together the sugar and cinnamon to make cinnamon sugar and spread on a flat plate. Roll the side of the frosted cupcake so that the cinnamon sugar mixture coats the edges just above the wrapper. Top with a cinnamon stick.

HI-TOP MERINGUE CUPCAKES

Chocolate cupcake with hi-top meringue frosting dipped in chocolate.

1 1/3 cups all-purpose flour
2 teaspoons baking powder
1/4 teaspoon baking soda
1/2 cup unsweetened cocoa powder
1/8 teaspoon salt
3 tablespoons butter, softened
1 cup white sugar
2 eggs
3/4 teaspoon vanilla extract
1 cup milk

Preheat oven to 350 degrees. Sift together the flour, baking powder, baking soda, cocoa, and salt. Set aside. In a large bowl, cream together the butter and sugar until well blended. Add the eggs one at a time, beating well with each addition, then stir in the vanilla. Add the flour mixture alternately with the milk and mix until smooth. Bake for 15 to 17 minutes. Makes 12.

Frosting: Hi-Top Meringue Dipped in Chocolate

1 1/4 cups sugar
3 egg whites
1/4 cup water
1/4 teaspoon cream of tartar
1 teaspoon vanilla extract

Chocolate Coating:

12 ounces semisweet chocolate
3 ounces vegetable oil

In a large metal bowl, mix sugar, egg whites, water, and cream of tartar. Set the bowl over a pan of simmering water and whisk the mixture, making sure the sugar dissolves and the temperature reaches 160 degrees Fahrenheit. Then return the bowl to the mixer, add the vanilla, and continue mixing on high speed until stiff peaks form, about fifteen minutes. Scoop the frosting into a pastry bag and, using a round tip, pipe thick swirls of frosting onto the cupcakes until they are about two inches high. Transfer the cupcakes to the refrigerator while making the candy coating.

To make candy coating: Using a double boiler, melt the chocolate and mix in the vegetable oil thoroughly. Once the candy coating is smooth, pour it into a deep bowl and let it cool to room temperature. Dip each cupcake frosting side down into the candy coating so that the meringue is fully covered. Place on a rack to cool completely for fifteen minutes, then store in the refrigerator.

MEL'S FONDANT RECIPE

Mel and Oz use a lot of fondant in their creations, so here is their tried-and-true fondant recipe so you can make fondant of your own.

16 ounce package of marshmallows
1/4 cup water
1 teaspoon vanilla extract
32 ounces confectioner's sugar
1/4 cup butter

Using a large microwave-safe bowl, pour in the marshmallows and microwave on high for 30 seconds. Stir in the water and vanilla until smooth. Using a mixer on low, gradually beat in the confectioner's sugar, setting aside one cup of sugar for kneading, until a sticky dough forms. Use the butter to coat your hands and then start to work the dough in the bowl until it becomes less sticky. Turn the dough out onto a large piece of parchment paper and continue kneading with the remaining sugar, about ten minutes, until the fondant is pliable. When it reaches its desired consistency, shape it into a ball and wrap it tightly in plastic wrap. Refrigerate overnight. When you are ready to use the fondant, let it come to room temperature and dust with confectioner's sugar while rolling it out.

ABOUT THE AUTHOR

Jenn McKinlay, the *New York Times* best-selling author of the Cupcake Bakery Mysteries (including *Wedding Cake Crumble, Caramel Crush,* and *Vanilla Beaned*), has baked and frosted cupcakes into the shapes of cats, mice, and outer-space aliens, to name just a few. Writing a mystery series based on one of her favorite food groups (dessert) is as enjoyable as licking the beaters, and she can't wait to whip up the next one. She is also the author of the Hat Shop Mysteries and the Library Lover's Mysteries. She lives in Scottsdale, Arizona, with her family.

The employees of Thorndike Press hope you have enjoyed this Large Print book. All our Thorndike, Wheeler, and Kennebec Large Print titles are designed for easy reading, and all our books are made to last. Other Thorndike Press Large Print books are available at your library, through selected bookstores, or directly from us.

For information about titles, please call:
(800) 223-1244

or visit our website at:
gale.com/thorndike

To share your comments, please write:
Publisher
Thorndike Press
10 Water St., Suite 310
Waterville, ME 04901